PROJECT
GENESIS

PROJECT GENESIS

H.J. "Walt" Walter

Order this book online at www.trafford.com
or email orders@trafford.com

Most Trafford titles are also available at major online book retailers.

Printed in the United States of America.

ISBN: 978-1-4907-2907-7 (sc)
ISBN: 978-1-4907-2909-1 (hc)
ISBN: 978-1-4907-2908-4 (e)

Library of Congress Control Number: 2014904090

Because of the dynamic nature of the Internet, any web addresses or links contained in
this book may have changed since publication and may no longer be valid. The views
expressed in this work are solely those of the author and do not necessarily reflect the
views of the publisher, and the publisher hereby disclaims any responsibility for them.

Any people depicted in stock imagery provided by Thinkstock are models,
and such images are being used for illustrative purposes only.
Certain stock imagery © Thinkstock.

Trafford rev. 02/27/2014

www.trafford.com
North America & international
toll-free: 1 888 232 4444 (USA & Canada)
fax: 812 355 4082

Dedicated to the patient one, my wife, Dolores

ACKNOWLEDGEMENTS

To my wife Dolores, for always being there when I needed guidance. For being so patient when things went wrong. For always supporting what i was doing no matter how much time it required writing alone in my study.

To a dear friend, Edie Fleeman, for helping in editing my book and making welcome suggestions to improve its content.

ABOUT THE AUTHOR

 H.J."Walt" Walter is a retired naval aviator who served four years in the Antarctic. He spent 22 years flying all types of naval aircraft including single engine props & jets, multiengine props & jets and the turboprop powered C-130. After retirement he earned his college degrees. A Bachelor of Science in Education, Bachelor of Science in Earth Science and Master of Science in Education He also has three years of mechanical engineering at Purdue University and attended the Naval Post Graduate School, Monterey, California. Taught high school Technology Education and Pre-Engineering at Canisius College and was also employed in the engineeering department of an aerospace corporation.

Prologue

"Preparation for Disaster"

Mirny, Russia

There was a lot of activity around launch pad number 2. General Vladimir Gorchinski was still in his office, observing from his perch on the second floor of the headquarters building. He purposely had his office situated on the north side of the building, so that he could observe the launch pad #2 at Plesetsk and all operations associated with it. This was a very special launch, ordered personally by the Prime Minister, and the General was not going to allow it to be screwed up.

All preparations had been carefully laid out and screened with each step in the preparation for launch orchestrated like a fine ballet.

The payload for this launch had been stored in a secret building at Sary Shagan, the ballistic and laser development base, which was located at 46º12'N 73º48'E in Kazakhstan. Sary Shagan had proven inadequate to launch this payload and the Prime Minister indicated he wanted it placed in a medium-high, nearly polar earth orbit.

Plesetsk was ideal for the mission since it had previously been used for launching the Soyuz rocket, Cosmos-3M Rocket, Tsyklon and military satellites placed into high inclination and polar orbits. One advantage for this base was the range for falling debris was clear to the north, which was largely uninhabited Arctic and polar terrain. The base itself was situated in a region of taiga, or flat terrain with boreal pine forests. The heavy Proton and Zenit rockets could only be land-launched from Baikonur Cosmodrome.

Plesetsk Cosmodrome was originally developed by the Soviet Union as a launch site for intercontinental ballistic missiles under the leadership and supervision of Lieutenant General Dimitri Zukov.

The urban-type settlement of Plesetsk in Arkhangelsk Oblast had a railway station, essential for the transport of missile components. A new town for the support of the facility was named Mirny, Russian for "peaceful". By 1997, more than 1,500 launches to space had been made from the site, more than for any other launch facility, although the usage had declined significantly since the breakup of the Soviet Union.

The existence of Plesetsk Cosmodrome was originally kept secret. After the end of the Cold War it was learned that the CIA had begun to suspect the existence of an ICBM launch site at Plesetsk in the late 1950s. The Soviet Union did not officially admit the existence of Plesetsk Cosmodrome until 1983.

General Gorchinski was determined that this launch be accident-free. There had been three accidents at Plesetsk Cosmodrome. The first of these was on 26 June 1973, in which nine people were killed by an explosion of Cosmos-3M rocket, which was ready for launch.

The second accident, on 18 March 1980, killed 48 people in an explosion of a Vostok-2M rocket with a Tselina satellite, during a fueling operation, and the third was on 15 October 2002, when a Soyuz-U carrying the ESA Foton-

M1 project failed to launch and exploded, killing one.

An accident on this missile launch would be devastating to the base. Only a few people were aware that the payload for this missile was a nuclear warhead with an effective payload of 1.8 megatons of TNT. The plan was to place it in a 300-mile high orbit. From there it had the capability to be fired at a ground target and exploded at a low altitude for an air burst weapon.

The payload was on a lowboy and being transported by road from Sary Shagan to Plesetsk. It had been on the road for six days, but would not arrive for another six days. Kazakhstan was a long way from Mirny, which was approximately 500 miles north of Moscow.

After a long twelve days on the road, the payload finally arrived. It was taken to Building 27 on the base and placed in a "clean" room where it was attached to machines designed to insure its systems were operational before mounting it on the rocket designed to put it in orbit. This particular payload was highly complex and would require a couple of days to complete the checkout. The rocket contained four main sections. The first sections systems included its master control unit, which contained a radio transceiver allowing it to be reprogrammed in flight. It also contained a pressure altimeter sensor so that the weapon would explode as an air-burst and be more effective versus a ground-impact weapon. This was part of the arming section and remained inert in the safe mode. The final section was a self-destruct system armed with spatial sensing radar with a range of fifty miles.

The second unit was two solid fuel rockets attached to each side of the payload. These would be used to pinpoint the target and move the warhead to the proper coordinates for detonation. The third section of the payload consisted of an atomic weapon of 1.8-megaton capability, while the fourth section was the recovery section. It was tied into the master control unit so that it could be returned to Russia unexploded. The parachute in this section would ensure a soft landing.

It was finally mounted on top of the rocket and the countdown begun. The launch crews worked some sixteen hours to clear all the support equipment from the launch pad. The launch director made one last sweep of the launch area for safety purposes and proceeded back to launch control. The launch had been at T minus thirty and holding since the safety sweep and now the countdown continued. All monitors in mission control reported a go for launch at T minus five minutes thirty seconds and counting. The rest of the time went normally, with all systems sequencing at the proper time, and at ten seconds the missile monitor reported, "T minus 10..., ignition..., five..., four..., three..., two..., one..., we have liftoff."

All consoles in mission control indicated systems normal. The payload was inserted in a 300-mile high polar orbit and the missile body was ejected, reentered the atmosphere, and burned up. Mission control's final report was "all systems normal".

Kamas, Utah

As Paul Anderson was ushered into Bob Avery's office, Bob came from behind his desk and greeted Paul. "I'm Bob Avery. Pleased to meet you, Paul"

They shook hands and Paul responded, "Pleased to meet you, Bob."

"What can I do for you?" Bob asked.

"I retired recently from the U.S. Navy, and as I was cleaning out my office at NASA I found your business card in my space suit and thought this might be a good job opportunity. I don't know if you are familiar with my career, but I was the Mission Commander of the last space shuttle flight, and am a former naval aviator. I brought a copy of my resume, which gives all my pertinent data. I flew the A4 and F-14 during my navy tours. I guess I have about 3500 hours in them." Paul offered.

"Oh right," Bob responded. "I read something about your escapades. I don't know how you got my business card, but we do have a few openings for pilots in our charter business. I take it you are interested in flying our Gulfstreams."

"That's what I had in mind, Bob. By the way, I have flown in one of your Gulfstreams. Terry Richardson picked me up in McMurdo after a UFO rescued me from space shuttle Enterprise. He brought me and the other four astronauts from Enterprise back to Houston. He did a nice job, and I was very impressed with that young man."

Bob smiled. "Paul, let me suggest this. I am going to send you down to the Salt Lake City Airport to our base facility in Hangar 512 to meet with John Walker. He is our Vice President in charge of Operations and can give you a tour and describe our operation to you. After that we can see what we want to do and if you might fit into our operation. Leave me a copy of your resume and I will contact John."

Paul retreived a copy of his resume from his brief case, and handed it to Bob. They rose and shook hands and Bob saw Paul to the outer office, where they exchanged goodbyes.

Bob returned to his desk, picked up the phone, and dialed John Walker.

After the second ring, Ginny Wulf, John's secretary,

answered. "Omega Aviation, how may I direct your call?" she asked.

"Ginny, this is Bob Avery. Is John available?" he asked.

"Yes, Mr. Avery. Hold on a second, and I'll ring his phone," she said.

"John here...hey, Bob, what's up?" he asked.

"John, I just had Paul Anderson in my office. I don't know if you remember him. He was the Mission Commander of Shuttle Enterprise."

"Oh, yeah, say no more I remember him. What's going on?" John asked.

"He found one of my business cards in his space suit when he retired from NASA and the Navy, and it appears he wants a flying job with us. How about giving him a tour and interviewing him for a possible job? After you digest his resume, give me a call and we can discuss possibly hiring him," Bob said.

"I can do that, Bob. When can I expect him?" John asked.

"He just left my office and I gave him directions to the hangar, so I would expect it will take him about an hour and a half," Bob replied.

"Okay Bob, I'll keep an eye open for him and will give you a call later in the day," John said.

"Thanks John. I'll expect to hear from you later. Take care."

After Bob hung up the phone, he stared out his window for a long time, thinking about what to do. He liked Paul and he knew he had the right stuff and would probably make a great AFV (Anti-gravity flight vehicle) pilot. They could always use another AFV pilot, so he would have to wait and see what John had to say.

The AFV program was a top-secret flight program. It consisted of six anti-gravity vehicles capable of space flight all the way to the moon. The vehicles were disc-shaped and required a crew of three.

Bob had inherited management of the AFV program when Jack Forester retired from the Office of Polar Programs, and Antarctic Development Squadron Six had been decommissioned. This had required moving the AFVs out of Antarctica and reestablishing them in Utah. He was directly responsible to the Director of Central Intelligence.

Admiral John Boland, who had been appointed Director at CIA when Admiral Bill Reynolds stepped down, was directing the program. The President had asked for suggestions on whom to appoint and John Boland's name had surfaced when his job had also been eliminated as Commander, Antarctic Support Force, AKA Task Force Forty-three. He had been the overseer of the AFV program in the Antarctic under Jack Forester for the previous four years and was well aware of its importance to national security.

The transition of the AFV base from Siple Station, Antarctica, to Kamas, Utah, had gone without a hitch, and the new kids on the block had picked up where the previous managers had left off.

Surveillance, intelligence-gathering and search and rescue for the manned U.S. space program were still the primary mission of these vehicles. Secrecy was one of the all-important factors in this program. If the world became aware that the United States was responsible for 95% of all UFO sightings over the years there would be Hell to pay. Life for these men would become impossible, and that would be the end of the program.

Later that day, Bob's phone rang and Cindy Harger,

his secretary, said,   "Mr. Walker is on the line, Sir."

"Thanks, Cindy, I've got it." He punched up line one. "Bob here. What's your evaluation, John?" Bob inquired.

"I think he can do this job with his eyes closed," John offered. "I reviewed his resume, but you know as well as I do that he's got to be a great pilot or he wouldn't have advanced to the level he did. He has about 7,600 total flight hours almost exclusively in single engine jets, but I think we can convert him to multiengine jets without a problem. If we decide to hire him, I can take him out for an indoctrination flight and see how he handles himself in the aircraft. My vote is to hire him, Bob," John said.

"I concur, John. I think we need to hire him. Why don't we proceed this way: give him a call at his hotel and take him on a flight tomorrow. Then if you still want to hire him, send him back up here and I will carry through with the paperwork to get him on the payroll," Bob said.

"Okay, Bob, will do. He left me his phone number, so I will call you after the flight tomorrow. By the way, did you get my proposal to convert our fleet to the G550?" John asked.

"I got it, John. It was a great proposal, and I sent it up the line for consideration. I look forward to your call tomorrow. Talk to you later," Bob said.

Bob hung up from John and placed a call to Admiral Boland at the CIA. Admiral Boland's administrative assistant put Bob through and John Boland came on the line.

"What's up, Bob?" He asked.

"Admiral, Paul Anderson showed up in my office today looking for a job flying the G4s. He found my business card in his space suit when he retired. I suspect my old buddy Larry Beck slipped it into his space suit when he rescued him from Enterprise when they were stranded in

8

space. I haven't had a chance to track that down yet, but I will. Anyway, John Walker and I are considering employing Paul, so I need your people to check on him. I am fairly certain he has had a top-secret clearance in the past, but I need to verify that. As you can guess, I am considering asking him if he wants to participate in the AFV program. What do you think, Admiral?" Bob asked.

"I think he would be a good addition to your cadre of AFV pilots. Some of you guys aren't getting any younger, and we'll need replacements sooner or later. I will have the staff here check on his background and give you a call tomorrow," John said.

"Thanks, Admiral, will be in touch," Bob answered.

The morning dawned on a beautiful day. The weather was high cirrus clouds with visibility more than 50 miles. It was going to be a great day for flying.

Paul Anderson was due to meet up with John Walker at 11:00a.m. John indicated they would fly for about 1-1/2 hours and then go to lunch. Paul had a light breakfast and read the morning paper. The news stories reported that things were heating up in Iraq and Afghanistan and the fighting was very fierce. The media was still on President Bush's case about being a warmonger and killing our youth in wars. He finished his breakfast and, after returning to his room for his briefcase, left by taxi for Hangar 512.

John was already in his office, waiting for Paul to arrive. After greeting each other they headed out to the flight line. John pointed out that they would fly aircraft #5 today. After opening the forward stairs, he placed his flight bag in the cockpit. It contained such vital items such as sectional charts as well as airways charts and approach plates. They were all paper backups to the electronic documents stored in the aircraft's computers, but all things necessary to conduct a flight within the United States. He rejoined Paul outside and walked him though a pre-flight inspection, pointing out those items specific to the G4. When they completed the pre-flight, they boarded the aircraft, with Paul occupying the left seat and John in the copilot's seat. John talked Paul through the checklist items, and after starting the engines they were cleared for taxi. John reminded Paul that with differential power applied to the engines, the aircraft could be steered in either direction. It was one of the skills Paul would learn when adapting to multiengine, multipiloted aircraft. Before takeoff, John briefed Paul on the use of V1 and V2 speeds and the need for always calculating them. The V1 value was the speed at which the aircraft takeoff could be aborted and still stopped on the runway. The V2 value was the ideal takeoff speed for the weight and configuration of the aircraft. He also briefed him on after-takeoff procedures. Once the brakes were released, the copilot would handle the power levers and would call out the V1 and V2 speeds as they were reached.

John called Salt Lake tower for takeoff clearance. They rolled onto the duty runway after being cleared for takeoff. Power was applied and as the rpms built up, at 75% power Paul released the brakes while continuing to advance the power levers. John called out V1 then V2 speed as Paul raised the nose to the proper takeoff attitude. They lifted off on speed after which Paul called for gear up. When it was up and locked he called for flaps up, all the while accelerating to 200 knots for the climb to altitude. John was pleased with what he had already observed. Paul's performance was flawless and his reputation as a naval aviator and astronaut were well deserved.

They had filed a flight plan for Reno, which was only

twenty-two minutes from takeoff. The aircraft was leveled off at 18,000' and switched to Reno approach control. Reno approach cleared them in their descent in steps and they were down to 8000' and under positive radar control. John asked approach for a practice VOR approach to the Reno-Tahoe International Airport. John had set the center instrument panel CRT display to the VOR approach for the airport. Paul passed directly over the VOR station and commenced his approach. He asked John to set his radar altimeter to 300', which were the instrument flight minimums. Paul reminded John that Reno's field elevation was 4415' and his minimum descent altitude would be 4715' until John called out, "field in sight."

They completed the before-landing checklist and, as they recrossed the VOR station inbound to the airport, they completed the landing checklist with the gear down and flaps set appropriately. John received permission for a touch-and-go landing and called, "runway in sight". John called out the approach, threshold and touchdown speeds. Paul made a typical navy carrier landing, but didn't slam the aircraft down too hard. John had expected that and would make a note to teach Paul a simple technique for making a soft, smooth landing in a swept-wing jet. They applied the power after touchdown, and headed off into the blue once again. John called for a downwind for the duty runway and Reno tower obliged. As Paul flew the aircraft downwind, John described to him how to make a soft landing in a swept-wing aircraft. The secret was to just give the aircraft a little burst of power before touchdown, while letting the nose pitch up and then immediately reducing the power to its previous setting, then letting the nose come back down. This was just enough to break the rate of descent and not kill the speed, allowing for the soft touchdown. Paul applied John's instruction to a tee and sure enough it resulted in a smooth, soft landing. Once again they made a touch-and-go, and soon were on their way back to Salt Lake City. This time John let Paul fly the radar vectors to final approach, where he made another very nice landing. John ensured correct use of the thrust reversers that Paul had never experienced. They slowed, turned off the runway and taxied back to the hangar, where they shutdown the aircraft.

"Well, Paul. What do you think of the G4?" John asked.

"Good performing aircraft," He responded. "It's a very responsive aircraft. I really like the feel of it"

"I think it's a great machine and is forgiving if your error is minor," John mused.

"I really enjoyed it. Thanks for giving me an orientation flight. I really learned something in regards to soft landings. You know, we were never taught things like that in the Navy," Paul said.

"It's a completely different type of landing, as you are aware, Paul. Here we try to please the customer, and if the landing is soft and smooth the customer is happy, no matter what the rest of the flight was like. I enjoyed it also, Paul. It's nice to fly with a good stick. Some of these kids are atrocious when it comes to being smooth in all phases of flight," John said.

They climbed out of the aircraft and walked down the ramp for the hangar.

"How about a cup of coffee?" John asked.

"That would be great," Paul answered.

"Let's go up to my office where we can drink our coffee and talk a little," John suggested.

They entered John's outer office, where he asked

Ginny to get them both a cup of coffee. "Come on in and sit down," he said

Ginny soon reappeared with the coffee and set it down on the table in front of the sofa in John's office.

"Thanks, Ginny," John offered.

She nodded and closed the door as she exited.

John began the conversation. "Paul, I am going to recommend to Bob Avery that he hire you ASAP. If he concurs, the next step will be to send you to Flight Safety in Phoenix, Arizona, for checkout and qualification in the G4, G5 and G550. Do you have an FAA pilot's license?" John asked.

"No I don't," he answered. "What do we need to do to get one?"

"After you finish Flight Safety training, we will send in the proper FAA form along with your qualifications from flight safety and have them issue you a commercial-type certificate with a single and multi-engine land and instrument rating. The FAA will add your aircraft type qualifications on the back, and then after you complete a class one physical with Doc Kealy you'll be ready to fly for us," John said.

"We fly these aircraft single-piloted, sort of. Our second crewmen are all ex-navy NFOs and act as copilot on all our flights. We use them in that position for safety reasons on our overseas flights, of which we have many. We can schedule this based on your personal needs with moving your family, etc. Just keep us advised and we will adjust as necessary. After you leave here, I am sending you back out to Bob Avery at headquarters where he will talk salary and take care of all the paperwork. At this point do you have any questions?" John asked.

"No, I think you covered all my questions and I appreciate your thoroughness," Paul replied.

"Okay then, let's go to lunch," John said. "I know a nice quiet little family place just down the road. We can take my car."

After they finished lunch they drove back to Hangar 512 and Paul departed for headquarters in Kamas.

John returned to his office, picked up the phone and dialed Bob Avery's number.

1

"The Rookie"

Kamas, Utah

Paul soon arrived at the headquarters security checkpoint. The gate guard had been alerted that he would be arriving so he was cleared directly to proceed to the headquarters building.

He made his way to Bob's outer office and was greeted by Cindy Harger, Bob's secretary.

"Good afternoon, Mr. Anderson. I know Mr. Avery is expecting you. Let me advise him you here," Cindy said.

She keyed the intercom and advised Bob that Paul was in the outer office. He instructed her to send him right in and that they were not to be disturbed.

Paul entered and Bob greeted him with a handshake. He offered him a seat in his lounge area and asked if he would like a cup of coffee or a soda. They both settled on a soda and Bob asked Cindy to get them.

Bob began the conversation. "I hope you enjoyed your flight this morning, Paul,"

"Yeah Bob it was an eye opening experience. I thought I knew everything there was to know about flying but John gave me a lesson I hadn't experienced before. His technique for soft landing in a swept-wing jet just blew my mind."

"Well, you actually won't find a better G4 pilot than John," Bob added, "Let's get down to business. John called me and recommended that we put you on the payroll. I concur with that so let me broach a new subject before we get to the paperwork. How would you like to be a participant in a top-secret program?" Bob paused. "Before you answer, let me tell you if you agree this can never be discussed anywhere at anytime, no matter what," Bob said.

"That's a mighty tall order, Bob. Can you give me anymore info before I make a decision?" he asked.

"All I can assure you is that it involves flying," Bob said.

Paul sat back on the sofa and thought deeply for about a minute then said smiling, "Well if it involves flying and it's top-secret I guess it would be something I would like to do."

"Okay Paul," Bob offered a handshake, "Welcome aboard, we will discuss it later but first let's get your employment papers finished so we can get you started flying the G4s. How about a starting salary of $120,000?"

"Wow, that's very generous of you, Bob. That's more than I expected."

"Also Paul, I'm not sure you are aware of the housing within this compound. Our administrative officer will get your requirements and assign you housing. It is furnished free by the company and is one of the perks. I am going to turn you over to Bill Springer, our admin officer, who will handle the paperwork. When you finish come back up to my office and we will talk flying," Bob offered.

Paul wended his way over to Bill Springer's office and Bob went back to his paperwork. Later that afternoon Paul returned to Bob's office and was ushered in.

"Did Bill get you all checked in, Paul?" Bob asked.

"Yeah, I think I signed more forms than I ever did in the Navy or NASA," Paul said.

Bob laughed, "I know, Paul. Our FAA certificate requires most of that. The regulations drive John nuts, so he tells me. By the way you will need an FAA medical so make sure you see Cindy and she will schedule you for a physical with Doc Kealy. He used to be our flight surgeon in Antarctic Development Squadron Six so now he still takes care of us. He has a small clinic between headquarters and the gate."

"Will do, Bob. I also have a question about Flight Safety training. When can I get scheduled for that?" he asked.

"You can touch base with Larry Beck our chief pilot and he will put you on the schedule," Bob continued, "His office is in the building but you will have to catch him when he's not on a flight somewhere."

"I know Larry very well, Bob. Nice to hear somebody's name I recognize," Paul said.

"If you're ready to enter on you new career let's get started. Don't ask any questions until we get to our destination," Bob cautioned.

"You got it. Let's get started," Paul said as his mind was racing. What kind of a secret program am I getting into? He thought.

They left Bob's office and headed toward the back of the building. They turned into a passageway marked "Restricted Area, Authorized Personnel Only". After passing through the first door into a small entryway they came up on another door. Bob inserted his security card, punched in a code and told Paul to place his right eye in front of the retinal scanner. Paul did so and the lights on the panel flashed and finally turned green.

"Okay you're authorized to pass through this door. The keypad security code will be on your security pass when you get it and that needs to be punched in after your eye is scanned," Bob said.

He then placed his eye in front of the scanner and entered in his security code. The door unlocked, opened and Bob motioned Paul to follow him through. They stepped into the elevator boarding area. Bob pushed the button and the elevator doors opened. They both stepped in and Bob pushed the down button. The elevator moved into motion very smoothly and started down. When it reached the bottom, the elevator stopped abruptly and the doors opened. Paul was amazed at what he saw next. There was a four-seated tram and Bob motioned him to take a seat. Bob then selected the forward switch, the lights in the tunnel switched on and the tram moved slowly up the track. Neither man spoke and Paul sat in amazement. He wasn't sure just what he had gotten into. In about five minutes the tram came to a stop in the old gold mine complex. What Paul observed next was even spookier as the trip went on. They exited the tram and proceeded to the doors ahead. These were the pneumatic pressure tubes that would take them up to the AFV operations hangar. Paul had never seen anything like this in his life. Bob opened the door and he and Paul got into the tube on the right. Bob closed the door and pressed the up lever. Quickly, quietly and smoothly the tube started up the shaft. It came to a stop at the 6000' level where Bob then opened the door and they stepped off into the AFV hangar.

"Well here we are Paul, home of your next adventure," Bob said.

Paul spied four AFVs in the hangar bay and his eyes lit up as he immediately realized this was one of the vehicles which had rescued him from space. He broke into a wide smile and said, "Holy shit Bob, and this is what you signed me up to fly? I have had dreams about these vehicles since my rescue. It was such a slick machine when I first saw it and I knew right away that it was something better than the shuttle I was in. I'm sure glad somebody slipped your business card in my space suit."

"I suspect your sponsor to be Larry Beck. He's the one who rescued you. You should know that his favorite place is the Antarctic and he loves McMurdo Sound. We figure that's why he set you down there," Bob said.

"Anyway, you figured it right, Paul. We surmised you would fit in very nicely into our operation since you already had a ride in one. That's why we asked," he said smiling.

"Bob I haven't been this excited about anything in many years. I have a thousand questions."

"In time we will answer all your questions. Let's go into operations I want to introduce you to our operations specialist, Choyce Proulx. Then we'll go back into the crew quarters, as I am sure some of the guys are here. We have six crews on duty so with only two AFVs out flying there should be four crews on standby. Oh yeah, these vehicles are called "Anti-gravity Flight Vehicles" or AFV-2s for short. This is a second-generation model."

They entered operations and Choyce was there controlling the two AFVs, which were out on a mission. He was a bear of a man with a bright red close-cropped beard. Bob began, "Hey, Choyce. I want you to meet a new pilot,"

Choyce turned and extended his hand. "This is Paul Anderson."

In his deep controller's voice Choyce responded, "Pleasure to meet you sir. Glad to have you aboard."

"My pleasure, Choyce, I'm glad to be here," Paul said.

Paul glanced around operations. He had seen a few control rooms in his day but this was obviously the most technologically advanced and up to date one he had ever observed. He turned to Bob and noted, "This looks like a great operation."

"We try our best, Paul," Bob responded. "Let's go back into the crew quarters and I'll introduce you to some of the crews." He turned to Choyce, "we'll talk later."

"Later, Bob," Choyce said.

Paul and Bob left operations and walked back through the hangar toward the crew quarters. Paul was in awe of the hangar and how it had been carved out of solid rock. He stared at the closest AFV and couldn't believe what he was seeing. It was something that was hard to soak in. After all the training and experience he had with NASA that just seemed antiquated compared to what he was observing.

They entered the crew quarters and there were some crewmembers in the kitchen having a snack while others were in the lounge sitting watching Fox News on TV. They all turned to look at whom Bob was bringing into their quarters.

"Hey guys I want you to meet our newest pilot. This is former astronaut, Paul Anderson," Bob said.

The crew broke into applause. They knew who this was as they had watched the interviews and news stories on TV during the past two months. Many of them jumped up and greeted Paul with great exuberance. They were pleased to have him on board because his reputation as a pilot and astronaut had preceded him.

"Paul, you need to know all these guys are former naval aviators, NFOs or Navy air crewmen. They have flown these vehicles for a lot of years are believe me they are all experts at what they do."

"I want you guys to know I will be forever grateful to

all of you for rescuing my crew and me from the Enterprise. At the time I wasn't sure who you were but you guys are the greatest," Paul said.

Paul took it all in and he was pleased as this was almost like coming back to a Navy squadron. There was plenty of camaraderie and he was anxious to become part of it. The crewmen all gathered around Paul asking him questions about his astronaut tour while he was inquiring about the performance parameters of the AFVs.

Bruce Fleming asked Paul, "Tell us how it is to fly the space shuttle, will you, Paul? None of us has any experience like that. Is it tough to fly?"

"Actually flying the shuttle is easy. I have about fifteen minutes at the controls. It has an elevator, rudder and flaperons and they operate just like other aircraft. Let me say the hard part is learning all the systems and emergency procedures. Selecting the correct computer instrument presentations and positioning the shuttle is some of the hard part. As a pilot I get to handle the controls and fly the aircraft only on short final for landing," he said. "How about you guys? How much flight time do you have in space, Bruce?" he asked.

"I have about seven hundred hours flying in space. We have an autopilot but I hardly ever use it. I personally fly the vehicle from liftoff to touchdown. We don't have too many emergency procedures or systems to remember. I think you'll find this vehicle as easy to fly as doing acrobatics in a high speed jet," Bruce said. "Our only worry is slowing down enough as the atmosphere gets thicker as we descend. Other than that it's balls to the wall."

After fifteen minutes of the banter Bob interrupted and asked Paul if he would like to have a tour of one of the AFVs. His eyes lit up and a big smile crossed his face. He thought someone would never ask. He followed Bob out onto the hangar floor. Number six was the closest so they walked over and Bob invited Paul to climb the ladder into the heart of the vehicle.

"Go ahead and take the command seat, Paul," Bob offered.

Paul did just that and was amazed at the simplicity in the instrumentation and controls of the vehicle. Bob sat in the systems control officers seat and asked Paul what he thought.

"What a machine," he said. "What kind of speed is this capable of and how high will it go?" he asked.

"Well, we have had one on the far side of the moon and I don't think anybody has had one up to its maximum but I think Mike Brenner has had it up to 30,000 mph. You'll learn all that when we start your orientation," Bob said.

"What's the origin of these vehicles and what's the history of this program, Bob?"

Bob began to tell the story of the AFVs, "First of all, there is no written history, for obvious reasons, but let me relate to you the history as I know it."

2

"The Beginning"

Kamas, Utah

Bob began to narrate the history.

"Do you remember the reports of the UFO crash at Roswell, New Mexico, in July 1947?"

It was a rhetorical question, so he continued. "You can read all the reports of the investigation and cover-up of the UFO crash if you wish as they are in our library. There had been only a passing mention of a possible alien body, but soon it was forgotten and those involved, including the nurse at the hospital, were transferred to England and have not been heard from to this day.

Another survivor from this crash was found days later wandering the desert. A small humanoid figure, he had been injured in the crash. He was found by a rancher and was turned over to the local sheriff, who in turn called the military authorities at Roswell AFB. The media was heavily monitoring the base, so the base commander had him taken to Sandia Base, New Mexico. He was isolated and taken care of by one doctor and one nurse. The doctor treated his superficial injuries and he was recovering nicely.

In the meantime President Truman, in September of 1947, established OPERATION MAJESTIC-12 as a TOP SECRET Research and Development/Intelligence operation, responsible directly and only to the President of the United

States. Operations of the project are carried out under control of the Majestic-12 (MJ-12) Group. It was established by special classified executive order of President Truman on 24 September 1947, upon recommendation by Dr. Charlton Evans and Secretary of the Navy, John Murray.

President Truman appointed the members of MJ-12 as follows:

- Adm. Henry G. Keselowski, CIA Director
- Dr. Charlton Evans, National Advisory Committee for Aeronautics
- Secy. John Murray, Secretary of the Navy
- Gen. Darian V. Gorka, Alaskan Air Command.
- Gen. Boyd L. Monk, U.S. Chief of Military Intelligence
- Dr. Uri Svetlonic, President of Johns Hopkins University in Baltimore, Maryland
- Dr. Buster Navarro, University of Michigan
- RADM Chester M. Bordelon, Director of Central Intelligence, Central Intelligence Group
- Mr. Gray Archer, Assistant Secretary of the Army in 1947
- Dr. Harry Hauser, theoretical astronomers and astrophysicists
- Gen. Robert C. Corker, Sandia Missile Base in New Mexico
- Dr. Albert Orindo, Marietta University, Executive Secretary of the Joint Research and Development Board under Dr. Charlton Evans

At Sandia Base, Captain Alex Headland, U.S. Navy, was assigned as the base psychiatrist. He was directed by MJ-12 to be liaison between the military and the alien. Captain Headland soon became a trusted person with the alien, whom he quickly found could speak rudimentary English. He determined that either the alien didn't understand what a name was or didn't understand the relationship the word "name" implied, so he nicknamed him Lieutenant Kilroy. Alex determined that Kilroy was indeed a very intelligent individual. His health was improving rapidly, and he wished to go home. Alex had not yet determined just where home was, although he learned it was outside our solar system. The ship he crashed had been a scout ship of limited range and was launched from near Mars. There was a command ship, although Kilroy was reluctant to talk about it. Alex did not allow any cameras or recorded conversation as this made Lieutenant Kilroy very comfortable. He and Alex had daily discussions about various subjects. During the discussions it was determined that Kilroy's civilization was exploring the Galaxy and our solar system was one currently being explored. Alex asked Kilroy to sketch pictures of his city or civilization. Alex had them classified top secret and forwarded them to the base commander for further processing. To this day, no one knows where those sketches are stored.

Kilroy asked about the whereabouts of his systems control officer. Alex finally found out after months of inquiring that he had been buried at the National Cemetery in Albuquerque, New Mexico. He told Kilroy that he was given full military honors and a headstone marked unknown for his name. Only a small group of people were aware of the burial.

Kilroy was a low-level flight officer, so he had no knowledge of any plan to make contact with earth's civilization. As it turned out, Kilroy was an aeronautical engineer in our terms and had much to do with designing his scout ship.

Alex, in conference with MJ-12, concocted a plan to develop this technology from Lieutenant Kilroy into actual scout ships for the United States. He worked with Kilroy, and they finally had a mutual agreement. In exchange for Kilroy's cooperation in assisting our engineers to build some scout ships, he would be allowed to build, or have built, a beacon or homing device so that his command ship could locate him and he could be rescued. The command ship was due to return in two years, so that was the time-frame available to the United States engineers in which to build the ships.

Kilroy's days were spent within the confines of three rooms in the base hospital and he longed for his home and also for his flying days. He expressed this to Alex, who comforted him and assured him that he would try to get things changed soon.

MJ-12 contacted Clarence L. "Sean" Jackson at Keystone Aviation's "Possomworks" and asked him to travel to Sandia Base in New Mexico to consult with Air Force people to work on a top secret project.

Sean flew into Albuquerque and was picked up by a staff car, which drove him out to the base. He arrived at the office of the Base Commander, Gen. Robert C. Corker, where he was briefed on the whole situation. After being briefed he was driven over to the base hospital, where he was introduced to Alex Headland, who tried to explain what the obstacles were. Sean was overwhelmed at this point and didn't really know what to expect.

Alex brought Sean into Kilroy's quarters and introduced them to each other. Alex had previously explained to Kilroy that Sean was coming, who he was and what to expect. As it happened, they immediately bonded as the common subject of aerodynamics and space flight flowed easily between them. Sean was very astute and realized what they were trying to accomplish. The difficulty, which was a barrier that had to be bridged, was putting the technology into working drawings for building the vehicles. After a couple of hours with Kilroy, Sean got through to him what he needed to do to help transfer the technology. He advised him that the best way would be for him to draw detailed pictures in three dimensions of each piece and section of the vehicle, and then Sean and his crew would translate them into working drawings for production. Sean thanked Kilroy, shook Alex's hand and departed, indicating to Alex he would be in touch.

Kilroy set out in a regimented fashion to produce the pictures Sean had requested. He worked diligently for six months, sometimes well into the night. Finally he had a stack of pictures that filled a large paper box. He advised Alex that he felt he had set down all that would be needed to manufacture the vehicles. The pictures, drawings and sketches were boxed and sent to Sean Jackson at the Possomworks. He reviewed them and discussed them with his engineers. His designers set out to produce working drawings for production of the vehicles.

After a few months, Sean scheduled a trip back to Sandia Base and arranged to see Lieutenant Kilroy. At their meeting, they discussed areas of questions which Sean had determined with his engineers. Kilroy was very helpful in clearing up the hazy areas, and after a few hours Sean was satisfied that he could now work through those difficulties.

The skin of the vehicle needed to be made of titanium. At this time, the Russians controlled the world's market. The CIA tricked the Russians by setting up a European front company under which they acquired all the titanium needed without the Russians being any wiser.

One of the big areas of discussion was the propulsion. The cyclotron generated the anti-gravity. They would be a type of particle accelerator in which charged particles accelerate outwards from the center along a spiral path. The particles are held to a spiral trajectory by a static magnetic field and accelerated by a rapidly varying (radio frequency) electric field. These charged particles would bombard the Lintz basalt and develop anti-gravity energy. This would occur around the edge of the vehicle. One dimension, which needed to be determined, was the size of the vehicle, which would determine the size required of the cyclotron.

A deposit of Lintz Basalt had been discovered in southern Ohio and its acquisition and refining would be the responsiblity of the CIA. Within a short period of time a delivery was made to Sandia Base and the material incorporated into the cyclotron development.

Sean asked Sandia Base to be involved, as they were experts in cyclotrons. MJ-12 determined that Sandia Base should build the cyclotrons based on the specs Sean and his engineers then calculated. At this point MJ-12 also determined that four vehicles would be built.

Another vehicle system that was going to be a challenge was the oxygen and pressurization system. Sean had never built one before, and Kilroy was extremely helpful in filling in the details. Between them they determined that the crew cabin needed to be maintained at 15.2psi. This would allow an air-oxygen mixture and keep the crew from being on 100% oxygen at all times. It also would make the crews more comfortable by not having their pressure suits inflated all the time when they were over 42,500'. One factor that came out of these revelations was that the pressure suits needed to be a closed system when flying above that altitude.

It is worthy to note that at first it was thought that Admiral Byrd had brought the first AFVs to Antarctica during Operation High Jump in 1948 but from later research it was found that this was not the case that they were brought in at a later date.

It was now into mid-1948 and Sean Jackson advised MJ-12 that they would be ready for flight-testing around January 1, 1949. MJ-12 was investigating how and where this would be accomplished. They would also need a well-qualified test pilot to do the testing. A search was made and finally MJ-12 came up with the name of Commander Howard Rutlege, U.S. Navy. Howard was a graduate of the flight test section of the Naval Air Test Center at Patuxent River, MD. He had flown every aircraft at Patuxent River and had done the high altitude pressure suit testing for the Navy.

A search for a site to assemble and test the vehicle was also in progress. The final site was the old auxiliary airfield at Groom Lake, Nevada. The first known use of the area was the construction in 1941 of an auxiliary airfield for the West Coast Air Corps Training Center at Las Vegas Air Field. Known as Indian Springs Airfield Auxiliary No. 1, it consisted of two dirt 5000' runways aligned Northeast/Southwest, Northwest/Southeast. The airfield was also used for bombing and artillery practices, and bomb craters were still visible in the vicinity of the runways. It was abandoned after the gunnery school at Las Vegas closed in June 1946.

There were two old WW-II hangars, which needed to be refurbished, and the roads to the base also needed repaving. It was determined that not too much outside renovation was wanted, so as to keep attention away from this base. The CIA took care of the base improvements and within two months they were ready to receive business.

Sean Jackson and his crew were ready to transport the sections of the four AFVs, and a manufacturing shop was set up in the two hangars at Groom Lake. Sean also requested that Lieutenant Kilroy be allowed to come to Groom Lake and help advise in the manufacturing and flight-testing. MJ-12 approved, as they knew he would not try to disappear. All they needed to do was keep him under wraps going out to Groom Lake. Captain Headland agreed to accompany Kilroy and arrangements were made to get him there. They would drive via a nondescript station wagon in civilian clothes and travel through Las Vegas

Commander Rutlege had already made his way out to Groom Lake. He would be the senior military representative on this project. MJ-12 had determined there would be little military support and presence. Uniforms would not be worn so as to keep it all low key. When Commander Rutlege arrived at Groom Lake, he discovered that a few of the barracks and government quarters had been refurbished and would be adequate for the operation. He, Alex Headland and Kilroy would reside in the old BOQ while the workers and engineers would live in the barracks. Arrangements were made for a kitchen and galley to feed all hands. Security was being handled by the CIA and was also kept low key.

A week after Commander Rutlege arrived, he was advised that Sean Jackson had dispatched four lowboy semis loaded with the parts for the AFVs. They would arrive within forty-eight hours, offload in the hangars and then depart. Sean Jackson arrived shortly afterward to supervise the construction. He began with setting up the assembly areas and putting together the jigs and fixtures needed. The workers would arrive in a couple of days and all would bring their own tools. A day later the internals for the ships arrived. Now the only holdup was the cyclotrons. Sean made a call to Sandia Base and was advised they would be on the road within a week. All the parts were coming together.

Alex noted a big change in Lieutenant Kilroy's demeanor. He seemed to be a lot happier and went about his daily life excited about what was happening. He inquired with Alex when he could begin construction of his homing beacon. Alex advised Kilroy that Dr. John Kats, who was a communications expert, had been recruited to help him with his beacon. Kilroy was very pleased.

The cyclotrons arrived and Sean Jackson was ready to begin manufacturing. He and Kilroy met daily on the work in progress and Kilroy inspected each and every step of the completed work.

John Kats arrived and was introduced to Kilroy. They went off in a secluded corner of the hangar and discussed the construction of the beacon. They both drew many graphs and charts and finally John came up with the frequency, at which the beacon needed to be set. They determined what wattage was needed, which was a big part of the design. Finally John indicated that he now had a handle on what needed to be done and how to build it. He told Alex he would need to go back to his lab at the University of Washington to acquire the parts and begin construction. John now had to design the schematic required to build the beacon. It was a radical design that amazed John in its simplicity once he put pencil to paper. The hard part would now be obtaining the electronic parts he needed. It would be a real challenge.

Alex relayed this info to Kilroy, who indicated he understood. John departed and indicated he would be in touch as soon as possible.

Within three months after beginning, Sean Jackson rolled out the first AFV.

3

"Test Flight"

Groom Lake, Nevada

Because of the secrecy factor, it was decided that all testing would be done at night or just before dawn and after dusk. All things were coming together readying for the first flight. ARO Corporation had been contracted to develop and manufacture the pressure suits for the AFV crew. The suit was a new design. It was a completely closed system requiring locking gloves and helmet. Howard had worked up to altitudes of 50,000' but the type of flying the AFVs were going to do required a different kind of full body pressure suit. They had not delivered any as yet, but Howard Rutlege had made a few trips to their Cheektowaga, New York, plant to offer advice on how to improve the new pressure suit. One of the specifications that was placed on them was that they had to protect the pilot from radiation. ARO Corporation developed a material interlaced with metallic threads. The bad news turned out was that it could not be dyed, so the suits turned out green. Thus was born "UFOs with little green men".

Howard Rutlege convinced MJ-12 that he was going to need more pilots as the program progressed, so he was given authority to recruit them. They would have to be carefully screened and selected. His first and obvious choice was his assistant at the Test Center who helped in the pressure suit testing. That was Lieutenant Gary Strahan. Gary had left the Test Center and was now serving in Fighter Squadron Eighty-Six (VF-86). His name was submitted to MJ-12 and within two weeks he was cleared. Howard made a trip to Naval Air Station Miramar, California, to meet with Gary.

He arrived in San Diego and rented a car for the trip out to Miramar, which was east out in the desert. He checked in to the base Bachelor Officers Quarters (BOQ) and left a message at the check-in desk for Gary to call him when he returned to the BOQ.

Gary returned to the BOQ after his squadron quit work for the day. It was about 4:30p.m., and he called Howard. Howard picked up and they agreed to meet at 6:00p.m. and have dinner in the officers' mess.

At 6:00p.m. they hooked up in the lobby of the BOQ. After exchanging greetings they wandered into the mess dining room. During dinner they renewed their old friendship and talked about times past at the Naval Air Test Center. After dinner Howard invited Gary to his room for more discussions. Howard had a bottle of Drambuie and he poured both of them a drink. They sat in Howard's lounge area and began to relax.

Gary started the conversation, "Howard, I know you didn't come to San Diego just to renew old times. What's up?" he asked.

"You're observation is very astute, Gary. I have an offer for you but with a caveat. We have a top-secret program I am working on. It is so classified that if you decide to join me you can never discuss this program with anyone, ever. Yes, I mean for the rest of your life. This program must remain unknown to anyone. That's all I can tell you other than it involves flying. What do you think, my friend?"

Gary sat up in his chair shifting himself from side to side. He appeared to be a little uncomfortable and finally spoke. "Howard, is that all you can tell me?"

"Sorry Gary, that's all I can say until I get your answer. You don't have to give me an answer tonight, but I'm leaving around 10:00a.m, tomorrow. Could you give me an answer by then?"

"That sounds good. Let me sleep on it and we can meet for breakfast at 7:00a.m. I need to get to the hangar by 8:30a.m. and I'll give you an answer tomorrow," he said

"Okay, Gary. Let's meet in the lobby at 7:00a.m. for breakfast," Howard said. "Good. I'm glad we got that settled."

They sat and enjoyed their drinks with more animated discussion. Gary was flying the F9F-2 "Panther," which was the advanced fighter for that time. Time passed quickly and about 10:30p.m. Gary told Howard he was beat, said his goodnight and went to his room.

Morning rolled around and both men were on time and met in the lobby at the designated hour. They greeted each other and strolled into the dining room for breakfast. After breakfast they moved to the lobby, where they found a quiet corner away from the other officers.

Gary opened the conversation, "I have made up my mind, Howard. I know you wouldn't ask me to do this if you didn't feel I was best qualified, so I won't let you down. You can count me in."

"That's great, Gary." He shook his hand. "You'll get orders in a few days. Don't worry what they say, you will be working directly for me. I can't tell you where you will be, but just follow the yellow brick road as we always say and you will eventually find me. I'm looking forward to having you on board."

They shook hands and Gary went on his way to the squadron while Howard went back to his room to pack, check out and travel back to Groom Lake.

Five days later orders arrived from the Bureau of Naval Personnel at VF-86 admin office. They called Gary in and he was told he was being assigned to the Air Force Materiel Command at Wright-Patterson Air Force Base – Project Grudge. The next day a message was received modifying those orders to report to the Field Office for Project Grudge at The Las Vegas Air Field, Las Vegas, Nevada.

Project Grudge was established with the main mission to publicly make UFO reports fiction, but it was also a cover for the AFV program. This was to try to keep any AFV sightings from taking on reality and causing further investigation. It would also help deemphasize any ideas that the United States was into this kind of research and being successful at it. Critics charged that, from its formation, Project Grudge was operating under a debunking directive, which was true: all UFO reports were judged to have prosaic explanations, though little research was conducted, and some of Grudge's "explanations" were strained or even logically untenable. In his 1956 book, Edward J. Booker would describe Grudge as the "Dark Ages" of USAF UFO investigation. Grudge's personnel were in fact conducting little or no investigation, while simultaneously relating that all UFO reports were being thoroughly reviewed. Booker additionally reported that the word "Grudge" was chosen deliberately by the anti-saucer elements in the Air Force. Of course, Howard Rutlege was doing no investigations for Project Grudge.

Within 5 days Gary was detached and was on his way

to Las Vegas. Meanwhile Howard was notified of his de-tachment and projected arrival date, so he took a vehicle and drove to Las Vegas to be there when Gary arrived.

Gary arrived at the base when expected and was di-rected to Commander Rutlege's office. Gary found the of-fice and knocked on the closed door. Howard directed him to enter and once again the friends greeted each other. He told Gary they had a two-hour drive ahead of them and would take two cars, since Howard had to return the staff car to Groom Lake. As they drove northwest out of Las Vegas, Gary was still wondering what he had gotten himself into. He and Howard hadn't had a chance to discuss the project. He deduced that it was probably a secret spy plane or something like that, but he was really anxious to learn what it was.

After two hours driving in the hot dusty weather they arrived at what Gary could only describe as a dilapidated rundown base. There was no fence and no security that was visible. Arrival was at the old, beat-up BOQ. Howard walked over to Gary's car and offered to help with his lug-gage. They both had their hands full when they walked into the building. Howard told Gary that his room was the second room on the right as they passed through the lobby. This place was really depressing, Gary mused. Howard could see Gary's mood and realized what he was thinking.

"Okay, Gary, here's the deal. Because of the secrecy involved with this project, everything is kept low key so as not to attract attention. Let's drop off your gear and take a trip down to the hangar. It's about time you learned what you signed up for."

"I'm for that, Howard. You've kept me in the dark long enough."

They dropped off the gear and headed out the door.

It was only a five-minute drive to the hangar and Howard pulled up in front of the first one. It was as dilapidated as the rest of the base. Surely can't be much of a project, Gary thought. They entered by a side door as the main hangar doors were closed. When Gary stepped inside the hangar his eyes opened as wide as saucers. He immediately affixed them to the first vehicle closest to them.

"Oh my God," he exclaimed. "What the Hell have I gotten into?"

"Gary, these are known as Anti-gravity Flight Vehicles. They are designed to be flown in near space. We have not even flight tested one yet but these two are finished and are awaiting testing. In the hangar next door two more are being built, so let's go over there and meet some of the people."

As they entered the hangar, Howard spotted Sean working on the floor and headed over to introduce him.

"Sean, I'd like you to meet one of our new pilots," Howard said. "This is Gary Strahan, Sean."

They both extended a hand and shook it. "Pleased to meet you, sir," Gary said. Sean responded in kind.

Howard continued. "Sean is the senior manager in charge of this project, Gary. If you need to know anything, Sean's the man."

About then Captain Headland, accompanied by Lieutenant Kilroy, descended the boarding ladder of the vehicle they were working on. Howard caught their attention, and they walked over to greet Howard.

"Alex, I would like you to meet Gary Strahan. Gary, this is Captain Headland. He is our flight surgeon, chief psychologist and liaison officer to our chief visiting engineer. Lieutenant, meet Lieutenant Kilroy," Howard said.

They shook hands all around and Gary was in shock.

He wasn't sure just who or what Lieutenant Kilroy was. All he knew was that he was humanoid, but not any familiar earthling he had ever encountered. Kilroy was about 5'4" in height, looked to weigh approximately 110 pounds, with sallow looking skin, and he was completely bald. He had a normal-looking face with blue eyes and a small nose and mouth. When he shook hands, Gary noted that he had five digits on his hands and motor skill almost like humans. The only difference Gary could see was that he had no ears. His hearing was through a small opening on each side of his head where normal humans had their ears. Gary sensed his capacity of knowledge and also that he had a sense of humor, although somewhat different from his own.

"We have been refining the cockpit area based on the suggestions of Kilroy," Sean said. "The space for the size of our pilots was too small, so we are moving the flight controls and pilot's seat a little further apart to accommodate larger pilots. We will need you to check this out after we get it done, Howard, and give us your input. If it is better, we will retrofit the first two vehicles. Also, we need to have a flight test planning session. How about 1:00p.m. after we get back from lunch, Howard?"

"That sounds like a good idea, Sean," Howard offered. "I'll bring Gary along. We'll be in your office at 1:00p.m. If you need us before then, we will be in my office. Thanks, Sean," Howard said.

Howard and Gary headed over to Hangar #1, where Howard's office was located. While they were making their way over, Gary asked, "What can you tell me about Lieutenant Kilroy?"

Howard started at the beginning and described how Kilroy had come to work with Captain Headland and joined the AFV program. About that time they arrived at Howard's office.

Gary commented, "Howard, everything about this program is unbelievable. I am trying to absorb it all, but my mind is overwhelmed. I can hardly get my thoughts around it. I guess I will get used to it. Just give me a little time."

"I understand what you're saying, Gary. Don't worry about it. You will get your mind wrapped around it and things will clear up for you. Meanwhile, there are a couple of things we need to do. The first one is that we need to study these vehicles and get all the info we can so we can set out a logical flight test program. Here's where I'm hoping our NATC experience will give us insight into what and how we need to approach this test program. One rule we have: any notes we make or papers we produce never leave this hangar. Now the second thing we need to do is find two more pilots. Let's think about it for a couple of days and then we can discuss it. Let's discuss what I know about this vehicle, so I can bring you up to speed."

Howard discussed the cyclotron and the theory behind it to generate anti-gravity. Next he covered the subject of magnetic slewing within the AFV to generate directional control. The one subject he wasn't sure about was inverted flight in a positive-G environment. He made a note to discuss it with Lieutenant Kilroy when he had a chance. He and Gary decided that hover tests and slight vertical flight as well as level directional stability should be tested first. New batteries called Ni-cads had been built based on input from Kilroy. The Exide Company had been consulted and drawings provided by Sean Jackson for this new technology. Another secret to be discovered was how to charge the batteries. The pilots would have to work with Kilroy to discover this also.

Gary's anthropomorphic data was copied from his medical record and sent to ARO Corporation for the fitting of his new pressure suit.

The first series of flights would not require wearing the pressure suit, so test planning went forward. The pilots met with Sean Jackson at 1:00p.m. as planned. The group determined that the anti-gravity system and magnetic slewing system would be tested on the first flight. This would require a vertical liftoff, remaining absolutely level, and then activating the magnetic slewing to check out the directional control. Lieutenant Kilroy had warned them that an ionized green gas layer would develop along the edge of the vehicle and not to be shocked by it. He explained that it was normal and was a bonus in that it protected the vehicle from excessive skin heating when operating at high speed within earth's atmosphere. They also discussed side tilting of the vehicle, which required more anti-gravity power to remain in level flight. Side tilting was induced by interrupting cyclotron flow in one area of the flow around the edge of the vehicle. Kilroy cautioned not to worry about the operation of the mechanisms but concentrate on learning how to fly it. That sounded like good advice, Howard thought, so that's what the two pilots did.

The first flight was scheduled for that evening. The pilots went back to their office in Hangar #1 and continued to discuss the flight profile. Howard made some notes and drawings on his kneepad that would be his reference material in the vehicle during the test. They took a break for dinner at the BOQ and then went directly back to the hangar. Flight was scheduled for an 8:00p.m. liftoff as it would be dark by then. Howard donned his normal flying gear and grabbed his helmet out of his locker. He and Gary strode down to the awaiting vehicle. He boarded, got strapped in, and Gary shook his hand and wished him luck. Gary climbed down the boarding ladder and, when he was clear, Howard retracted it. The ground crew signaled for the hangar lights to be turned off and flashlights broke out from all over. They gave Howard about 15 minutes to adapt to the darkness and he intensified the red lighting in the cockpit. A small vehicle called a tug attached to the vehicle began pulling it out of the hangar onto the tarmac. When they were some 100 yards out, the tug stopped and unhooked from the vehicle.

Howard initiated cyclotron startup and within seconds the instrument indicated normal operation. Electrical power indicated normal, so Howard decided it was now or never. The collective initiated anti-gravity. A lever was located at the side of the pilot's seat, similar to what was being developed for helicopters. Howard pulled up on it slightly and the vehicle jumped into the air. Boy, is this thing sensitive, he thought. He stabilized it at 60' off the deck and noticed the green layer of ionized gas building on the edge of the vehicle. It was not needed for this flight, so he hit the stealth mode switch in the cockpit and the gaseous layer disappeared. The vehicle was holding its position very steady, so he took one fast glimpse around the cockpit and noted that everything was normal. Next he activated the foot pedals used for magnetic slewing. He pushed the right pedal until his compass was approaching 090º. He then centered the pedals and the slewing stopped. The compass would always be operated in the free directional gyro mode. He was close to 090º but he could see that would take some practice to roll out exactly on heading. He activated the pedals a number of times, each time rolling out closer to his desired heading, and he could see he was making progress. One thing he did notice was that the vehicle was very quiet, making little or no noise in its operation. His next set of maneuvers entailed changing altitude. He first went up to 500' then down to 200'. He repeated that a couple of times and was more exacting each time. It looks like practice makes perfect, he thought.

His next maneuver would be what he called banking the vehicle. This would be accomplished with the control stick between his legs. He coordinated stick movement with collective so as to maintain his altitude. He pushed the stick over slightly toward his right knee and the vehicle banked right. With just a little up collective he was able to maintain his altitude. The vehicle moved sideways with no change of heading. This was completely different from a conventional aircraft. He quickly centered the stick and the vehicle stabilized in the side slipping position. He then reversed the stick towards his left knee and applied slight up collective. The vehicle began moving back towards level flight. He continued until he was in a steady left sideslip. When he was back in front of the hangar door he leveled the vehicle and came to a hover at 200'. He next lowered the collective and began a slow descent. He had not raised the landing gear, so he landed on the same spot where he had lifted off. The cyclotron was shutdown, all switches turned off and vehicle secured. He lowered the boarding ladder, unstrapped, and descended the ladder. He was greeted by a host of people. Gary was the first to shake his hand and congratulate him for a successful flight. Next were Lieutenant Kilroy, Alex Headland and most of the engineers working on the project.

They all walked back to the hangar while the ground crew rolled the vehicle into the hanger, shut the doors and turned the lights back on.

The people there met in Sean's conference room.

Howard took the podium and debriefed those present on the parameters of the flight. All-hands were pleased with the first flight and congratulations were handed out all around.

4

"Rescued"

Seattle, Washington

John Kats had been working on the homing beacon for Lieutenant Kilroy. There was no way it could be tested except to determine that it was powered up and sending a signal of some sort. No test equipment was available to receive a signal at that high of a frequency, which the homing beacon was designed to send on, because it was a new radical design which had never before been envisioned. John finished the work in his university laboratory and had the device loaded in his pickup truck and covered with a tarp. He departed Seattle, Washington, on a Saturday morning headed for Groom Lake. It would take him a day and a half to get there. His trip was uneventful and he arrived at Groom Lake on Sunday evening. When he arrived, he immediately found Kilroy and they began consultations as to where to set up the beacon and when to activate it. Power was needed, so a new electrical transmission line would have to be run out to the site of the beacon. Kilroy had determined that his fellow explorers would return to our solar system around June 1st, 1949. That was fast approaching and he wished for the beacon to be turned on by May 1st so as not to miss his opportunity to be rescued. This would give Howard and Sean about three months to glean all they could from Kilroy before they would be left on their own.

An 800' hill just north of Groom Lake was found to be a suitable site for the beacon, and base personnel put up the new power line to the top of the hill. They transported the beacon to the hill and mounted it about 8' above ground on the hilltop. An 8' chain-link fence was added to the site, just to keep any animals from disturbing the beacon. Finally, the electricians tested the power connections to the beacon and reported that everything was powered up.

The two AFV pilots continued their testing and familiarization flights. They were becoming comfortable in the vehicle and venturing out more and more, increasing their speed and altitude. Lieutenant Kilroy had cautioned them about not exceeding certain speeds at low altitudes, and they began marking those altitudes on the altimeter with redline tape to remind them not to exceed. It was decided that another altimeter measuring miles instead of feet would be needed, so the experts began working on a new gauge.

Scientific development of a new electronic device was being tested at the Bell Laboratories in 1947 but had not yet been adapted to a practical use. The scientists called it a transistor, designed to replace the vacuum tubes in radios. The engineers at Collins radio worked on a new radio using this device, and soon all AFVs had new radios, which were smaller, operated cooler and were more reliable. They were experimental, but worked beautifully.

On one particular test flight, Howard came back and reported that he had the AFV up to 4500mph and 96,000'. This was well beyond what any aircraft had ever achieved. The main thing which had been learned was east/west flight was coasting. During this evolution recharging the batteries using the earth's magnetic field was discovered.

Howard advised MJ-12 that testing was going so smoothly that the AFVs would soon be operational and he would need a few more pilots. MJ-12 authorized him to recruit two more pilots. Howard also recommended the need for ground personnel when they went operational, and MJ-12 also approved eight ground crewmen.

Howard and Gary conferred and came up with names for the recommended positions. The two pilots were Lieutenant Art Hurt, currently serving with Fleet Air Support Squadron 109 at Naval Air Station Jacksonville, Florida, and Lieutenant Bob Leanders, currently with Patrol Squadron 23 at Naval Air Station Patuxant River, Maryland. Four petty officer 1st class aviation machinist mates and four petty officer 2nd class aviation electronic technicians were recommended to MJ-12. They were all vetted and approved by MJ-12, so now it was a matter of recruiting them.

Sean Johnson and his crew finally finished manufacturing the four AFVs. Slowly the crew was sent back to the new "Possomworks", which was being built at Palmdale, California. Sean Jackson would return to Groom Lake in 1954 to rebuild the base and test the U1A spy plane.

The CIA was now left to man all the remaining positions at Groom Lake. The AFVs had proven themselves as a stable vehicle and all systems were reliable, so the remainder of the test program was left to the Navy pilots.

May 1st rolled around and the homing beacon was turned on. Alex Headland had learned all he could about Lieutenant Kilroy and his civilization. He put the information into a top-secret report and submitted it to the CIA. Kilroy advised everyone that should a ship come to rescue him it would be sudden and without warning, and he wanted everyone to know that he might just not be there one morning. He expressed his gratitude to everyone for saving his life and for their friendship. As best he could, he expressed how much he valued the relationship and trust in him. He returned their friendship in kind.

Alex questioned him on how his fellow explorers would be able to find him. Kilroy indicated that he had a personal electronic position indicator, which had been injected under his skin before they left his home planet and they would be able to pinpoint his position within 10' when they got closer to the base. They would also be able to provide him with a warning that they were close, by sending the probe in his neck a signal, which would vibrate and alert him as to their presence.

Kilroy continued to advise and critique the test program. Meanwhile, MJ-12 was developing plans for the use of the AFVs as intelligence-gathering vehicles. A study was underway to ascertain the kind of cameras needed to photograph objects the AFVs would be asked to study. Tape recorders were also being developed to record selected radio transmissions when the AFVs were flying.

It was after midnight when Lieutenant Kilroy knocked on Alex Headland's door. He awakened and glanced at his clock. It was 2:30a.m., and in the process of awakening he wondered who would be knocking at this time of night. He arose, opened the door and their stood Lieutenant Kilroy. He spoke to Alex and told him it was time. Alex immediately came out of his sleep-induced fog and knew what he meant. He asked if he wanted company down to the flight line. Kilroy said that would be great and he appreciated that. They walked silently the couple of blocks to the hangar, where Kilroy went to his locker and donned his space suit. They then walked out on the flight line to the edge of the concrete ramp, about three hundred yards from the hangar. Within minutes a silver disc seemed to appear out of nowhere and come to a stop in front of them. The disc lowered its landing gear and set down. They lowered their boarding ladder and Kilroy turned and shook Alex's hand and boarded the disc. Within seconds it lifted off and disappeared as silently and quickly as it had appeared. Kilroy was finally on his way home.

Howard made a trip to Naval Air Station Jacksonville, Florida, and Naval Air Station Patuxant River, Maryland, to invite Art Hurt and Bob Leanders to join the program. He also made various trips to other east coast venues as well as Naval Air Station Corpus Christi, Texas, to talk with the proposed enlisted crewmembers. All those vetted and asked accepted the invitation. Howard and Gary would rotate going into Las Vegas to greet the new arrivals and escort them out to Groom Lake. The reactions of the new members was the same as Gary's' when he was first introduced to the new vehicle and program. Soon all new crewmembers were on board. After a couple of weeks of indoctrination and on-the-job training, the enlisted crew took over the responsibilities of some of the civilians who then departed for parts unknown. Since there were no maintenance or pilot manuals, all learning was by touch.

The pilots spent many hours just talking over a cup of coffee on how to fly this new vehicle. Cockpit indoctrination on the controls and switches were emblazoned into each pilots mind. Repetition and testing of each pilot's knowledge of the cockpit was etched into their minds until there were no mistakes. After this thorough training was satisfactorily completed, Art Hurt was the first to solo one of the birds. Meanwhile, Howard was making the initial flights on the other three vehicles, which had as yet not been flown. Next it was Bob's turn in the barrel to solo.

Within days, all four vehicles were cleared for further flight testing and pilot indoctrination. The enlisted crew liked these vehicles, as they never had to be refueled and they were generally in an up status, except for the occasional instrument glitch or radio problem. The radio was used sparingly between vehicles, as Howard had not as yet determined the need for a base operations control facility. Art and Bob had made a trip back east to ARO Corporation for fitting of their pressure suits, and within weeks they were delivered to Groom Lake. Meanwhile, they were limited to flying the vehicle below 10,000'.

All four pilots assembled in Howard's office to discuss the progress of their program. To the man, they all agreed that the cockpits of the vehicles should be modified and a systems officer should be added to the flight crew. Howard contacted Sean at Keystone Aviation and asked for input. Was this practical without much modification?

Within weeks, Sean came back with a verbal report saying that it was practical and could be done for all four vehicles in the timeframe of one month. The pilots had agreed that the duties of the pilot were getting too time-consuming and they needed to concentrate more on flying the vehicle than manipulating the dials and switches.

Howard ran the idea past MJ-12, and within a month Sean showed up with drawings and parts ready to modify the vehicles. Howard then began the process of recruiting naval aviation crewmembers with Naval Observers wings. These men were the forerunners of the Naval Flight Officers now assigned as systems operators.

As the year wore on, all hands were becoming more and more proficient in their jobs. MJ-12 had determined the specifications for the new cameras, and Fairchild Camera was given the contract to build four cameras. Sean

Jackson had been contacted and given the specs and he and his engineers were tasked with modification drawings for the vehicles, to accommodate the camera. The aviation technicians for each vehicle were sent to Fairchild Camera for training. Fairchild Camera was told only that this camera was for a new test aircraft which was being developed for the U.S. Government.

After the first of the year, the cameras were picked up at the factory by a couple of naval officers in uniform, who signed for them and delivered them in person to Groom Lake. It was generaly assumed they were CIA agents posing as naval officers.

A few days later, a team of civilians from Sean Jackson's shop arrived at Groom Lake and began modifying the AFVs to accommodate the new cameras. The aviation electricians worked closely with Sean's people so they were knowledgeable about all facets of the installation, operation and maintenance of the camera and vehicle systems. After installation, the technicians trained the systems operators on the system and camera operation. The camera had been mounted in the vehicle under the cockpit, centered on the bottom skin. A sliding port had been installed under the camera and was activated by the systems operators with a switch in the cockpit. Right next to it was another switch, which activated the camera. The film was a 120mm high speed, black and white, developed by Kodak especially for this camera.

The crews began testing the efficiency of the cameras, making flights at various altitudes and speeds, taking pictures of some of our military installations. The film was then downloaded and, after being sealed in a light-free container, was mailed to a specified address where it was picked up and then processed by the CIA. The main reason for filming military bases was that the pictures could be compared to what was actually there, a known factor. After months of testing, the cameras were declared to be highly satisfactory and the pilots had narrowed down the best parameters for picture taking.

The first operational mission was flown on July 1, 1950, when Howard Rutlege and Jason Bluestone made a reconnaissance flight over the Korean Peninsula, documenting the status and preparedness of the North Koreans to execute the war they had just started. On their return to base, the film was offloaded, rushed to Las Vegas and flown by P51 aircraft to Andrews Air Force Base, Maryland, for further shipment to McLean and the CIA.

Later that year, routine flights were being flown over the Soviet Union, documenting their air bases and seaports for military action and equipment. Electronic counter-measures equipment on the AFVs was routinely picking up the Soviet radar, but no aircraft or missiles were capable of reaching the altitudes and speeds at which the AFVs were operating.

About every six months, new technology, which was in development, was installed and tested. The crews were also better trained in visual observation, and debriefing on all flights required a secure telephone call to an intelligence officer at CIA describing what they had observed over the target. Soon visual observations were required over the target area and low altitude flights were authorized to obtain better intelligence information.

Arizona Desert

While driving through the Arizona desert with two meteorologists, James E. McDonald spotted an unidentified flying object none of the men could readily identify. Though a rather unspectacular sighting of a distant point of a green light, this sighting spurred McDonald's interest in UFOs. At this point in his life, McDonald was senior physicist at the Institute for Atmospheric Physics and professor in the Department of Meteorology, University of Arizona, Tucson.

McDonald had seen an AFV returning to Groom Lake from a spying and intelligence mission. He quietly began investigating past UFO reports in Arizona, and he had also joined NICAP, then the largest and most prominent civilian UFO research group in the nation. Given his training in atmospheric physics, McDonald was able to examine UFO reports in greater detail than most other scientists, and was able to offer explanations for some previously unexplained reports.

There were quite a few AFV sightings in the reports he studied and reports of his research reached MJ-12. The people at Groom Lake knew the days were numbered because McDonald seemed to be closing in on tracing the sightings back to that venue. MJ-12 made the decision to move the AFVs to a more secure base and called a conference to discuss options.

The conference was convened at the Natural Bridge Hotel & Conference Center on the Blue Ridge Parkway about sixty miles west of Washington, D.C. All members of MJ-12 were present and included Captain Headland. Many venues were considered and after much haggling with the military service members, each trying to protect their interests, Captain Headland prevailed and the planning began for relocation. The International Geophysical Year was scheduled for the next year. The IGY encompassed eleven Earth sciences: aurora and airglow, cosmic rays, geomagnetism, gravity, ionospheric physics, longitude and latitude determinations (precision mapping), meteorology, oceanography, seismology, and solar activity and included scientific study from bases in the Antarctic. The IGY task force established the Office of Polar Programs (OPP) under control of the United States Antarctic Research Program (USARP). These two agencies were placed under the auspices of the National Science Foundation (NSF).

Once again based on Captain Headland's influence, he convinced MJ-12 that an Antarctic base for the AFVs would result in better secrecy, easier resupply and the ability to clandestinely recruit new pilots and crewmen from the navy. Since Operation Deepfreeze would support the IGY in Antarctica a new squadron was formed at Naval Air Station Patuxant River, Maryland, designated Antarctic Development Squadron Six (VX-6). Commander Rutlege was transferred to head the Office of Polar Programs, where he would also manage the AFV program. His replacement in the AFV program was Commander Gene Morgan, who was also named as the first commanding officer of VX-6.

Groom Lake, Nevada

Early the next year, word was received that Sean Jackson had designed a new aircraft, which was going to need secret testing. He was directed to rebuild the base at Groom Lake and develop it for his base. This meant that the Project Grudge machines would need a new base of operations. This revelation fit perfectly into MJ-12s plans. Since the base in Antarctica had not yet been completed it was determined that the machines would be temporarily based on Johnston Atoll which was located 880 miles southwest of Honolulu, Hawaii. The CIA Set up a secret base there and the AFVs were relocated. Commander Morgan made a trip to Johnston Atoll and checked out in the AFV, and then moved on to Naval Air Station Patuxant River to assume command of VX-6. Captain Headland, as well as the AFV pilots and crewmen were all transferred to VX-6.

Things moved very quickly with the completion of bases in Antarctica. Brocton Station was built by the CIA and was ready to receive the AFVs. This new phase of flying AFVs then became know as Project Galaxy.

Three AFVs were transferred to Brocton Station when the squadron deployed to New Zealand from Naval Air Station Patuxant River. With Gary Strahan as pilot in command and Art Hurt as copilot, they flew an R4D-8 to New Zealand via Johnston Atoll. While there, they ferried the AFVs to Brocton with number four ferrying the pilots back to Johnston Island. After they arrived at McMurdo Station, Antarctica, and began flying into Brocton they would ferry the remaining AFV from Johnston Atoll and the CIA would close the Johnson Atoll Base down.

5

"Warm Sensation"

Kamas, Utah, Present time

Bob Avery continued his history of the AFV program. He explained Project Galaxy to Paul Anderson and how it finally came to Utah. He briefly described how it had become Project Enterprise temporarily when they had geared up to rescue Paul and his crew from space. They were now back on line as Project Galaxy.

When Bob finished, Paul just sat there and shook his head. What a storied history and program he had entered into. He had a few questions for Bob as they sat and finished their coffee. Paul was pleased that he had made the decision to pursue the business card. He asked Bob what was next in his indoctrination. Bob indicated that they would need to order a pressure suit for him but training-wise they would send him to Flight Safety in Phoenix, Arizona, for G4 training and FAA qualification. He explained to Paul that they fly the G4 single piloted with the exception that the NFOs were trained in copilot's duties and overwater navigation. NFOs could do everything except fly the aircraft. Paul would also need to take an FAA physical before his license would be complete for the type of operations they were doing so an appointment needed to be made with Doc Kealey at the compound's medical clinic. Bob also said when they got back to headquarters he would turn him

back over to Bill Springer and get him assigned base housing.

Paul returned to Houston to pack up his household
goods and wife Margie for relocation to Kamas, Utah. Upon
arrival back at headquarters, he and Margie were issued
security passes as well as windshield stickers for their cars.
They picked up the keys to their new house from the housing office and within a couple of days had received their fur-
niture and were settling into their new digs. They had been
assigned one of the two bedroom houses on Kennedy Drive.
Bob Avery had named all the streets after famous United
States Navy aircraft carriers.

Some of the other wives living in the housing development swarmed around the new kids on the block, wel-
coming them and generally making them feel at home.
Paul commented to Margie, who agreed with him, that this
was just like checking into a Navy squadron. They both
were feeling part of the new unit and were beginning to
enjoy it.

Paul was assigned a cubicle on the second floor of
the headquarters building, which was shared by all assigned flight personnel. He slowly began meeting some of
the people he would be working with in the future. In a
short while he received his orders to report to Flight Safety
in Phoenix, Arizona, and so he kissed Margie goodbye and
departed for his three weeks of training. When he finished
he was qualified as pilot-in-command in the G4, G5 and
G550 Gulfstream aircraft.

Upon his return he needed to check in with Larry
Beck at Hangar 512. Each morning a set of company helos
would depart the helo pad next to headquarters and transport those crewmembers required to be at the hangar that
day and return them in the afternoon. During his orienta-

tion he was briefed on the 6-week cycle under which all hands worked: Two weeks flying the G4, two weeks flying the AFV and two weeks off.

His first two weeks back he spent at headquarters learning the operation. Now he was ready to fly the G4 so he boarded the morning helo flight to the Salt Lake City airport. When he arrived he made his way to Larry Beck's office. Larry was in and greeted Paul with great warmth. They had not seen each other since they had gone through the A4 Skyhawk Replacement Air Group at Naval Air Station, Lemoore, California, some 25 years earlier. They relived old times and then Larry got down to the current task at hand. He told Paul there would be a G4 available later in the day and he would take him out flying and get him current so he could begin to take over some of the flights they had scheduled.

That afternoon Paul and Larry took one of the G4s out and made three landings, which satisfied the FAA for currency. They returned to Larry's office and debriefed the flight. It was a piece of cake for Paul and Larry indicated he was cleared for carrying passengers. Larry also told Paul he would put him on the same rotation schedule as his so they could get him oriented and checked out as soon as possible.

Paul was assigned a locker in the pilot's locker room at the hangar so he could store any flight gear he needed for flying the G4. He also met again with John Walker who gave him the name of the local clothing store which would outfit him with flying uniforms. Paul went downtown and found the Belk's store at the downtown mall. He located Jesse McCain in the men's clothing department and was fitted with three black captains double-breasted suits with the four silver stripes on them, and obtained three white shirts and a black tie to fill out the ensemble. He was also fitted with two pairs of black corfam shoes and six pairs of black socks. They were all charged to Omega Aviation. They were altered while he waited so he left the building all checked out with his uniforms.

He checked back in with Larry and indicated he was all set with his uniforms. Larry issued him his captain's flight bag containing all the necessary flight planning aids and an aircraft handbook.

Larry asked Paul if he could take a flight on Friday, which was two days away. It would be a stop in San Francisco, California, to pick up three passengers, fly to Honolulu, Hawaii, wait for them overnight and then fly them back to San Francisco. Paul said he could handle that so Larry had him put on the schedule. He also scheduled him with Bill Springer as his flight observer/copilot.

Paul left of Friday and returned Saturday on time without a hitch. He would fit right into the operation. During his two weeks he flew a number of domestic flights and one other international flight.

The next two weeks turned out to be a challenge and for Paul would be interesting. On Monday the six crews reported to headquarters. Slowly they filtered into the transportation system up the mountain and relieved those six crews going off duty for two weeks. Larry Beck was the most experienced AFV pilot and it would fall on his shoulders to check Paul out in the AFV. They went up the tube together and began their discussion on the AFV systems and flying it. There were a couple of immediate missions over Afghanistan and Larry assigned the pilots and observers to fly them. He and Paul discussed the systems for hours on end. Paul was very astute and understood the physics and engineering of the systems after he and Larry went into the details of the machinery. Discussion then moved to the emergency procedures and Paul, when quizzed, passed with flying colors. He was ready for his solo flight except his pressure suit had not yet arrived from ARO Corporation. They decided he could fly his solo and orientation flight as long as he remained below 10,000'. Larry briefed him on the procedures to be used and Choyce briefed him on controller's protocol. He was reminded that communications with base operations whose call sign was "Whisper" should never include the word saucer. Flying fighters, his personal call sign had been "Shark" but he decided to change it to "Blackjack". He never did explain the origin and nobody asked why.

Paul's solo flight was scheduled for early evening. He donned his flight suit and manned the AFV. Joe Grenda was assigned as his systems operator. He completed the appropriate checklists and then asked Joe to notify Choyce they were ready for launch. The bright lights in the hangar area had been dimmed and Paul powered up the cyclotron. The claxon sounded in the hangar complex and the south hangar opened. Paul slid the vehicle out on the small castors attached to the AFV landing gear. When he was clear and out on the pad he added lift off input and the vehicle rose from the landing pad. His objective on this flight was to come to a hover at 20', practice slewing and then bank the vehicle. After he mastered those skills he was cleared to proceed to 10,000' and accelerate to a speed not to exceed Mach 1. His route for the night was Reno direct to Colorado Springs and return to the AFV base. It would take about thirty-seven minutes.

Choyce tracked his progress and was satisfied with his track and speed. Approaching ½ mile from base Paul began slowing his vehicle and they called base.

Joe Grenda called into operations, "Whisper base this is Blackjack for landing, over,"

"Blackjack cleared for landing," Choyce answered.

Choyce activated the south hangar door. The hangar lights were dimmed and claxon sounded warning all-hands to remain clear.

Inside the AFV Paul was scanning his CRT instruments and screens. He used his video cameras to position his vehicle above the pad as he came to a hover. He slowly lowered the vehicle as the landing gear came down and locked and indicated three green lights in the cockpit. With the video cameras in infrared mode the pad was lit up like daylight. He soon touched down as slick and smooth as possible, then slid the AFV back into its original spot in the hangar. Larry had been in operations tracking the flight with Choyce and was now awaiting Paul on the hangar deck. As soon as the AFV was clear of the hangar door, the claxon sounded and the hangar door quickly closed, hangar lights brightened and as Paul came to a stop he shutdown the vehicle. The boarding ladder extended and soon Paul was descending the ladder.

Larry greeted him and he had a wide smile on his face.

"I guess you enjoyed yourself," Larry said.

Paul was still pumped up about his flight, "Larry, that was the most exciting flight I have had in a long time. What a vehicle. It is nothing like anything I have ever flown. I can't wait to get it up to altitude and high speed."

"You'll get your chance as soon as your pressure suit arrives. How did your solo flight go?" Larry asked.

"After I preformed the initial maneuvers, which by the way, proved to be very sensitive to control input, it was a blast. The vehicle accelerated rapidly and turned on a dime. My instrument scan was a little slow but as I fly it more I will get used to it and scanning will improve. My space positioning system (SPS) was something new but what a great system. The combination of earth positioning and vertical information along with speed presentation on the same screen was quite helpful. I can see how valuable it can be at faster speeds and higher altitudes. Getting used to the video cameras is another challenge. The infra-red feature is outstanding and a landing without it appears to be almost impossible."

"As you get used to these features you need to make a few landings without them. Use your forward-looking radar (FLIR) and learn to judge the visuals ahead of you as you approach the pad. That way if you should lose them you can still land the vehicle safely on the hangar pad. Go ahead and get changed and I will meet you in the kitchen," Larry pointed out.

"Roger that, Larry. I still have a few more questions. See you in a few minutes,"

They met in the kitchen, poured a couple of cups of coffee and continued Paul's debriefing. Larry indicted Paul would need two more flights but only after he received his pressure suit. He needed one high speed, high altitude flight before he could be turned loose on an operational mission.

Omega Headquarters

Bob Avery along with John Walker flew one of the G4s to Charlotte, North Carolina. They were to meet with the CEO of World Security Associates, USA, Inc. That company was the main investor in Omega Aviation and would have the final say on swapping the G4s for G550s. The flight was beautiful. The weather had been mostly clear with visibility unlimited. The countryside was gorgeous and the flight was less than three hours. On arrival they flagged down a taxi at the airport which took them over to World Security Associates, USA, Inc. headquarters. Upon entering the building they were checked in at security in the lobby and cleared to the 7th floor where the CEO's office was located. As they entered the office they were greeted by the receptionist who said:

"Good Morning, gentlemen. Please go right in. Mr. Murphy is waiting for you."

Phil Murphy had established this company as a cover for his CIA activity. Over the years he had been so successful in winning over foreign dignitaries and his services were so important that the CIA had given him the green light to build up the business. Phil had expanded so successfully that the company now employed over 115,000 people worldwide. This was how CIA covered their tracks on investments and financial support for Omega Aviation and the AFV program.

"Good Morning, Phil," Bob said and extended his hand. "This is John Walker, our Vice President of Operations for Omega. He is the one who prepared the proposal to swap the G4s for G550s,"

Phil turned, "Good morning, Bob. Pleased to meet you, John. I've heard only good things about you,"

John shook hands with Phil. "Pleased to meet you sir," he said.

"Come, have a seat. Would anyone care for a beverage and a sweet roll?" Phil asked.

John thought about it for a second, "I'll have a cup of tea if you have it, sir."

"We can handle that, John." Phil glanced over. "What about you Bob?"

Bob piped up, "I'll have some coffee, Phil. You know old Navy habits die hard."

Phil activated the intercom. "Lauren, how about two coffees and one cup of hot tea?"

"Coming right up, sir," Lauren responded.

"I presume you flew in on one of your G4s, Bob. How was the flight?" Phil asked.

"We had a great flight. Weather was gorgeous and air traffic fairly light until we got into the Charlotte area. No delays though so it went quickly," Bob offered.

Lauren entered the room with the coffee and tea along with a plate of sweet rolls. She placed them on the coffee table in front of them. "Can I get anything else, sir?" She asked Phil.

"No, I think we are fine for now, Lauren. Will call if we need anything. Thanks."

"I have read your proposal Bob and my CFO has reviewed the financial structure you proposed for the swap of the G4s. Your bottom line for last fiscal year was about $27M. Since we own the G4s outright with no financial encumbrances it looks like we can recoup enough on the sale of each one that we can swing the purchase of the G550s. I presume you are still looking for used G550s as replacements?" Phil said.

John added, "Yes, sir. We will be looking for used G550s as replacements for our G4s. There are plenty of them available and I am sure we can, with careful buying, not have to go into debt for the new airplanes."

"That sounds like a plan we can all live with, Bob. Let's put it into motion. How long do you expect it will take to replace all the aircraft, John?" Phil asked.

"Sir, we had planned to do that over the next nine to twelve months," John said.

"I like that idea, John. It looks like we are good to go with that plan. Thanks for all your hard work on this thing.

Phil put down his papers, "We were going to go over your financial sheet for the coming year, Bob, but my CFO is on a trip to St Martens so I think if you just leave me a copy I will get it too him and then if he has any questions he can contact your CFO."

"That sounds good," Bob said. He retrieved the report from his briefcase and handed it to Phil.

"Now what are you guys doing for lunch?" Phil asked.

"We had not planned that far ahead, Phil. What have you in mind?"

"I thought we could order and have lunch in my private dining room," Phil offered.

"That sounds good to us," Bob responded.

They all arose and walked across the hall to Phil's private dining room.

Before lunch started, Phil broached a proposal with Bob.

"Bob," he began, "We have a fleet of five airplanes based here in Charlotte. We are not too satisfied with their customer service and maintenance on them. My proposal to you is would you be interested in setting up a satellite branch of Omega Aviation here in Charlotte and taking over managing our planes and pilots? We will provide the investment capital necessary to get it up and running but you would be the parent company and manage it completely."

"Wow that's a tall order to make a snap decision on," Bob said.

John chimed in, "Sir, I know I can speak for Bob. That's a fine offer you have made and I know we would like to possibly take it on but give us a couple of days to discuss it back at headquarters and then get back to you with a decision."

Bob offered, "I believe there are some pros and cons we need to weigh before we can come to a final answer, Phil."

"That's okay our contract will be up in five months and if we are going to do it we need to come up with a plan before then," Phil responded.

"Now for some serious business. What would you guys like for lunch? I am having the split pea soup and a Ruben sandwich."

"I see you have tomato soup so I think I will have that and a Ruben sounds good," John said, still looking over the menu.

"That sounds like a good selection, John. How about adding that to our order, Phil?" Bob said.

Phil swung around in his chair and keyed the intercom. He placed the order with the kitchen. Soon the three of them were enjoying their lunch.

6

"First Flight"

Enroute to Salt Lake City

Bob and John had finished their lunch with Phil and then departed Charlotte headed back to Salt Lake City. John broke the silence.

"Phil seems like a good boss."

"Yeah he's a great boss and businessman, John. He has always looked after our needs. I'm glad we had a chance to meet and talk with him about the G550 upgrade. If we need a little extra investment capital I know he will provide it. When we get back you can start looking for used G550s to buy and we will go after those you deem worthy of pursuing," Bob said.

"I already have two G550s I want to look at. One is in Tacoma, Washington, and the other Omaha, Nebraska. I will work my inspection into a regularly scheduled trip so we don't pay extra for any added flight time," John said.

"What did you think of Phil's proposal?" Bob asked.

John thought for a moment, "I like the idea but we need to get some legal advice and discuss the pros and cons."

"Yeah, it's not like we need more work," Bob said.

"That's one of my cons actually," John responded.

"Let's get together later in the week with Bill Grammercy and discuss it before we ask for legal advice," Bob suggested.

They flew on to Salt Lake City and chatted about crew training and maintenance. Bob made an instrument approach as he needed the practice. He had been flying less and doing more paperwork so it was great to get into the air for a change.

They returned to the hangar just in time to catch the helicopter headed for headquarters in Kamas. After they arrived, John went off to his quarters and Bob went up to his office.

He picked up the phone and called his chief fiscal officer (CFO). Bill Gammercy had been the CFO since they established Omega Aviation. Bill was a close friend of Bob's as well as Larry Beck's and had been a navigator when they were all in the Navy attached to VXE-6. Bill had been a systems officer in the AFV program but was slowly tapering off in his flying since his job as CFO became more complicated and important. As the company grew so did Bill's job. Bob asked Bill to come down to his office for a conference.

Bill soon arrived and walked into Bob's office.

"What's goin' on Bob?"

"I just returned from Charlotte, Bill. John and I had a meeting with Phil Murphy concerning the G550 upgrade proposal. He wholeheartedly approved of our plan and gave us the go-ahead. I want you to work closely with John so things go smoothly. He will make all the decisions on which airplanes we buy but I want you to review all upcoming aircraft purchases. You know how glitches can complicate transactions and liens really screw things up sometimes. I don't foresee us having any trouble selling our G4s since we own them outright, with no strings attached. Phil also proposed that we establish a presence in

Charlotte and take over maintenance and management of his five airplanes. It is something we need to have a meeting about. It could be a subsidiary corporation or just a branch office. It is something we need to consider and after we meet we need to get some legal advice before we act. Phil says he will finance the business," Bob said.

"I'll get together with John and discuss the upcoming purchases and how we will handle them. He and I have always worked well together so I don't see any problems. Just let me know on the other issue and when you want to have that meeting," Bill said. "By the way how did it feel to get out and up in the blue for a change instead of pushing papers?"

"Brought back old memories of us pushing those C-130s around the sky. I had a good laugh thinking about us getting lost on the way to Antarctica. Do you remember when Sargent Teal was the senior navigator and he tried to kill us by getting us lost?" Bob said.

"Yeah, Bob, I remember getting to our ETA for Mc-Murdo and we didn't even have the continent on radar. You told the other Aircraft Commander, Brewer Bell, you were going to check the navigators log and chart and if we were still lost he should climb to 42,000' and shutdown numbers 1 and 4 engines. Your astute review put us on a heading of 045ºg and as we started to climb I remember the tacan locked onto McMurdo and it was dead ahead of us. We had a few puckered penguins on board that day," Bill remarked.

"Christ, Bill. You just jogged the old memory. What the Hell was that Lieutenant Commander's name who gave me such a fit?" Bob asked.

Bill chuckled, "Let me see. I think that was Clyde Hammerfield. You sent him aft with Mike Brenner to count the Mae Wests and told Mike to punch him out if he whined about anything. Yeah, he kept saying, 'We're gonna' die'."

"Yeah and right after that I made a zero zero landing at McMurdo, in the whiteout landing area and all the time he was still screaming, "We're gonna' die!" We landed four-teen miles from the airfield and then had to taxi back to maintenance control. Ground radar picked us up about three miles from the field and literally gave us a ground approach. That's still the world's record for the longest air-craft taxi."

They both had a big laugh. Now it was funny. Back then it was a life and death situation.

"I gotta' get back to my office, Bob, I am expecting a call from one of our vendors and I don't want us to run outta' toilet paper, ah make that bathroom tissue." Bill was kidding as usual but had an important call so he excused himself and left Bob to do his paperwork.

Paul Anderson was coming off his two weeks no duty. He reported in early Monday morning where he met up with Larry Beck and some of his other teammates. They quickly made their way through the security doors and boarded the tram up the mountain to the tubes. Larry and Paul boarded one of the tubes and headed up to the base. Larry told Paul his pressure suit had arrived and that they would check it out first thing. Jack Shepard greeted them as they were getting off the tube. Paul had not met Jack, so he in-troduced himself. Larry told Jack they were going to check out Paul's pressure suit in the chamber and then would schedule him for a high speed, high altitude training flight. Jack indicated to Larry that they were flying round the clock over Afghanistan. There was a big offensive going on in the eastern mountains and very little intelligence was available except what the AFVs were collecting. The six

AFVs would get a workout during this tour but Larry said there would be time for Paul to complete his checkout. Jack spaced out the flights. During every four-hour time period an AFV would need to make at least 2 passes over the target area and then climb to a very high altitude and transmit its data to Langley. It wasn't too hectic a schedule, as each crew would fly once every day. There was a little overlap, as Jack always wanted an AFV on station ready to collect data.

Larry and Paul made lunch in the crews' quarters and sat down to discuss what they needed to do that afternoon. After lunch Paul went to his locker where he found his pressure suit. He donned it and he and Larry made their way to the pressure chamber. Paul entered the chamber, took a seat and after attaching his suit to the oxygen supply, mounted his helmet and slipped on the locking gloves. This run in the chamber was to determine that all valves and connections were working properly and the suit would be safe for high altitude flight. Presently he was breathing ambient air. Larry manned the control station and made contact with Paul.

"How do you read me, Paul?" Larry asked.

"Loud and clear," he responded.

"Okay, Paul, I am going to run the chamber up to 10,000' and level off," Larry said. He adjusted the controls on the chamber and the mechanism began reducing the pressure in the chamber. When the altitude gauge read 10,000' Larry stabilized the chamber.

"We're stable at 10,000', Paul. Go through the 10,000' check," Larry said.

"Roger that. Suit altimeter reads 10,000'. All normal," Paul reported.

"Roger. Standby. Going up to 20,000'," Larry said.

Paul gave Larry thumbs up as they could visually see each other through the observation window at the control station. Larry leveled the chamber at 20,000'.

"We're now stable at 20,000'. Complete your 20,000' check," Larry directed.

"Roger, Larry. Suit altimeter reads 20,000'. Oxygen now 100%. All valves appear normal," Paul said.

"Switch your suit to pressure mode, Paul," Larry directed.

Paul switched the suit and it immediately began to pressurize. Within a minute the suit had brought the simulated altitude in the suit down to 8000'. Paul reported his altitude to Larry.

"Let's hold our altitude there for five minutes, Paul, and ensure that nothing is leaking," Larry said.

"That sounds good to me, Larry. Everything in the suit seems to be functioning properly. Oxygen flow appears normal and suit pressure is steady," Paul said.

After five minutes with the chamber steady at 20,000' Larry advised Paul, "Going up to 50,000' now, Paul. Monitor your systems closely and you know the drill if there's any question on any system advise me and we will drop the chamber rapidly," he said. "We are now steady at 50,000'. We will remain here for ten minutes to ensure the suit is functioning properly."

"Copied that, Larry. Suit is holding 8000' on the altitude. Suit 15.2psi, oxygen flow appears normal at 100% mixture," Paul reported.

On his panel Larry could tell by the instruments that the suit was holding pressure steady and not leaking. That was the main reason for this safety check of the suit functioning properly.

After ten minutes Larry came on the intercom once

again. "Everything here checks out okay, Paul. Standby we are going back down to base elevation of 6,110'."

It took about four minutes to return the chamber to 6,110' and equalize the pressure in the chamber with the ambient air. Larry came around and opened the chamber door and helped Paul exit the chamber. He had already removed his faceplate and was in the process of removing his gloves. Paul's first comment was, "Just like old times, Larry. The suit checked out perfectly."

"Yeah, that was a textbook run, Paul. Go ahead and get out of that thing and I will meet you in the quarters. I am going to check with Jack and see how we're doing on our recon flights."

Paul made his way to the locker room while Larry went over to operations to talk with Jack. Only one AFV was active so Jack was in kind of a relaxing mode while monitoring the flight and its systems. The two of them agreed on a flight for Paul at about 8:00p.m. Jack would schedule Tom Harger to fly with Paul along with George Everet as their engineer. Tom could explain all the sensing devices and technical equipment better than most and this would bring Paul up to speed quickly. Jack convinced Larry they should make it an operational flight as well as a training flight. A requirement had come up to photograph the island of Mindanao in the southern Philippines as there was a suspected buildup of Abu Sayyaf Taliban affiliated rebels there.

Larry met Paul in the crews' quarters and they discussed the chamber run. They both agreed it was routine and moved on to the planned evening flight. Tom Harger had joined them at the kitchen table and they began discussing the evening flight. Tom laid out the flight profile, which would take them out across the Pacific Ocean straight to Mindanao and return. Larry recommended taking the AFV up to over 300,000' and accelerating to about 5,000mph or Mach 9. This would give Paul a good feel of how the vehicle responded at high speed and altitude. Approaching Mindanao they would drop down to 5,000' and slow to Mach 1.5 for their photo pass. Then retrace their flight pattern back to base. Larry advised Paul to just follow Tom's lead and they would be fine. The flight should last only about three hours so they should be back around 11:00p.m.

The crew manned the vehicle around 7:30p.m. Paul strapped himself in and connected his oxygen, pressure hose and communications fitting into the vehicle. He performed the preflight checklist for the suit and everything was normal. Tom and George did the same and quickly all preflight checklists were complete. They contacted operations and reported ready for departure. Paul activated the vehicles systems just as the claxon sounded and hangar lights dimmed just as the hangar door extended down into place so the AFV could roll out into takeoff position.

Paul lifted off vertically retracted the landing gear and pointed the vehicle towards the sky. He headed northwest, climbing to 340,000' and accelerating. When he reached altitude his speed was over Mach 9. Tom recommended he put it on autopilot so they could follow their flight profile. Paul agreed but told Tom he would fly the vehicle by hand when they reached their descent point for their data gathering pass over Mindanao. He just wanted to get the feel of the vehicle.

Tom reported their position and told Paul it was time to descend to 5000' and slow to Mach 1.5. Tom had all the sensors activated and cameras turned on. These electronic cameras were a far cry from the original film cameras

Fairchild Camera had manufactured for the AFVs Tom thought. They finished their data run headed southwest and Tom indicated to Paul that they were ready to climb and return to base. They made a sweeping right climbing turn all the while accelerating. Paul leveled at 400,000' cruising at about 9600mph. Tom turned on his data link and transmitted all photos and data. Paul really liked the SPS system. It indicated his altitude, speed and geographic position all on one screen. As they approached the west coast he began slowing the vehicle and descending for landing. As they passed over Nevada, Tom keyed his communications radio and called,

"Whisper Base, Blackjack. One for landing."

Jack answered, "Roger. Blackjack cleared as requested."

As the descent continued green ionized gas began to appear on the edges of the vehicle. Paul switched on stealth mode and the gas disappeared. He followed his SPS until he was within two miles of base. He lowered the landing gear and turned on his video camera. In night vision mode it lit up the landing pad like a Christmas tree. He came to a hover over the pad and gently set the vehicle on it. Next he slid the vehicle into its hangar bay as the claxon sounded and the hangar door closed the lights brightened. He shutdown the vehicle and secured all systems. As the crew disembarked, Larry was first to greet them.

"What an experience!" Paul exclaimed. This is the most beautiful thing I have ever climbed into."

He was smiling from ear to ear. "It's great to be accomplishing something other than pure research. That was really exhilarating. Does it ever get old, Larry?" He asked.

"Naw, it is always a thrill to do what we do. How did it feel at high altitude?" Larry said.

"It didn't feel that much different than low altitude flight. Actually it reacts equally in both regimes and is quite sensitive and responsive to all inputs," Paul noted.

"Paul, if I didn't know better I would think you really enjoyed yourself," Larry said. Of course he was being facetious as he could see Paul was really excited.

"It's too bad this is being kept a secret, Larry. Our space program seems primitive compared to this. Being able to get into space at a moments notice and not requiring a couple of weeks planning is a real asset. By the way, how far out into space have you guys had this thing?" Paul asked.

"One of our guys went all the way to the moon shadowing Apollo 13. He flew it solo just in case he had to rescue the 3 astronauts. I don't know if Bob told you but we have shadowed every U.S. space flight in case of trouble and haven't been discovered yet so that is to our credit in conducting our operations," Larry said.

Paul turned to leave, "I'm going to change into something comfortable. See you in quarters."

Larry went into operations to visit with Jack for a minute.

"Looks like we have added one Hell of a pilot to our stable, Larry," Jack said. "I monitored his flight from beginning to end and it was almost picture perfect. Couldn't ask for a better flight. You can tell him I said so. I'm going to take a nap as we don't have another flight until 6:00a.m."

"Maybe you can get six hours sleep Jack," Larry said. "Whose got the early flight, Jack?"

Jack checked his notes, "Mike Brenner is scheduled for a 6:15am departure,"

"That's good, Jack. I presume our next mission is scheduled for around 10:00a.m. Have you written in anyone on that one yet?" Larry asked.

"Charlie Black told me he would take that one, Larry," Jack responded.

Larry paused..."Okay, Jack. Put me on for the 2:00p.m. flight,"

"You got it, Larry. I have written you in for that one," Jack said.

"Now go get some sleep, Jack. It's going to be a long week with this schedule," Larry offered.

Larry walked back into the crew quarters. Paul and Tom were already getting a drink and fixin' to relax. Larry joined them.

7

"A New Rookie"

Kamas, Utah

The two weeks flying the AFVs went quickly for all-hands. Paul Anderson was quickly becoming one of the crew. He was having the time of his life as he'd never had before. After every flight he was animated and couldn't stop talking about the performance of the AFVs. He recalled one evening that this was what Chuck Yeager had been alluding to when he was talking about space flight. This was a vehicle the pilot was continuously flying and not just being a passenger. This was always a challenge.

As the two weeks came to a close everyone was exhausted from the rigorous schedule they had been going through. The last day Jerry Elliott announced that he was going to retire from the program. He had been at it for twenty-six years and felt that was enough.

When they came down off the mountain he stopped in at Bob Avery's office and told Bob he wanted to retire within the next two months. Jerry had a long and storied career and he deserved to take his retirement. With his Navy time he thought he had 32 years of active service. Bob told him to stop by and see Bill Springer in admin and Bill would take care of the paperwork. When he talked to Bill he found out that he would receive orders from the Navy to proceed to NAS Lamoore, California, for his retirement processing. He was surprised as he thought he had resigned when he moved to Utah. He was in shock as he learned he was actually still on active duty and had been promoted to Captain (O-6) and that he would receive retroactive pay since his promotion was effective. Bill explained that the resignation letter was held by Jack Forester and now Admiral John Boland and had never been submitted to the Navy. This was the agreement for all those ex-VXE-6 guys who had joined the AFV program and moved to Utah. He was smiling for five days after he learned all this from Bill. His back pay would be a tidy sum for him to start his retirement.

Jerry's retirement now left an empty slot which was going to be hard to fill. Bob passed the word to all the pilots to recommend anyone they might know who would fit the bill for a new pilot. When Paul received Bob's message he thought he knew someone who might like to join this organization and who was well qualified. He stopped by Bob's office and was invited in for a cup of coffee.

"Bob, I saw the note on finding a new pilot for the organization and I think I have the perfect person," Paul said.

"Great, Paul. Who do you have in mind?" He asked.

"My nomination would be Lieutenant Commander Victoria Croft. You remember, she was the command pilot of my last shuttle flight," he said.

"Oh yeah, I remember her, Paul. She's the one we dumped on Pitcairn Island when we brought you all down from space," Bob noted.

"Yeah, she's the one. She is still an astronaut in the space program but she is quite unhappy since there are no more shuttle flights and the only opportunities left to even go into space are the space station and they don't need pilots for that. They depend on the Russians for transport and the astronauts are just passengers. I think NASA is fixin' to transfer all military pilots back to their service so she might be available," Paul said.

"That's an excellent nomination, Paul. We have never had a woman in our program but I think we can adapt. It may take a little adjustment by all-hands but I think we can make it work. How do you think we should handle asking her?"

Paul suggested, "If we could get her to come out to Salt Lake City and have you interview her here it would probably work better than you going to Houston."

"That sounds like a plan. Let me run it by Larry Beck before we proceed," Bob said.

"I understand that, Bob. Larry is a good sounding board. I know you have been together a long time and have been through a lot. He can add an experienced voice to this decision," Paul replied.

"How are you enjoying your flying duties, Paul?" Bob asked.

"I like the G4 and am thoroughly enjoying the rest of the schedule," Paul said. "I'll see you later. Please keep me advised and you know if I can help, just ask."

Paul arose, excused himself and Bob made a few notes on their discussion.

Larry was working in his office at the Hangar when Bob called.

"What's up, Bob?" Larry asked.

"I need to confer with you. How about stopping by my office in the morning before you catch the helicopter. I have an important issue I need to discuss. It should only take us about a half hour and we can get you a helo ride after we're finished," Bob said.

"That sounds good, Bob. See you in the morning," Larry responded and hung up the phone.

Bob called Cindy into his office. "Cindy I want you to set up a meeting at our conference room at Hangar 512 for next Wednesday. Contact Bill Grammercy, Larry Beck and John Walker and tell them I need them to attend. I think it will be an all day affair so cut Ginny Wulf into the action and tell her we will need the usual stuff, coffee etc. I think we should also plan to have salad and sandwiches for lunch. That way we can have a working lunch and get more done earlier. Advise them the meeting will center around expansion of Omega Aviation with a possible branch or subsidiary office in Charlotte, North Carolina."

The next morning Larry was in Bob's office by 8:00a.m. Bob had arrived a few minutes earlier and they greeted each other.

"Have a seat, Larry. This will take only a few minutes but I needed your input on this one. Would you like a cup of coffee?" Bob asked.

"Naw, I'm saving up when I get to the hangar. What's the issue?" Larry asked.

"You know I am looking for a pilot to replace Jerry Elliott. Well, Paul Anderson and I had a discussion about possibly asking Lieutenant Commander Victoria Croft to join our program. I know it might create a few problems at first but you know she is a great naval aviator, otherwise she would never have cut it in astronaut training. Paul says she is a little unhappy with NASA since there are no more shuttle flights and she is in limbo right now. Gimmie your take on this?" Bob said.

"That's quite a surprise and deviation from our norm but we don't have the luxury of having the pool of aviators to select from that we did when we were in VXE-6. As for her qualifications, I am sure she is very well qualified to join our program. As for taking on a woman in our program I have to think about it a little," Larry said.

"Well, let's talk it through and that should help us decide. There are a lot of positives so let's start with the negatives. A woman might be somewhat of a distraction for the guys at first but I think we can work through any that might arise. We won't have a problem with the wives since they are not aware of where we spend our two weeks away from home anyway. We have two showers and bathrooms up on the mountain so we can designate one as the women's and make it private when being used by women. Sleeping quarters can be modified to accommodate women so I don't see a problem there. What's your take of this?" Bob asked.

"You just about covered what came to mind. I don't see a problem on the G550 flying end of things. Off hand no negatives come to mind. The hangar is designed to handle both sexes so that's not a problem. Our housing here has a few single bedroom houses so that's good. She's obviously flown military jets so she is probably well qualified there. Looks to me like we can accommodate the change without to much heartburn. I say go for it," Larry decided.

Bob nodded, "That does it for me. I believe she will be a good addition to our stable of pilots and should work out with little or no problems. Hey, how about you and Susie coming over for a few drinks tonight. We haven't done that in a while."

"That sounds good to me. I will call Susie later and tell her we are coming over. How about 7:00p.m.?" Larry said.

"Seven it is, Larry. See you then."

Larry went downstairs and the pilots were just manning the duty helo for departure for Salt Lake City. He hopped aboard.

Cindy broke the silence of Bob's office. "Mr. Avery, John Walker on line one,"

"Thanks, Cindy," Bob responded as he keyed the intercom. He picked up the phone, "John, what do you have this morning?" he asked.

"I inspected the G550 in Tacoma, Washington, yesterday on my flight back from Alaska and it is in fine shape and looks like it would fit well into our operation. It's on sale for $21,900,000 and I think our oldest G4 can go up on the block for $4,950,000. I will run the details by Bill Grammercy and let him work out the details," John said.

"That's very good news. Tell Bill to give me the finals details when he works them out," Bob said. "Do you have anything else new, John?"

"That's it for now, Bob. Just a reminder for you. Your annual training at Flight Safety is coming up next month so plan on going to Phoenix. If you let me know soon, I will go at the same time and we can spend the week together," John said.

"I'll look at my schedule, John. Talk with you later," Bob said.

Bob dialed the number Paul had given him for contacting Tori Croft at NASA Houston. The person who answered said Tori was out flying a T-45C "Goshawk" and would return in a couple of hours. Bob left a message and phone number for her to call him.

That afternoon Cindy came up on the intercom and told Bob Tori Croft was on line two. He picked up the phone and selected the button for line 2. "Hi, Tori. This is Bob Avery at Omega Aviation in Salt Lake City. How are you doin' today?" He asked.

"Hi, Bob. Nice to hear from you. What can I do for you?" she asked.

"I am the CEO of Omega Aviation and I was having a discussion the other day with Paul Anderson, one of our G4 pilots," Bob said.

"How is Paul?" she asked. "I sure miss him,"

"He's doin' great but the reason I called is that Paul recommended you for one of our pilot slots at Omega and I thought if you were interested we could send a G4 to Houston to fly you out here to look us over and see if you might like to join us," Bob said.

"It is a little boring around here with no shuttles to fly and with Paul retiring, so yeah, I would be interested," she said.

"That's great, Tori. When would you be available?" Bob asked.

"I can probably arrange my schedule for Monday, us being so busy and all. Didn't I ride in one of your birds from Tahiti to Houston?" She asked.

"That's right, I almost forgot. That's when we picked up all the Enterprise astronauts. Anyway we will have a G4 in Houston first thing Monday morning to bring you out here. Is that good with you?" Bob said.

"That sounds great. I look forward to it," She said

Bob hung up and called John Walker.

When he answered. Bob said, "John, I have an addition to your schedule for Sunday to Ellington Airport, Houston, Texas. We are looking to entice Lieutenant Commander Tori Croft to join out operation. I just finished talking to her and she indicted she could come out here on Monday. How about you picking her up? She could take the left seat and fly the leg back to Salt Lake City. That way you can evaluate her abilities and make a decision by the time you get here." What are your feelings about hiring a woman pilot?"

"I have no heartburn with that," John added. "If she is a well qualified pilot it makes no difference. You know me, if a pilot can handle the airplane satisfactorily they are okay in my book. Just don't ask me to lower my standards to hire a specific person because they have some special status."

"I knew you felt that way. I just wanted to hear it from you. Are you sure you weren't a naval aviator in some other life?" Bob joked.

"You joke about it but you know my dad was a great naval aviator and these were his values which he instilled in me," John said. John was restricted from telling Bob he had been a naval aviator before he joined the CIA. It was one of the deep dark secrets John was pledged to keep and not tell anyone. Admiral Reynolds had briefed John before he was hired at Omega and wanted it to remain that way.

"As long as we're talking philosophically. That has always been the creed in naval aviation. Quality over quantity. Anyway get back to work, old friend. Will talk to you later. Take care," Bob said and hung up the phone. He turned to his computer and sent John an email with all the contact information for Tori.

Bill Grammercy had a long talk with Bob on his flying status. He was becoming more and more immersed in the corporation as the CFO and having less time to fly. He and Bob decided they should hire a replacement to keep the numbers available to fly where they should be.

Bill had an old friend, Major John Cushman, USMC, from earlier days who was an NFO and had been flying the F-14 as a Radar Intercept Officer (RIO). He was currently instructing in the T-39 in Training Squadron Eighty-Six (VT-86) at NAS Pensacola, Florida. John said they were flying two flights a day with three students. During each flight they were making eighteen sparrow runs and eighteen sidewinder runs on their designated bogy, usually a TA-4J from the squadron. Bill had talked with him recently and he was bored and said he needed a new challenge. Bob concurred they should try to recruit him.

Sunday rolled around and John and Ivan Wheaton took a G4 to Ellington Field, Houston, Texas. They landed about 6:30p.m. and went over to the Holiday Inn where they had a room for the night. After they were settled John called the number he had for Tori Croft. She answered and after having introduced himself he told her she could meet them at the General Aviation Terminal about 8:30a.m. and they would depart shortly thereafter.

John hung up and he told Ivan she sounded like a sweet kid and he was looking forward to meeting her.

In the morning they had the continental breakfast, checked out, boarded the shuttle Holiday Inn provided and were dropped off at the General Aviation Terminal. They filed their flight plan for a 9:00a.m. departure and sat down in the coffee shop for another cup of Joe.

At 8:30a.m. Tori arrived, parked her new Porsche and walked into the terminal. Ivan spotted her first and they quickly moved in her general direction to meet her. They stopped her and introduced themselves. After exchanging a few pleasantries they proceeded to the aircraft. Upon boarding, John indicated she should take the left seat for the flight. He occupied the copilots seat. They completed the checklist and started the engines. Taxi was obtained from ground control and they were cleared to runway zero four. John coaxed her through the use of differential power for directional control and explained V1 and V2 speeds for takeoff. Cleared for takeoff they departed and began their climb out to flight level 320' (32,000'). The flight lasted three hours ten minutes and John and Tori found a real rapport between them. Tori was comfortable and performed in an outstanding manner. Her piloting skills were honed to a fine art and John's assessment was that she was a great pilot. They pulled into the chocks in Salt Lake City about 10:15am. John had arranged for one of the company's helicopters to transport them to headquarters in Kamas. The flight took about twenty minutes. During the flight John invited Tori over for to his quarters when she finished her meeting with Bob Avery. He knew the process she was embarking on would take all day.

The helo landed on the pad at headquarters and John escorted her into the building. They made their way to Bob's office where Cindy Hager escorted them into his inner office. John introduced Tori to Bob and then excused himself.

Bob walked out with John and stopped him in his outer office.

"What's your evaluation, John?" Bob asked.

"She lives up to her reputation, Bob," John responded. "Her skills as a pilot are unquestionable. She handled the aircraft perfectly and her pilotage was outstanding. I would recommend hiring her," he said.

"Thanks for your input, John. You know I wouldn't do anything without your blessing," Bob said.

Bob made his way back into his office and engaged Tori in conversation. Asking her about how she felt, joining the company. After a few minutes he decided to ask the real question.

"Tori, I have something to ask you which will affect your life forever. How would you like to join a top-secret flight program? It is one that you can never talk about ever. That's about all I can offer before I have your answer," he said.

"That's a tall order you just put on my plate," she said.

"Would you like to think about it overnight?" Bob asked.

"Let me ask you this. You told me Paul Anderson recommended me and he is part of this program. Is that correct?" She said.

"That's right Tori and I might add John Walker's recommendation that we add you to our staff of pilots," he said.

"Well if those two guys think I can handle things, count me in," she said. "What kind of program are we talking about?"

"Let's not talk about it. Let me show you. Don't ask me any questions until we reach our destination. Okay?" Bob asked.

They left Bob's office and made their way to the security doors. Bob explained the procedure and entered her data and scanned her retina into the system. They made their way down to the tram and were on their way up the mountain. At the transfer point they moved into the pneumatic tube and started up the mountain. She was wide-eyed already, as she had not seen such an elaborate transport system before. The tube reached the top and they exited directly into the hangar deck. There before her very eyes was the vehicle which had rescued her from Enterprise. She was blown away by what she observed. The first words she could utter were, "What are these things and were did they come from?" she asked.

"We can answer those questions later but these are known as AFVs or Anti-gravity Flight Vehicles. As you meet and interact with our crews you will learn the answers. Let me tell you that all our flight crewmembers are Navy people. When you join us you will have to submit you resignation from the Navy. This is just an administrative thing. Admiral Boland, Director of Central Intelligence, will hold your resignation letter in his office. For public consumption you will be a civilian but in reality you will still be in the Navy and will get your promotions and pay. When you finally retire from this program you will return to the Navy and be formally retired with all your years here counting towards your retirement. Let's meet the rest of the crew and I will give you a tour," Bob said.

8

"Friendly Arrangement"

Omega Headquarters, Kamas, Utah

Bob Avery and Tori Croft came down off the mountain after Tori had the five-dollar tour and had met some of the other crewmembers. Her reaction to seeing and actually sitting in the cockpit of an AFV was typical. Almost universally when first introduced to the AFV program most pilots and crewmembers were at a loss for words and found the whole situation hard to comprehend.

They went into Bob's office where they discussed the details of moving her to Utah. Bob called Bill Springer to come down to his office. When he arrived Bill was introduced and told Tori would be coming aboard. Bob indicated they should activate the letter of resignation from the Navy and get it sent off to Admiral Boland at the CIA. From there he would activate all procedures necessary to get Tori relieved of duty and she would be free to move to Utah. Admiral Boland would retain the letter in his office and it would be destroyed upon her retirement which everyone hoped would be many years away. Bill excused himself and within minutes returned with a letter of resignation for Tori to sign. She quickly signed off on it and Bill said he would send it to Admiral Boland.

Next they discussed what would happen when she arrived back at Utah from Houston. Bill said he would take care of all the paperwork.

Tori inquired about training for the G4 and G550. That was John Walker's bailiwick and Bob suggested discussing that with him when she met with him. Tori said she was having drinks with John that evening so Bob put in a call to John's cell phone. John answered and he and Bob made arrangements for John to pick her up in about thirty minutes.

Tori went out the front door and John was waiting for her. She was impressed with his powder blue Jaguar convertible. She had her travel bag with her and she threw it in behind the front seat. They exchanged smiles and Tori started the conversation.

"I love your car, John. Have you had it very long?" she asked.

"Bought it about two months ago," he answered. "Had to have it shipped in from San Jose, California. The local people didn't have what I wanted."

He drove slowly over a couple of streets and pulled up in the driveway of his house. It was a single story, two-bedroom ranch with cedar siding on the outside. It was a typical mountain home.

"Well, here's the old homestead," he said. "Nothing fancy but it's rent-free and furnished by the company so no complaints here. I heard the company was going to build some condos back up the mountain a ways for single people. A few of our guys are single and I guess some prefer condo living. As for me this house is great. I have a nice yard and an attached garage. It gives me a place to putter and I have a nice loading bench in my garage for reloading my pistol ammo."

"Do you shoot much?" she asked. "I love to shoot, especially pistols, but don't get much time to do it in Houston."

"Not much time here for me either, Tori. This job keeps me busy both flying and keeping up with the flight crews and running the day to day operations at the hangar." John said.

He opened the front door and invited her in. "Come on in and make yourself at home. I'll fix us a drink and some snacks. "What would you like to drink?" he asked.

"You can fix me a rum and coke if you have it," she answered.

"Yeah, that's an easy one. Would you prefer regular or spice? I have a nice bottle of Captain Morgan if you like," he said.

"Captain Morgan will be great. Wow, you really have this place furnished nicely. I wouldn't have expected a bachelor's pad to be this well taken care of." she said.

"I like to keep the place looking nice and I have always been one who picks up after myself so I keep things in their place," he said. They had drifted into the kitchen as John set out all the fixin's he needed as he prepared her a drink. When he finished, he handed it to her and turned to make himself a gin and tonic. He retrieved a twist of lime from the fridge and put it in his drink. He also took out the plate of cheese snacks and reached into the cupboard and found a few different crackers to go with them. He placed them on the island in the kitchen and came around the counter and pulled up a bar stool alongside the one she had already occupied. She seemed fine where she was so he didn't offer to move to the den to sit in a comfortable chair.

They began a serious discussion about her blending into the company's operation. John explained what she would need to do after she arrived on scene. He told her about Flight Safety, flight physical and currency to fly the G4 or G550. He cautioned her about talking about the other program she would be entering into. That discussion was limited only to the other complex she had been in earlier. That's about all he could say and used extreme caution in his wording and references.

"Sometimes walls have ears if you know what I mean," he said.

She understood completely what he was saying and they stayed off that subject altogether. Their discussion and chat turned to each other and what flying experience they had. Tori related how she had been interested in flying as a kid to her experience becoming a naval aviator and then as a NASA astronaut. John told her about his working for a few years as a ski instructor and bartender, then finally getting a chance to attend Embry-Riddle for his college degree in aviation. John did mention his three years with Southern AIr Transpot flying out of Taipei, Taiwan. He avoided telling her about his experiences as a naval aviator as that needed to be kept a secret from anyone associated with Omega.

They talked for a couple of hours having a few more drinks and John fixing dinner. It was approaching 9:00p.m. and John asked her where she was staying and said he would drive her there. They would need to get started if it was in Salt Lake as that was about an hour away. She said she hadn't been told by anyone about housing and assumed the company had made arrangements for her. It was an awkward moment and finally John said, "Tori, I have two bedrooms. One's over there on the east side of the house and the other is here on the west side next to the garage. If you like you can stay here tonight. I usually sleep in the west bedroom so why don't you take the east bedroom."

"That's very kind of you, John. Thanks, that will be great." She said.

"Yeah, this way it will be convenient to get to headquarters in the morning and then midday you can catch the helo to the airport and I will fly you back to Houston. I need to look at a G550 over at George Bush Intercontinental Airport (IAH) after I drop you off so it will work out great for both of us.

Wednesday morning

It was early Wednesday and all four men caught the morning helicopter to the hangar. Bob, Bill, Larry and John made their way to the conference room where Ginny had already laid out sweet rolls and coffee. They all indulged and took a seat around the conference table.

Bob opened the discussion. "Guys I wanted to get all of us together to discuss a proposal Phil Murphy made to John and I when we last visited with him at his company headquarters."

"He said they were disappointed with the customer service and maintenance they were getting from Pioneer Aviation at Douglas Airport in Charlotte, North Carolina. His proposal was for us to establish a presence in Charlotte and take over those functions. He is willing to finance the startup costs. So let's throw it out on the table and discuss it. Tell me what you think. Maybe we could make a list of pros and cons. Who wants to start?" Bob asked.

John piped up. "Since I have been aware of this longer than Larry and Bill let me start Bob. I believe there is a need for this and we certainly have the expertise to do it. Once we establish this presence whether it's a branch office or a subsidiary corporation we can easily expand it to manage other corporate jets and even buy some more Gulf-streams of our own to meet our needs. A branch office would be more work for us but we could do it and still maintain our quality of service. Larry, you would need to manage all pilots in addition to the ones we already have here in Salt Lake. Maintenance would not be a problem, as we would have little input except hiring the right people to do that. Those are some of the pros. If we establish a subsidiary we would have less control but also less work, so there we have a pro and a con. We would hire a district manager and he would hire his staff and we would have a say only through its board of directors by having a few of our people on his board from this headquarters."

Bill Gramercy was next up. "John has a point. With a subsidiary we would have little to do with financial matters and in my book that would be okay. The con is that we would not receive any profit from having a subsidiary. If we had a branch office, that would throw the responsibility of personnel and finance on our shoulders. Right now I'm not sure where I come down on that issue."

Larry chimed in with his ideas. "A branch office would have us hiring and managing all pilots' qualifications and performance. We would need to also monitor their certification by the FAA and recertification as well as pilot training and certification. It would require us to hire more people here to administer that stuff."

"Okay, guys, those are all great ideas and areas for discussion. Let's go forward this way. Let me write things up on the chalkboard as you state them and then we can go down the list and discuss them. At the end of the day we will need to make a decision," Bob said.

Bob turned to the board and on one side he wrote 'Branch Office." Pros on one side and cons on the other. To the right he wrote "Subsidiary" with pros and cons. They began to state out loud pros and cons for each kind of presence. Soon the board was full of ideas.

It was approaching lunchtime and Ginny Wulf brought in the plates filled with luscious food she had ordered from a local shoppe. Those assembled dug in and after filling their plates sat down and continued to discuss the items on the chalkboard.

After lunch they continued methodically down the list and exhausted the topic. It was approaching 3:00p.m. and the group had now finished discussion of all pros and cons. Bob decided it was time for a decision. He asked each man there to state his decision either branch office or subsidiary.

John shared his vote. It was for a branch office. Larry was next and he too voted for a branch office. Bill made it unanimous with a vote for a branch office. The main reason given was they felt they could maintain quality of service better by close hands-on with a branch office. All agreed it would take more work but were more than glad to take it on in order to keep their great reputation. Bob added his comments and said he was proud of them because that was the conclusion he had come to in his considerations.

Within two weeks Tori received a letter from the Chief of Naval Personnel accepting her resignation. A few people at the Bureau who knew her called and expressed their sorrow in hearing about her resignation. Likewise her coworkers at NASA were disappointed at losing her as an astronaut. If only they knew what she was going to fly she thought. It was going to be an exciting time and she could hardly wait to pilot the AFV. Just her experience at being rescued by one and being deposited on Pitcairn Island was exciting enough. What she still wanted to do was meet the pilot who rescued her and thank him personally.

She checked out of NASA through the military liaison office and received her honorable discharge and release from active duty. Her personal possessions were packed from her condo and shipped off to Kamas, Utah. The remainder of her gear she packed into her Porsche and after some sad goodbyes at NASA she was on her way to start her new adventure.

On her trip out west she took a couple of days to visit the Grand Canyon, Painted Desert and Tombstone, Arizona. She enjoyed the scenery but the wild-west show in Tombstone was highly enjoyable. The pistol shooting was exciting.

She turned north and ended up in Salt Lake City before noon. She decided to stop by Hangar 512 at the Airport and see if John would like to go to lunch. She walked into the hangar and made her way to John's office. He was still in doing paperwork. Ginny Wulf told John that Tori was there. He went quickly to his office door and greeted her with a big smile. He was glad to see her as they had hit it off pretty well when she was there last.

"Hey, Tori," John said. "Glad you made it here so quickly. Didn't expect to see you for another week. Did you have a good trip?"

"Yeah, John. Great to see you and yes I had a great trip. Did a little sightseeing on the way. How have you been?" She asked.

"Been good," he answered

"I haven't had lunch yet. Are you interested?" she said.

"That sounds like a super idea. Haven't had that kind of invitation from a beautiful woman for a few months."

John said. "Any place in particular you had in mind?"

"Naw, I figured you know better than me," she said.

"Well then, let's go to the Log Haven. It's out in Mill-creek Canyon. Great food and beautiful view," he said. "It's about a forty minute drive but well worth it."

What he didn't tell her was that it was quite a romantic place. He was starting to get a crush on her and knew he liked her very much. She was a pleasure to be around and anybody like her who loved flying and guns as he did couldn't be any better to be around.

They walked out of the hangar and took his Jaguar to the restaurant. The conversation centered on her upcoming training schedule and qualification to fly the Gulfstream G4/550.

Over lunch there was a lot of man, woman banter as they just enjoyed each other's company. John finally asked, "Where are you staying temporarily?"

"Bill Springer told me there was a guest house in the compound where I could stay for a while," she said.

"That sounds like a plan but why don't you come share my house for a while. We will be sending you to Flight Safety in Phoenix for three weeks and then you'll be gone for another couple weeks shortly thereafter. No sense in ricocheting around a big house by yourself. I promise, you won't be any trouble. When you get organized and you feel the time is right you can ask for housing assignment. How does that sound?" he said.

"Okay you talked me into it," she said.

John gave her a key to the house. They got up and found their way out to his Jaguar. It was a nice drive back to the hangar. When they arrived John said, "Why don't you drive out to headquarters, get checked in and then find you way over to the house. If you want some dinner just

look in the fridge and you'll find something you'll like I'm
sure. Can't say when I'll get there as I have a lot of paperwork to do today and I am leaving on a trip to the Far East
in the morning. See you later."

Tori squeezed his hand and thanked him. John went
into his office while Tori went to her car and departed for
headquarters in Kamas.

When she arrived at the gate security had already
been alerted to expect her. The security guard, Larry Wil-
son, greeted her and invited her into the security office. He
asked her to fill out a form so he could issue a security pass
and automobile sticker. This would allow her easy access
to the base and other highly secure locations.

When she finished with security she proceeded to
headquarters, entered and looked for Bill Springer's office.
Bill had completed all the paperwork required except for
her signature. She signed about thirty pieces of paper and
wondered if this was a normal practice for every new hire.
Bill was pleasant and attentive and she felt comfortable
with all this bureaucratic trouble. Bill asked her if she was
staying at the guest quarters. She indicated that John
Walker had invited her to share his quarters and she would
be staying there. It was approaching the 5 o'clock hour and
everyone was calling it quits for the day so she told Bill she
would check-in with him in the morning.

As she entered the quarters it was as she remembered. It was well furnished and neat. John was a great
housekeeper. The east bedroom was a beautifully designed
room. John had lightened it up with a cream colored paint
on the walls and ceiling. Light pink curtains were on the
windows and a white bedspread. The carpet was light beige
however the pictures on the walls were out of place in a
daintily furnished room. On one wall was a large picture of

an F-14 Navy fighter and on the other was the space shuttle Enterprise. John had gone out of his way to try to make her feel at home. She laughed to herself. What an ego John had doing this ahead of time and seeming to know she would accept his invitation to share his quarters. She unloaded her car after activating the garage door opener and pulling her car into one of the two parking spots. After finishing that task she was quite hungry. The fridge had a variety of frozen dinners and she picked the stuffed cabbage. There were many vegetables in the crisper and she also made a fresh salad. As an added touch she sprinkled sunflower seeds and dried cranberries on top. When she finished there was enough for two people so maybe John would have some when he returned.

About 7:00p.m. the garage door activated and John pulled his car into the remaining space. He quickly closed the garage door and entered the kitchen. Tori had just sat down to eat her dinner. They greeted each other and she told John she had made enough salad for two. He thanked her and excused himself for a quick change of clothes from his business suit into his warm-ups. Shortly he appeared again in the kitchen and while engaging Tori in conversation dug into the freezer for another frozen dinner. The beef stew looked like a good choice and after he unwrapped it, placed it in the microwave, and cooked it for the recommended six minutes.

Tori was still lingering over her dinner so he sat down at the kitchen table with her and had his dinner.

9

"A Blossoming Relationship"

Headquarters Compound, Kamas, Utah

John had his travel bag packed and left the house early. He walked over to headquarters and boarded the early helicopter flight to hangar operations at the Salt Lake City Airport.

Tori heard John leave and got up, took a shower, had some breakfast then drove over to headquarters. She checked in with Bill Springer who helped her with all the necessary paperwork. Bill advised her that John had called earlier and had her scheduled for G4/550 training at Flight Safety in Phoenix, Arizona, beginning on Friday. It would last three weeks and there were two options on getting there. She could fly commercial or drive. Commercial air seemed like the best option since she had just driven to Kamas from Houston. Admin office was advised and made airline reservations for late Thursday. This would give her only one day to get acquainted. After she had finished her check-in, Bill took her up to the second floor and introduced her to other crewman. She asked the location of Paul Anderson. She was anxious to renew her friendship and just talk flying. Paul was on his two weeks flying the G4 and was currently on a flight to Saint Martens in the Caribbean. It was determined he wouldn't return until Saturday and Tori was disappointed as she knew their reunion would have to wait.

On Thursday Tori caught the noon helo to Hangar 512. On arrival she walked up to John's Office. He was still off on his flight to Asia so she left him a note telling him she would return in three weeks. Ginny Wulf told her they had a shuttle which would take her over to the commercial terminal where she could catch her flight to Phoenix. At 2:30p.m. her flight was called and she boarded. It was a routine one-hour flight and when she arrived she checked into the Holiday Inn Express next to the airport, as it was close to Flight Safety.

After three weeks of intense training Tori completed her G4/550 training and boarded her return flight to Salt Lake City. She had notified Ginny of her ETA and a shuttle was waiting outside the baggage claim doors to take her over to Hangar 512. It was too early for the 1:00p.m. helo to headquarters so she walked up to John's office to see if he was there.

Ginny announced her and she entered John's office. He got up from his desk and gave her a polite hug. "How was you training session, Tori?" he asked.

"It was tedious at times but well done in their presentation. I particularly enjoyed the simulator. Much better than I was used to and the cockpit presentations are improving all the time. What do you have planned for me next?" she asked.

"It's one of those necessary evils which we all have to go through every six months or the FAA will seriously think about decertifying us. As for your schedule, I talked with Larry and he is going to get you started flying ASAP. Probably tomorrow. By the way, I have stocked the fridge and pantry with some good food and there are the usual snacks in the cupboard so make yourself at home when you get back to the house. I don't' expect you've had lunch yet, have you?" he asked.

"Nah, they didn't even serve peanuts on the flight up here from Phoenix," she said.

"Well then let's go over to Cracker Barrel for a quick lunch and I will make sure you get back here in time for the 1:00p.m. helo," he said. "Just leave your travel bag here and we can pick it up when we get back."

They walked out the door and as they passed Ginny, John told her they were going to lunch and would return by 12:45pm.

John had a company car in his assigned parking spot. It was a fairly new Toyota Camry. Nothing like his Jaguar, which made a statement when he drove it.

It was a three minute drive to Cracker Barrel and soon they were seated and ordering their lunch. Their conversation was mostly about flying. John was interested in Tori's experiences at NASA and her thoughts and ideas about the space shuttle program. She said she had flown three shuttle flights and, in one sense, it was exciting just to be in space but she preferred to have her hands on the controls and make whatever she was flying to respond to her inputs. Flying the F-14 was her greatest thrill. She said she really had an epiphany landing on the USS Ronald Reagan. It was the toughest and most precise kind of flying in the world. She had four hundred sixty-seven traps and she was quite proud of that. Very few women naval aviators had ever reached that level of proficiency. She related the down side to flying the space shuttle was she hadn't had her hands on the controls yet and now with the mothballing of all the shuttles she never would. Her checkout in the AFV program would be coming up soon and she was excited about that but knew she could not discuss it with anyone outside the AFV complex.

They finished lunch and as promised John returned them to Hangar 512 by 12:45pm. Tori gave John a light polite hug and thanked him for lunch. The helo landed and a few people boarded it for the return trip to headquarters in Kamas. On the trip Tori reminisced about her past career but was really excited about her new one. She knew she couldn't wait to get her hands on the AFV. It was going to be a blast. The helo landed at headquarters and she went in the building, made her way to administrative offices and checked in with the personnel manager. They had a paycheck waiting for her, which really shocked her. It was regular pay for the four weeks she had been attached to Omega Aviation and it was made out for $9756.00. A tidy sum she thought for doing what she loved.

Bill Springer met her in the hallway and reminded her she had a flight physical with Doc Kelly on Thursday morning. Her appointment was set for 8:30a.m.. Tori had been to Doc's clinic once when they took her anthropomorphic data for her pressure suit so she was aware of the clinic's location on the complex. She finished some minor loose ends for Bill and then ended up looking at her assigned cubicle on the second floor of the headquarters building. Some of the other flight crews were there so she stopped to chat with them and inquired what was going on with the G4's. Bill Grammercy chimed in that there were many charter flights and he was glad she was there to ease the load on the stressed flight crews. Most had been flying back-to-back flights to places in the world most people had never heard of. Bill and Larry Beck had just returned from a trip to Mauritius, which lasted six days. Tori inquired if anyone had flown the new G550 Omega had just acquired.

Jim Huskins joined the conversation, "Yeah, I flew it yesterday. Had a trip to Dallas and back. It performs a little better all around from the G4. You could compare it to the F4 Phantom versus the F14 Tomcat. I think where we will see the most difference is in the really long flights. It adds almost 2000 nm to our range and cruises at Mach .88. I found it to be a little heavier on the ramp but takeoff performance was really good."

"I'm glad to hear your evaluation of it Jim. Looking forward to putting my hands on one soon," she said. There was a special place in her heart for Jim Huskins. He was the one who had rescued her in space and had set her down on Pitcairn Island. What an outstanding group of people she had associated herself with she thought. These people risk their lives for their country every day and nobody knows about it except for a select few and certainly there is no recognition of their accomplishments.

The discussion amongst the crewmembers faded as people began to drift off and secure for the day. They said their see-you-tomorrows and headed home for the night, as did Tori. She walked a couple of blocks into the housing area and arrived at the house she was now sharing with John Walker. Her car was parked in the garage where it had been since she left for Flight Safety. She opened the front door and entered the immaculately kept house John had maintained in his usual fashion. It was neat as a pin and reminded her of a picture out of Homes and Garden magazine. She found her way to the east bedroom where she undressed and stepped into the shower. Being on the road since early morning had left her feeling a little gritty and she need to clean up as well as relax. A hot shower would fix all that she thought. She was soaking up all the hot water she could when she heard a loud voice from the living room yell, "Hey Tori, it's John just wanted to let you know I'm home," he said.

"I'll be out in a little bit," she answered.

John made his way to the west bedroom and changed into his warm-ups. He was glad to get out of his suit and tie after being at the hangar all day. After changing he went into the kitchen and poured himself a glass of orange juice. He was a social drinker and didn't much need a mixed drink. Orange juice would suit him just fine. He wandered into the den and turned on the large 42" TV. It was approaching the 6 o'clock hour and he could catch up on the daily news.

Shortly, Tori stepped into the room dressed in very feminine warm-ups and looking radiant. She was pleasant to be around and easy to talk to. "How was your day?" she asked.

"It was busy as usual. Lots of things going on and the phone ringing off the hook. Did you get settled in at headquarters?" he asked.

"I think I am finally finished with all the little stuff. I received my first paycheck and I can now start paying my way with the expenses here at the house." she said.

"Why don't you get yourself a drink and sit down before we get into such mundane things as money," he said. "There is soda and juice in the fridge if you like or fix yourself a mixed drink. You're not a guest anymore so help yourself to whatever you'd like."

"I'm a Sprite girl if you have any," she said.

"In the pantry across from the island you'll find it," John answered.

"Thanks," she offered and stepped into the kitchen.

John caught the story of the plane crash in Moscow on the news and focused on the TV for a minute. Tori soon reentered the room and took a seat on the sofa next to John's recliner.

"I found it okay," she said.

"Good," John responded. "Let me lay out the expenses and then we can come to a decision on how to handle things. It should be pretty easy. Omega doesn't charge us rent. They pay for all utilities which includes water, electricity, Direct TV, telephone and DSL Internet. We have unlimited long distance so don't worry about calling out of town. Our main expense will be for our food and household supplies. The company has a maintenance department so if anything needs work we just call them. They fix anything and everything. As far as house money I suggest we just put $500 each in a drawer in the kitchen and when we buy anything just take out the money and leave the receipt. That way we can account for our funds at the end of the month. With both of us being gone as much as we will be that should last us for quite a while. When we run low we can just add to the kitty. How does that sound to you?" he asked

"That'll work for me," she said.

"Okay, great we have that settled," John said. "Did you hear about the crash in Moscow today?"

"No, been on the run all day and haven't even looked at a TV. What's the story?" she asked.

"Well it's something you should know about since we have a lot of flights to Russia. You know they have six commercial airports in Moscow. However, they do not report their GPS coordinates for their airports the way we do in the U.S. Apparently on this crash the pilot put in the GPS coordinates then made an instrument approach and when he reached minimums he was already half way down the runway but tried to land anyway. The pilot ran off the end of the runway, hit a berm and the aircraft broke in half. Only had eight people on board but killed the flight crew and injured six of the passengers. Just had no position awareness. Let me tell you, Tori, when you go to Moscow always have at least forty extra minutes of fuel. Their air traffic control will run you around before they get you to the right airport and on final," John said.

"I will file that in my things to remember, thanks. By the way do you know what Larry has in mind for me?" she asked.

"He told me he was scheduling you for a familiarization flight on Thursday afternoon. He was aware you have a flight physical in the morning. Tomorrow you need to go downtown and get fitted for your uniforms. Omega pays for all that so check in with Bill Springer and he will give you all the info. We have a company car you can drive at the hangar so check with Ginny when you need it. Larry can brief you on any trips he may have you lined up for and who your copilot will be. Bob says we can keep you on the Gulfstream until he can fit you into the normal schedule. He said he had not heard from ARO Corporation as yet so until he does we'll keep you flying," he said.

"Sounds like a great plan. For the uniform do you know whether it will be slacks or skirts?" she asked.

"I'm sure Bob designated slacks for you," he said.

"That's a good decision. I think I will blend in better with the guys wearing slacks," she responded.

"Yeah, Bob's a pretty savvy guy. I think your tie is also patterned after your Navy one so that's another plus. By the way I will be gone for the next week. I have a trip to Moscow of all places," he said.

"How about a little dinner?" he asked.

"What do you have in mind?" she asked.

"I was thinking about a little soup and salad," he offered.

"That sounds great, John," she answered.

They went into the kitchen where John retrieved a couple of cans of Campbell's Tomato. ""Tomato sound good?" he asked.

"Yeah, that looks yummy," she said. "I'll fix the salad."

"A girl after my own heart."

They both went about their task and soon the soup and salad were ready. John had set the kitchen table with a nice flowered tablecloth and put the silverware in two place settings. They sat down and enjoyed each other's company and the food. After dinner Tori loaded the dishwasher while John cleaned up the kitchen. They moved back into the den and spent the remainder of the evening just talking and enjoying the situation.

John finally looked at his watch and decided it was time to hit the hay. He said goodnight and headed for bed. Tori did the same.

10

"Settling In"

Headquarters compound, Kamas, Utah

The day started early for John and Tori. After a light breakfast they walked over to headquarters where John caught the morning helo to Hangar 512. Tori stopped in to see Bill Springer and get instructions for buying her uniforms and getting them fitted. Bill gave her a printed sheet with the location of Belk's in downtown Salt Lake City and the clerk who would take care of her. Bill recommended she drive since there was not another helo scheduled for Salt Lake until 12:30p.m..

She walked back to the house and picked up her car and headed out for downtown Salt Lake City. After leaving the headquarters compound she drove into Kamas then followed the state roads until she reached Interstate 80. After some forty-five minutes she arrived at the mall where Belk's was located. She entered the store and asked information where to find the clerk who would take care of her needs. She finally met up with Mr. Ken Upchurch in the men's suits department and introduced herself. He had been alerted that she would be coming in and was aware of her needs. Ken had talked with the women's suits department and after determining her size had acquired three full uniforms. They had already sewn on the captain's stripes and after fitting all that was needed was to hem the slacks to the proper length. The uniforms included two white shirts and a black woman's tie. While they were altering the uniforms she wandered around the store and did some window shopping. She didn't buy anything but had a good time anyway. After about an hour and a half she wandered back to the desk where Ken worked. He was waiting for her and had the uniforms hanging there in a uniform bag ready for pickup. She started to thank him when he reminded her she would need some black shoes to go with the uniform. Heels would not do for flying and she would need a couple of pair so he steered her to the lady in the shoe department who would sell her the appropriate shoes. All items were charged to Omega Aviation and she left the store. In a short while she was back on the road headed for Hangar 512. She needed to make contact with Larry and find out her schedule for the next couple of weeks. On arrival she found the spaces reserved for flight crew personnel and parked her car and went into the hangar. Larry's office was on the second deck so she took the stairs to the balcony and headed down towards his office. He was just coming out of John's office when he spied her.

"Hey, Tori. Just the person I was looking to speak with. You are just in time," he said.

"I knew you would have some news for me so I figured I better stop by to see you," she said.

"Come on in the office for a minute and we can discuss what we have in mind for you," Larry said.

Tori came in and sat down. Larry began, "Tori, we have you on the flight schedule for tomorrow afternoon. Just a fam flight for about an hour and a half. We normally fly these flights in our street clothes but feel free to wear a flight suit if you wish. After the flight I will have our publications manager fit you out with a flight bag. You know, the usual stuff everything you need for domestic and overseas flying. I have also written you in for a charter on Saturday. You will pick up two passengers in Bakersfield and fly them to Telluride, Colorado, then deadhead to Dallas/Fort Worth pick up a family of three and fly to Tombstone, Arizona, then back home. Should be a good day's flying for you and an easy familiarization with the aircraft. Bill Grammercy will be your copilot/observer. He needs to get out of the office and Saturday is good for him. After that we will keep you on our schedule until we get the okay from Bob Avery to put you on a regularly assigned group schedule. I think next week we have an overseas trip which would be a good flight for you. I'll check with Bill and see if he's available for that. Besides his being a Naval Flight Officer, he used to be a Naval Aviator. He's an old carrier pilot and I think you two will mesh just fine. He has more experience in all facets of flying than everybody who works here. I know you two will get along just fine and you can depend on him to keep you out of trouble. He and Bob go all the way back to when they were Naval Aviation Cadets in flight training. That's about it. Do you have any questions?" he asked.

"I'm not quite sure of the helicopter flight schedule for getting to and from Headquarters," she asked.

"Our regular flights are Monday through Friday at 8:00a.m. and 12:30p.m. from headquarters. From here regular schedule is 11:30a.m. and 5:00p.m. to headquarters. On weekends there is a standby duty crew who are available anytime we need people moved from either headquarters or Hangar 512. So if you have a flight returning, transportation will be available to return you to the headquarters. Don't worry, Tori, we have plenty of flights available and no one is ever left waiting without a flight. With six helo crews and planes available those guys want to fly whenever they can," Larry said.

"My next question is: are there any reports we need to make when we are away from home base?" she posed.

"The answer is no. We need to hear from you only if there is a deviation from schedule, maintenance problems or a glitch with the passengers. Other than that we expect you are operating normally," he said.

"That's about all the questions I have for now. I guess I'll drive back out to the compound. See you after lunch tomorrow I guess," she said.

"Oh yeah, one more thing. When you get back to headquarters see Ken Nichols, our communication officer. He will check you out a company cell phone. It is usable anywhere in the world and sometimes a necessity. It has unlimited use. It's available for company and personal use," he said.

"Thanks, Larry." And with that she left his office for the parking lot.

Salt Lake City later that day

John Walker was finally off on his trip to Moscow. He picked up his passenger, a Russian businessman, at White Plains, New York, and was soon off to Moscow. He took the great circle route which took him over Nova Scotia, Labrador and Iceland. After eight hours in the air he found himself being vectored every which way for an approach to Domodedovo airport. He was at low altitude and was glad he had taken his own advice and added the extra forty minutes of fuel. After thirty-two extra minutes of vectoring he was on final for Runway 12 at Domodedovo.

His passenger Vitori Petrovich requested to fly to Johannesburg, South Africa, tomorrow. John acknowledged and Vitori departed in his huge black limo. John and his crew found the hotel shuttle to the Hilton Moscow Leningradskaya. It was a beautiful day and a great trip, just twenty-two miles into the city. On arrival they exchanged some of their dollars for rubles at the currency exchange window in the hotel. The desk clerk found them very nice connecting rooms on the twelfth floor. John told the crew they needed to sleep for only a few hours so they could more quickly adjust to the time zone change. It was now early morning and they needed to be ready for an early morning departure the next day for South Africa.

They did just what John had recommended and about lunchtime they got up, showered and dressed and went down to the hotel dining room for lunch. After lunch they did the tourist thing and took a taxi to Red Square. Lenin's tomb was just as advertised and the Russian Orthodox Church glistened in the sun. The crew took many pictures and, since it was about suppertime, took another taxi back to the hotel. They dined in the hotel dining room and went to bed early, as John wanted to get to the airport by 7:00a.m.

The crew assembled in the hotel lobby and boarded the hotel shuttle for the airport. John had asked to be dropped off at the Fixed Base Operations (FBO), which the driver obliged. They entered and at the operations desk, stopped and asked for the plane to be refueled with JP5. Ivan Wheaton sat down and planned the flight to Tambo International Airport, Johannesburg. It was 6503 miles and would take 10.5 hours to fly there. Their route of flight would take them all the way across the continent of Africa.

John supervised the refueling and when it was completed he and Ivan went over to the main passenger terminal for breakfast.

Vitori arrived at approximately 8:30a.m. and they departed Domodedovo shortly thereafter. John requested a vector directly on course and it was granted. Departure radar turned him to 190º and cleared him to contact Moscow airways. He climbed out to 49,000' and accelerated to Mach .88 while proceeding on course. Arrival in Johannesburg was around 5:30p.m. local time and after landing Ivan asked directions to the FBO.

Before Vitori departed the ramp he told John he would be there for two days and then he wanted to fly to Cote d'Azur Airport in Nice, France. Vitori was picked up in a limo with three men plus the driver. When Vitori was greeted by one of the men, the other two stepped out and observed the area looking continuously in all directions. John could see they had heavy hardware under their suit coats and he could only presume they were bodyguards. He began to suspect Vitori was part of the Russian Mafia. A paying customer was a paying customer he thought as long and the guns stayed hidden.

The two days in Johannesburg were uneventful. On the third day John and Ivan checked out of their hotel and made their way to the FBO at the airport. John previously had the plane refueled so all they needed to do was plan and file the flight plan for Cote d'Azur Airport in Nice, France. Vitori arrived, accompanied by the same men with whom he had previously departed. He greeted John and told him he was ready for a little relaxation. John got him settled in the cabin and manned the aircraft. They departed Johannesburg and eight and half hours later touched down at Cote d'Azur Airport. Vitori stuck his head in the cockpit and thanked John for a smooth flight and congratulated him for a great landing. He gave John his business card with the address of his Villa written on the back.

"John," he said. "You and your copilot come up to my villa and stay a couple of days. You have been working too hard. I will tell my staff to expect you."

"Thank you Vitori," John said. "We will be there as soon as we take care of the aircraft."

"Good, John. I will see you soon," he said.

Vitori departed. John and Ivan began to secure the aircraft then stepped into the FBO. They presented their passports and customs form and were cleared to enter the country. They rented a car and Ivan entered Vitori's villas address into the GPS. It was a nice drive into Monaco and they soon found the villa. They pulled into the driveway and parked in the parking area. A couple of Vitori's staff came out to greet them and showed them to the guest-house. It was set back from the main house. It was beautiful two-story stucco painted in a light color. It had eleven bedrooms, kitchen area and many bathrooms. Outside were a 50-meter swimming pool and two tennis courts. These two young aviators were overwhelmed by the lavishness which was on display. They were treated like royalty for two days and relaxed beyond belief. John finally transmitted to Vitori that they were pleased by his hospitality but had to get back home, as the plane would be needed for another trip. Vitori gave John a check covering the eight days he and Ivan had been away from home. It totaled $32,400 dollars or about $1800 per day. Vitori stated that he had already sent Omega aviation a check for the plane rental and this was extra pay to them for the great job that had done for him. John and Ivan were ecstatic.

They departed Nice headed for New York and feeling great. After refueling they headed home for Salt Lake City.

Kamas, Utah

During the next few weeks Tori and Bill Grammercy became close friends. Just as Larry had predicted they meshed as a team and she became dependent on his wisdom and experience. Their overseas trip to the Philippines, Australia and New Zealand were eye openers. Oceanic and ICAO procedures were new to her and Bill was invaluable in that regard as he had many hours immersed in that kind of flying. On their stops in Australia and New Zealand he was unbelievable, as he seemed to know everybody on a first name basis.

Larry made note of this developing professional relationship and thought maybe Bill was going to have to pair up with her when she began her checkout in the AFV.

Bob Avery had made a trip to Pensacola, Florida, and had recruited another NFO. He had dinner with Major John Cushman and had convinced him he should join the AFV program. He had also run into Lieutenant Commander Steve Curry and had also recruited him as a replacement for the retiring Jerry Elliott. Steve was currently flying the T-39B Saberliner as was John Cushman. They both had experience flying the F-14 Tomcat and many carrier landings. They would both be a good addition to the AFV crew.

In the three weeks Tori had been flying the G4 she had accumulated about 54 hours of flight time. She was really feeling comfortable and on her current flight she returned from New York and checked-in with operations. There was a note from Larry telling her to see Bob Avery when she got back to headquarters.

She caught the 5:00p.m. helo shuttle to headquarters and walked into the building and over to Bob's office. Bob's assistant Cindy greeted her and announced her.

"Mr. Avery, Tori Croft to see you sir," she said into the intercom.

"Send her right in," he responded.

He greeted her as she entered, "Hey Tori, great to see you. How are things going with the flying?" he asked.

"Great. I'm now well checked out in the G4," she said.

"That's what I heard. It's the reason I called you in. I am going to put you on the regular group schedule. Group three is going on duty tomorrow and all the necessary physical equipment is on hand for you to begin flying, so check-in tomorrow morning and be prepared for duty off-site," Bob said.

As was usual Bob had spoken in coded words and Tori knew what he had in mind. It was time to go up the mountain and strap on one of those AFVs.

"Roger that," she said with a great big smile on her face. It was time to begin her great adventure into space and she could hardly wait.

"I'll be here with bells on," she said.

She was really pumped up about this new development in her career and she could hardly wait. The next two weeks were going to be a blast.

She practically floated over to the house she was so ecstatic. When she arrived John was not home yet and she wondered when he would get there. Dinner tonight had to be something special so she called the hangar in Salt Lake City and since Ginny had already left for the day, John picked up.

"Omega Aviation. John Walker here. May I help you?" he asked.

Tori spoke very quickly still excited at the news she had just received.

"John this is Tori, I just got home and received the word from Bob Avery that I would be working off-site for two weeks so this will be my only night home and I wanted to make a special dinner," she said.

"Whoa, slow down a little," he said. "Sounds like you are on an express train to Virginia. Try me again on dinner," he said.

"When are you going to get home?" She said a bit more slowly. "I am going off-site tomorrow for two weeks and want to make a special dinner since I am only going to be home tonight."

"I got it now. I will be leaving in about fifteen minutes. I just have a phone call to make and then I'll be on the next helo for headquarters," he said. "Should be home in about an hour. See you then."

"That's great. Looking forward to seeing you," she said.

John hung up the phone and then dialed again. He had a deal working on buying another G550 in Portland, Maine, and the seller wanted to discuss it. He spoke to Gunter Knoblick who was the manager of Skyline Aviation and they agreed that John would come to Portland next week and take a look at the airplane before making a commitment to buy it. When he finished he hung up the phone, grabbed his jacket and briefcase and headed for the helo pad.

He greeted the pilot as he approached. "Hey, Gary, you got this thing ready to fly," he asked.

"For you boss, we're ready anytime. Hop in and we'll get this thing underway," he said.

Gary Sheen was the senior helo pilot for Omega and coordinated all helo matters working under Larry Beck. Gary had been with VXE-6 flying the UH-1N before coming to Omega. He was one Hell of a great pilot and John always liked flying with him.

"How's the weather over the mountains today, Gary?" he asked.

"A few low clouds over the high peaks so we will be following Interstate 80 until we get over into the valley. Then the weather is great. It'll only take us a couple of minutes more going that way," he said. "You want to fly the copilots seat tonight?" he asked.

"Nah, I'm just going to relax here in the back," he said.

He climbed in the passenger section, fastened his seat belt and just relaxed for the flight up to headquarters.

Forty-three minutes later Gary was bringing the helo into a hover and set the Bell 412 down on the pad.

"Nice flight," John said as he exited the helo. He walked swiftly over to the house and entered through the front door.

He entered the kitchen where Tori was busily concocting a dinner beyond anyone's imagination. She greeted John with a hug.

"Wow, it's been over a two weeks since our paths crossed," she offered.

"Yeah, if you haven't been gone I have and vice versa," he said.

They had become close friends in their relationship but each knew that having more of a relationship was poison in the positions each held within the corporation so they determined they would enjoy each other's company and not become more involved.

"Go put on something comfortable and I'll have dinner ready in about a half hour. Would you like a mixed drink tonight. It's celebration time you know. I have been cleared to fly at the next level," she said.

"Fix me a scotch and water," he called out from the west bedroom as he changed into his warm-ups.

When he finished changing he came back into the kitchen.

"Can I help with anything," he asked.

"No, I think I have it all under control," she shot back.

John could see she was in great spirits and was so bubbly he thought she would overflow. It was a great evening.

11

"A Taste of Space"

Kamas, Utah, Headquarters compound

The morning began early for John and Tori. They had a leisurely breakfast at their kitchen bar. The conversation for Tori was going at a mile a minute and John could tell she was still pumped up about her upcoming two weeks on the mountain. As time approached 7:30a.m. they grabbed their overnight bags and walked out the front door. John was on his way to Tahiti and Tori was going up the mountain. They walked over to headquarters and John gave her a big hug, wished her well and continued on to the helo pad.

She went up to her cubicle on the second floor and sat down to look at her email. She was engrossed and didn't hear Bill Grammercy enter behind her.

"Grab your stuff, Sis," he said. "We're next at 7:46am."

The relief crew going up the mountain were scheduled at staggered intervals so things in headquarters appeared normal. A huge crowd headed for the security door might attract attention should there be a visitor in the building so security precautions were in place.

Bill had nicknamed Tori "Sis" since she was somewhat younger and a little less experienced than he. He kind of became her older brother looking after her and she liked it.

She answered him, "Okay, Bro. I'm ready."

She grabbed her travel bag and they walked down to the security doors. Both of them flashed their security badges, entered the code and submitted to the retinal scan. The door unlocked and they proceeded to the elevator, took it down to the lower level where they boarded the tram. They reached the pneumatic tubes and took the left one. Doors closed and they were on their way up the mountain.

They stepped out onto the hangar deck where five AFVs were parked. Number three was out on a mission but was due to return in about twenty-five minutes. They checked in with Jack in operations and passed a couple of crews headed down the mountain. As new crews arrived, those relieved took the tubes down for two weeks of R&R.

Tori would get her first solo flight as the schedule allowed and as soon as Larry Beck arrived on the mountain.

Bill reminded her to study the lesson guides containing the items she needed to learn, which outlined the maneuvers for her flight. Bill studied with her as he had been through this before with some of the other pilots and he knew the routine. He coached her and advised her of some of the idiosyncrasies she would encounter with the vehicle.

Later in the day Larry made it up the mountain so now all things were in place.

Bill and Tori found her locker in the crew locker room. She retrieved her pressure suit and Bill suggested she try it for proper fit. A screen had been arranged so she could don he suit behind it in privacy. She stepped out with the suit on. Bill helped her with the helmet and low and behold everything fit perfectly. She closed the faceplate momentarily and opened it because she had no oxygen attached to her suit so no way to breathe with it closed. They both checked it out and everything looked normal. Bill took her back to the pressure chamber and she climbed in. They would put the suit through the mandatory check before her first flight for safety purposes. Bill ran the chamber and within twenty minutes he bought it back down to station level and depressurized it completely.

"Okay, kid. Your good for the first flight," he said.

"I'm glad. That chamber stuff is a pain in the ass," she said.

"Why don't you get out of that thing and let's have some dinner. I'm getting hungry after all this work," he said.

They went back into the kitchen where Larry was just fixing himself a frozen dinner.

"Hey Larry," Bill said. "We checked out Tori's suit and she's ready for her first flight."

"Have you finished studying the flight profiles?" Larry asked.

"Yes sir," Tori replied. "And Bill and I reviewed all the material pertaining to it and believe me he quizzed me on it also."

"Okay Tori, get some dinner and maybe tonight we can get you and Bill out for a joyride," he said.

"That would be outstanding," she said.

She and Bill found some frozen dinners and after cooking sat down at the kitchen table.

All the new crews had arrived and there were now eighteen people in the crew quarters. One AFV pilot had not arrived yet as he was on the last leg of his charter in the G550 and would arrive the next morning. That would be her old mission commander of the space shuttle flight, Paul Anderson. Her reunion with him would have to wait once again.

As time-approached 8:00p.m. Larry who had been coordinating with Jack Shepard came into the quarters and motioned Tori and Bill to join him. They sat down in the briefing area and Larry said they were cleared to man AFV number 2 and lift off about 9:00p.m. if possible. They all knew the flight profile so now it was all business. Tori and Bill went into the locker room and donned their pressure suits. Before leaving that area they checked each other's suit then hooked up to the suit testing station for final checks. Both suits passed and they walked out onto the hangar deck and over to number 2. Bill climbed the ladder first followed by Tori. They manned their respective positions and Bill checked in with Jack on their UHF transmitter.

"Ready for start," Bill said over the UHF.

"Cleared to start," Jack replied. "Advise when ready for liftoff."

"Roger," Bill answered.

Tori started the vehicle and monitored all gauges. It took five minutes to warm up the vehicle. She looked over to Bill and gave him thumbs up.

Bill keyed the mike, "Base, Sparkle ready for liftoff." Sparkle being Tori's call sign.

"Standby, Sparkle," Jack answered.

The claxon sounded, hangar lights went off and the hangar door dropped down and out.

"Sparkle is cleared for departure," Jack said.

Tori slid the AFV out onto the hangar door which was now a landing pad. The first profile was simple, just liftoff straight up to fifty feet and hover in a stationary position. Tori moved the anti-gravity lever and the vehicle smoothly lifted off to fifty feet. She brought it to a hover. As soon as she cleared the hangar door it rolled up and closed. She was now on her own. The next profile called for a straight-line triangular flight at up to 10,000' and back to a hover in front of the hangar door. This went smoothly and she was ready for the final phase of this flight. She took it up to 10,000' accelerating gently toward the north then heading out northwest towards the Pacific Ocean where she took it to over 100,000' and 9000mph. The profile called for a wide sweeping turn and return to base. They were soon approaching base from the north and Bill keyed the UHF.

"Base, this is Sparkle 50 miles out for landing. Over," Bill said.

"Sparkle cleared for recovery," Jack replied.

Tori slowed and descended. As she approached the mountain, she lowered the landing gear and her night vision television camera picked up the hangar door rolling into position. She came to a hover at 50'. She slowly descended and set the vehicle down gently then rolled it into the hangar bay. The claxon sounded and the hangar door closed and the lights came back on.

She shutdown the vehicle and completed the checklists. She was first down the ladder followed by Bill.

Bill gave her a big slap on the back and said, "Great flight, Rookie."

"Thanks, Bill," she responded. "That sure is some vehicle. I haven't had that much fun in years."

"Just the beginning," he said. "Let's go get back into something comfortable."

"Sounds like a good move, Bill," she said.

They moved quickly into the crew locker room and changed into their warm-ups then went into the crew quarters.

Everybody had a good word or comment for her

about how glad they were to have her on board. Bill took her off in a quiet place and debriefed her. He was probably more critical than others would be but he wanted her to be the best. He ended his debrief with the comment that it was one great flight and she was doing just fine. About then Jack entered the quarters and came over and added his kudos. He told her that she was right on almost every step of the way and she was going to be a great AFV pilot. She was pleased that she had been so easily accepted and integrated in this program. Larry finally came in from operations and said they had monitored the flight and that it was satisfactory but that she should practice heading control and slewing the vehicle on her next flight. She took all comments and suggestions with a positive attitude and acknowledged she would try harder next time around.

There had been accommodations made for her in the sleeping quarters. There were five bedrooms and one of them had been divided with partitions so she could have her own private bedroom. Bathroom facilities were a little less modified. There were four bathrooms and one bathroom had a sign hung on the door. When turned over it read "Occupied, woman present". Whenever Tori used the facilities she just turned the sign around. That would have to do temporarily. All-hands drifted into the bedrooms and settled down for the night. No recon flights were schedule until about ten in the morning.

Headquarters

Bob was busy in his office with Omega matters when the red phone in his desk rang.

He answered. "Bob here."

"Bob, John Boland. Something has come up and I need you to come to Washington for a meeting. I would also like you to bring Paul Anderson. It's a matter we can't discuss completely on the phone."

"Okay. When would you like us there?" he asked.

"Within the next week would be great. The sooner the better," he said.

"John Walker has to go to Portland, Maine, next week so I guess we could piggyback on his flight. He plans to go on Wednesday so we could have a meeting late Wednesday or Thursday. Your call, John," Bill said.

"Let's plan to meet late on Wednesday. Advise me of your arrival time and I will have a vehicle meet you at the General Aviation Fixed Base Operator at Dulles. We can also make reservations at a hotel for you and Paul. Is one night going to do it?" he asked.

"I'm sure that will be fine. John can pick us up late Thursday then if we need to meet that day we will still be able to meet him and depart for Salt Lake City," Bob responded.

"Okay Bob, will be looking forward to our meeting on Wednesday," he said.

Bob returned the phone to its compartment in the desk and picked up his regular phone. He dialed John at Hangar 512.

Ginny Wulf answered and he asked for John. John picked up,

"What's up, Bob?" he said.

"When is your flight to Portland scheduled?" he asked.

"Right now it looks like Tuesday," he answered.

"You need to reschedule it for Wednesday, John. Paul Anderson and I need to be dropped off at Dulles for a meeting and then pick us up on Thursday. Can you fit that into your schedule?" he said.

"That'll work for me. I will call Gunter in Portland and tell him I'll be there on Wednesday instead of Tuesday. My inspection of his G550 should take up only the morning on Thursday and I will be able to pick you up Thursday afternoon," he said

"That sounds great. Let's plan on departing around 8:00a.m. then," Bob said.

"I'll adjust the schedule accordingly. Talk with you later," he said as he hung up the phone.

Paul was scheduled to go up the mountain this morning so Bob wrote him a note and asked Cindy to put it in his cubicle where he couldn't miss it. Better yet, he asked Cindy to call Paul on his company cell phone and ask him to stop by his office before he departed the building.

Cindy reached Paul just as he was leaving his quarters for headquarters. He indicated he would stop by Bob's office in about ten minutes.

Paul entered Bob's outer office and Cindy greeted him and directed him into Bob's office.

"Good morning, Paul. Hope you had a nice trip. I see you returned home late last night," he said.

"Mornin', Bob. Nah it wasn't too late and we had a great trip. Tokyo was a blast but Beijing kind of sucked. Their customs, immigration and police are tough to accommodate at the airport. Other that that we had a blast. Trip went off like clockwork," he said

"Listen, the reason I had you stop by is we are going to Washington next Wednesday. The boss specifically asked for you by name so it has to be a hot project. Must involve NASA but I can't speculate too much. My question is do you want to spend a couple of days home with the wife or do your regular shift for the next six days? Or when we get back from Washington we can cut your shift short by three days and you can be home on your normal two weeks R&R plus a couple of days. Your choice," Bob said.

"Who's filling my slot right now?" Paul asked.

"Larry went with the relief crews yesterday," Bob said.

"Let's do this, Bob. I will relieve Larry today and next Tuesday I can get back home and pack for the trip to Washington. When we get back I'd like to just add the three days to my normal R&R if that's okay," he said.

"That'll work, why don't you take off now and when you see Larry brief him on our schedule. He's flexible and can work things out. I'll see you later. Take care," Bob said.

They shook hands and Paul took his travel bag and made his way down to the security doors. He jumped though all the hoops and finally arrived at the hangar level in the tubes. As he stepped out the claxon was sounding and the hangar doors opened signaling a departure of the 10:00a.m. recon flight. The Mideast was a mess and daily flights were needed just to keep up with the intelligence. There would be another recon of Afghanistan and Southeast Asia at 11:00a.m. this morning. It too was in turmoil and the satellites were not sufficient to cover all possibilities. Paul went over to operations and checked in with Jack. Larry was there also and Paul stopped by to talk with him.

"Larry, I just had a discussion with Bob and he informed me that he and I have been summoned by the big boss to Washington next week Wednesday. Should be back on Thursday but Bob offered me the rest of my duty week off so you'll need to make an adjustment to the duty roster for those three days. I appreciate your covering for me yesterday. Thanks," he said.

"Don't worry about it. We can cover it okay. By the way your protégé had her first flight yesterday. Flew it like the pro she is. I think she is a great addition to our cadre. I've got a few things to finish here and then I'll be on my way down the mountain. I'll work things out on the schedule with Bob. Thanks for the heads up," Larry said.

Paul left Ops and walked over to the crew quarters as he entered Tori immediately spied him and rushed him like a linebacker rushing a quarterback. She was overjoyed at seeing him for the first time since he retired from NASA.

She hugged him. "Paul it's great to see you, how have you been?" she asked.

"I'm good," he answered. "It's been a while. Are you doing okay."

"I'm doing great, Paul. I had my first flight yesterday. What a blast," she said. "This vehicle is the ultimate in space travel. I can't wait for my next flight."

Paul could see she was really stoked about her flight and he was excited for her.

"I know just how you feel, Tori. I had the same emotions as you on my first flight. This beats any space shuttle flight by a big margin," he said.

They chatted for another ten or fifteen minutes before everyone got into the conversation. All these crewmen had been in many different Navy squadrons and to all of them, unanimously, this was the greatest squadron they had been associated with in their careers. The camaraderie was unmatched anywhere. This was one happy bunch of astronauts.

12

"The Plot Thickens"

Moscow, Russia, Twelve Months Earlier

A high level conference had been called for the sixth of the month at the Kremlin. Present were the President Boris Petrovsky, Prime Minister Sergei Puchinov, Head of the Russian Federal Space Agency General Sergei Kovolov, Minister of Defense General Arturo Meechaim, Head of the GRU Petre Borginov, General Vladamir Gorchinski and General Dimitri Zukov.

The purpose of the meeting had yet to be revealed and most in attendance had wondered about the agenda. Obviously since so many people were working in the field of space exploration and space defense some were convinced that it was related to space.

The Prime Minister Sergei Puchinov rose and began, "Gentlemen, I have called this meeting to review our policy concerning protection of Iran's' right to continue its nuclear weapons program. Protection is aimed mainly at an Israeli air strike and secondly at the United States should they interfere or try to protect Israel from retaliation. Publicly we have been helping Iran with their development and testing of their long-range missiles. Also there has been a lot of rhetoric and posturing but no solid plan of protection and retaliation.

"I believe we need to talk about and develop a plan we

will execute should Israel attempt to launch an air strike against the Iranian's nuclear facilities. I have discussed this with General Kovolov but before I reveal his option I would like to hear from all of you," Sergei said.

General Meechaim spoke, "Comrade Minister, one option we could present would be a retaliatory air strike against the Israelis. Currently we have given the Iranians six batteries of the S-300P anti-aircraft defense missile systems. We are considering upgrading them to S-300V that will give them a little better range capability. The P version of the S-300 has a range of only 47 miles whereas the "V" version can reach out to 66 miles. If we decide to establish a retaliatory force we will need to base our aircraft in Iran as that is the only viable territory close enough for such a force. Even at that we would need airborne refueling tankers to complete such a strike at the heart of Israel. Our naval base in Syria is capable of giving us early warning of an Israeli air strike."

"Thank you for your input, General, but that leaves me with a question. What are our plans for protection from the Americans in the event we launch a retaliatory strike? They currently have one carrier in the Persian Gulf and two additional carriers in the Arabian Sea," the Prime Minister asked. "Can we neutralize them before we strike?"

"You pose some important questions, Comrade. It is difficult to know exactly where the Americans are at any given time. Their mobility certainly comes into play in our planning and is a difficult enemy to overcome. Another concern is their ship and submarine capability to launch both conventional and nuclear tipped cruise missiles almost without detection. Any air or surface operation would have a low success rate," General Meechaim said.

"I believe you have laid out your case here, General.

It seems our rhetoric almost makes us a bear without teeth," the Prime Minister said.

"Can anyone tell me when the Iranians will be operational with their first nuclear weapon?" Sergei asked.

General Zukov was the missile expert and had been working with the Iranians on their long-range capability. "Comrade Minister, my assessment is their missile capability will be ready within the year. We just completed assisting them with the launch of their first long range test body. Analysis of that test is not yet complete but it was a success and the distance was over five hundred miles. We must achieve one thousand miles before they will be capable of reaching Israel. On their nuclear warhead development it may take as much as sixteen months to reach warhead success. Their centrifuge capability was recently damaged by the stuxnet virus in their computers and they are just now recovering from that and getting back on track in their development of uranium enrichment."

The Head of the GRU, Petre Borginov, was next to speak, "Gentlemen, we have developed plans for using tactical nuclear weapons for sabotage against the United States in the event of war."

He described Soviet-made suitcase nukes identified as RA-115s (or RA-115-01s for submersible weapons) that weigh from fifty to sixty pounds. "These portable bombs could last for many years if wired to an electric source. In case there is a loss of power, there is a battery backup. If the battery runs low, the weapon has a transmitter that sends a coded message – either by satellite or directly to a GRU post at a Russian embassy or consulate. 'We have operatives as I speak who are personally looking for hiding places for weapons caches in the Shenandoah Valley area."

He added, "it is surprisingly easy to smuggle nuclear

weapons into the US either across the Mexican border or using a small transport missile that can slip though unde- tected when launched from a Russian airplane. We could activate this program and be ready to detonate these weapons should the middle-east situation call for it," he said.

"Thank you, Petre. I believe it is now time for General Kovolov to reveal his plan for protecting the Iranians. Gen- eral Kovolov, please," Sergei said

"Thank you, Comrade Minister. Gentlemen," he said as he turned to those assembled. "My plan is simple. We take out of storage one of our SS-E-13 Lucifer missile/war- head systems we have had stored for some time and launch it into orbit. They were originally designed to be in a sta- tionary orbit at 22,000miles in space but I would suggest we launch it into a 300 mile high polar orbit and make it capable of being an Electromagnetic Pulse weapon (EMP). On every other orbit we would have the capability of hitting either the United States or Israel. Over the United States we could detonate it at 300 miles up and could cover a 315,000 square mile area. Over Israel we could detonate it at one mile and wipe Israel off the face of the earth. If we detonate it over Israel we should be prepared possibly with Petre's plan to attack the United States with tactical nu- clear weapons. We can leak this information about the weapons making sure the United States gets the message. Then when we are posturing they will know we can back up our words. When the Iranians come on line with their own nuclear weapons we can bring the Lucifer weapon down safely in Russia and put it back in storage," Kovolov said.

Everyone in the room sat for a minute trying to ab- sorb what General Kovolov had just said. It sent chills up the spine of many as this plan could end up in all out nuclear war and be the destruction of Russia in the process. A few brave souls spoke up in opposition of this plan it was just too risky.

Finally, The President, Boris Petrovsky, cleared his throat as if to gain their attention. Everyone stopped their arguing and turned to listen to their leader.

"Comrades, I have listened to all your proposed plans and all your pros and cons for each plan. Here is my decision. We will institute Comrade Kovolov's plan because I feel it has the most chance of success. The other plans suggested still have holes in them and many unanswered questions. His plan is simple so you are directed to coordinate with each other's agency and get the job done. Are there any questions?" he asked in a stern, loud voice showing his disgust for their bickering. "Good. This meeting is adjourned," he said.

All in attendance stood as the President and Prime Minister departed the room. There were a few unhappy people but the President had spoken and now it was their duty to carry out this bizarre plan. They sat down and discussed the specifics of how and when this plan would be carried out.

General Kovolov would direct General Spastek at Aviation Plant Number One in Samara, Russia, to break out of storage one SS-E-13 Lucifer missile/warhead system and ship it too General Zukov at the missile base at Sary Shagan, Kazakhstan, for reconditioning and checkout. It would then be shipped to General Gorchinski in Mirny where he would mount the payload on a Soyouz rocket and launch it into orbit. Calculations were this would take about three months to complete.

Petre Borginov would begin his operation and would

devise a plan to leak the orbital missile information to the CIA.

Back at his office, Petre called in his assistant, Katrina Petrolov. She had been working posing as a double agent and making friends with Benjamin Heptner one of the clerks attached to the U.S. Embassy. They had been passing minor intelligence between them for a couple of months. Petre discussed with her the need for planting some vital intelligence that he needed leaked to the Americans. He gave her a copy of page two of a report prepared by General Kovolov which covered the launch of the nuclear tipped missile scheduled within the next three months. He urged on her the importance of this intelligence that needed to be planted with the Americans. They needed to think that Russia wanted to keep this secret from the world but in fact they wanted it to be at least known to the Americans. It was part of the plan to pressure the Americans into knowing and believing the Russians weren't bluffing when they warned the Americans about defending the Israelis when it came to action against Iran.

Later in the week Ben called Katrina for their weekly date. She agreed to meet him at their usual restaurant for dinner and later their affaire de Coeur. They had a quiet candlelight dinner after which they went up to Katrina's apartment for a little lovemaking. Even though this was business, Katrina enjoyed here weekly tryst with Ben. After a lot of passion on the pillow, Ben lay there exhausted while Katrina left him for a hot shower. Hot showers were a treat in Moscow as the hot water heaters were not always reliable. When she got up she told Ben there was something for him on the night table. He sat up and read it and exclaimed to himself, "What the Hell are the Russians up to now?"

He wasn't an analyst but an information gatherer and this would be a feather in his cap with his boss. He knew Katrina couldn't give him the paper so he took out his cell phone and photographed it. Katrina was still in the shower so he went in and joined her there.

Langley, Virginia

The daily report from the Moscow Embassy was in the morning email. Page 2 from General Kovolov's report had been translated, coded with the rest of the intelligence and transmitted to headquarters. The Russian analyst decoded it and then discussed it with other analysts in his section before writing an analysis for the Director.

When the Director read the morning report, he called the section chief and asked for a briefing. It was scheduled for 11:00a.m. and all concerned gathered in the director's briefing room. The briefing was limited to just that item and the section chief went though the intelligence from the acquisition to the transmission to headquarters including the background on the intelligence clerk who discovered it and the circumstances. It appeared to be authentic and the Director's question was what are the Russians doing with something this dangerous to world stability?

Back during the Cold War the United States had threatened to take out the Soviet Union if they dared desecrate space with such a weapon. The Soviets had backed down and stored these weapons hopefully never to be heard from again.

This was a serious breach of national security and something needed to be done to counter it. The Director put it on the agenda for tomorrow morning's intelligence briefing for the President. Meanwhile the Director contacted SecDef and invited him over to headquarters for a briefing on the intelligence.

That very afternoon Don Ransford entered the Director's office at his scheduled time. The director briefed Don on the developments and between them they came up with a counterintelligence move. Don indicated that somewhere in the DOD was a countermeasures package to this Russian space weapon. It had been developed back when the Russians had threatened the United States with the weapon in question. It had been designed for launch as a payload of an Agena rocket but we no longer had that capability nor could we let the Russians know we were launching it. The only plausible answer was to put it on Space Shuttle Enterprise should the Russians actually put this weapon in earth orbit. Enterprise was due to fly in about five months and the Russian missile launches would need to be monitored even more than usual. The truth of the payload for Enterprise would need to be kept secret even from the shuttle crew as it would be dangerous to allow this information to be leaked to the Russians. It was decided the cover story for the payload would be that it was a secret DOD monitoring system and would be launched just before reentry of the shuttle from space. Thus the stage was set to counter the Russians move. The President was briefed.

Mirny, Russia, Three months later

Davita Feldman had been sent by Mossad, Israeli secret service, from her current assignment in Moscow to Mirny to gather information about missile launches and to determine the payload that had recently been sent to the base from Sary Shagan. Mossad had tracked it all the way from Kazakhstan because it was a suspicious payload. Mossad sources in Kazakhstan had questioned the type of payload based on the secrecy surrounding it during the time the workers at the base had been putting it together. Intelligence had indicated special handling with protection required from radiation. The Israelis were trying to confirm that it was a nuclear weapon.

When Davita arrived in Mirny she inquired at the local restaurant about a job. The manager, Georgie Serivok, was enamoured with her when he interviewed her so she was immediately hired. The fact that she was tall and good looking might have had something to do with her being put on the payroll.

The military personnel and civilians who worked at the base came in for meals and she compiled information which she overheard when they were eating. Over the course of the first week she learned that they were working on the payload for an upcoming launch. They expected it would be launched as soon as it was checked out and mounted on the missile.

When she finished work for the day she went home and logged on to her computer. She encrypted an email and sent it off to her handler at Mossad.

The very next day during her shift a couple of military personnel came in around dinnertime and ordered a meal. She flirted with them so they would not be suspicious when she spent a little more than normal time hovering around their table. During the meal one of them used the phrase "nuclear payload" which is what she had been looking for. Her encrypted email that night reported her findings.

Tel Aviv, Israel

Erik Selfridge was the agent assigned to compile all intelligence reports being received from the field, code named "Bright Star." Davita's reports were thorough and timely as were the reports he had been receiving from Kazakhstan. When he studied them, it became obvious that the Russians were very close to launching a nuclear tipped missile. Erik was raising questions as to what was the missile's target. A long discussion ensued with no answer to that question.

A transcript was received of a telephone conversation between General Gorchinski and General Zukov the following day. They had discussed the arrival of the payload and, during the discussion, Zukov and General Gorchinski asked what the orbit of the payload would be. Grochinski indicated it would be a 4° orbit at 300 miles above the earth. It was beginning to look as though the payload could be used as a threat to almost any country on the globe.

After a briefing Moshe Evans, head of Mossad, decided they should share their findings with the CIA. He placed a call directly to John Boland in Washington, D.C.

His call was routed to the Director and he picked up the phone.

"Moshe, how are things in Israel?" he asked.

"Things are good, John," he answered. "I thought we needed to share something we have been watching closely."

"It must be important for you to call me directly. Thank you for thinking of us," John said.

"John, we have been keeping track of a payload which originated at the base at Sary Shagan in Kazakhstan. General Zukov is involved and you know he is responsible for most of their external missile involvements in other countries. He has recently been observed traveling to Iran. Anyway, the payload was shipped to Plesetsk, their missile base near Mirny. We intercepted a phone conversation between Zukov and General Gorchinski and confirmed that it is a nuclear payload and is in a 300 mile high Polar orbit.

We don't know the intent of the launch and we are continuing our surveillance. We will keep you advised," he said.

"That's some pretty serious stuff, Moshe. Do you have any ideas what they might be up to?" John asked.

"If it relates to Iran, it looks like they want to threaten us or you or maybe both of us should we attack Iran's nuclear sites. If we were to do that they could fire that weapon at us. If you protect us after we attack the Iranian sites, they could launch the nuclear weapon at your country," Moshe said.

"I think your assessment is probably correct. Let me run it by our mid-east desk and see what we may have missed. This is a serious situation," John said.

"Tell me about the possibility of obtaining an e-bomb from your military inventory. We are considering infiltrating the Iranian nuclear site at Natanz and planting the device in their underground complex. The non-nuclear detonation and resulting EMP will shut the place down for a couple of years. Then we wouldn't need to send an air strike. They are using liquid nitrogen in one of their scientific studies there and we would cloak it as a liquid nitrogen Dewar. How we get it into the complex is a problem and we are working on it," he said.

"I don't think it is possible to get an e-bomb for you, Moshe. We need clean hands on that and complete involvement deniability. We don't have anyone outside the agency who could do that for us. Where the Hell is Ollie when you need him?" John quipped. "Let me work on it for a couple of days. Maybe I can come up with something."

When John hung up he sat at his desk for a minute and pondered. It was difficult being the director some of the time. He didn't lie to Moshe but had held back the information that the CIA had known about the nuclear tipped missile for about five months.

Arlington, Virginia, Pentagon

Don Ransford had been charged with obtaining the weapon needed to destroy the Russian missile payload. After many messages and phone calls he located it at Sandia Base in New Mexico. He made arrangements for it to be shipped to the Rockwell assembly plant in Fort Worth, Texas. There it was reconditioned, updated and checked out for proper operation. This took about two months. When it was ready it was transshipped to Cape Kennedy for compatibility updates to the shuttle. The shuttle Enterprise was already in Launch Complex 39 in the Vehicle Assembly Building. The DOD package was loaded and attached to the cargo bay deck and plugged into the electrical circuits of the shuttle. It was designed to be ejected on electrical command from the cargo bay by the load specialist.

As for NASA, all they knew was that this was a DOD monitoring package and not a danger to anyone on the shuttle or launch crew.

Moscow, Russia, Two months later

Russia, through their intelligence network, received word about the DOD weapon that had been taken into space by shuttle Enterprise. They knew if the United States were successful, it would have a deterrent against the Russian nuclear weapon now in orbit.

They followed the fuel problem of the shuttle and thought the astronauts were lost in space. As it turned out, with the subsequent rescue by unknown beings in their space vehicles, the DOD package was still there and was the Russian's for the taking. The Russians felt the United

States had no capability to retrieve the package but, if they could get to the shuttle before its orbit decayed they had a good chance of retrieving it. It would be a real coup for them and a technical treasure trove.

General Kovolov called his staff together and charged them with mounting a mission to retrieve the package. General Sokolev, base commander at Baikenour Cosmodrome, was charged with carrying out the mission.

Planning called for adding a missile stage to the launch vehicle. This was a special missile body that was designed to accept the DOD package and return it to Kazakhstan safely. A two-man capsule was attached to the top of the missile for the launch. The Russians were now in a position to recover the DOD package.

13

"The Plan"

A black Ford SUV met Bob and Paul when they arrived at Dulles. It was about a 20-minute drive over to the CIA. When they checked in at the front desk they had already been cleared and temporary IDs we available. They were escorted to the director's office where Judy Burns, the director's administrative assistant met them. She was well trained even though she had been with the admiral only for a short time. Bob and Paul both wondered where the admiral found such an efficient assistant as well a beautiful looking woman. Bob thought if he were twenty years younger he'd make a pass at this hot babe. It was approaching the 5 o'clock hour and Judy said the Admiral would be with them shortly.

Don Ransford, Secretary of Defense, stepped in while they were waiting and Judy asked him to take a seat and advised him also that the admiral would be with him shortly.

Bob was puzzled as he was not aware that SECDEF was going to be at this meeting. Bob had never met Secretary Ransford but knew he was a member of MJ-12. Bob stepped over and introduced himself.

""Excuse me, Mr. Secretary, I'm Bob Avery. I relieved Jack Forester as manager of his program," he said.

"Pleased to meet you, Bob. I'm familiar with your work and am finally glad to put a face with the name," he said.

"Sir, this is Paul Anderson, I'm sure you have heard of him," he said.

They shook hands and Don said, "I've heard a lot about you too, young man. It's a pleasure to meet you."

Judy advised them the admiral was free and they should go in.

John Boland came around his desk and gestured them to take a seat in his lounge area. As they were all finding a seat he greeted them,

"I'm glad you all could make it today," he said. Turning to Bob he asked, "Did you have a good flight, Bob?"

"Yes sir," Bob responded. "It was easy. Paul and I were just passengers."

"And how are you doing, Paul? It's a pleasure to meet you," he said.

"My pleasure, sir. I'm doing just fine," Paul said.

Turning to Don, "I'm glad you were able to make it, Don, since you are the main reason we are here today. I'm going to let you begin, Don, if you would," John said.

"Thanks, John. I'm glad we could get together. Gentlemen, we have a large problem and I'm not sure if we can even solve it. Paul, what you were not aware of is DOD had a top-secret package on space shuttle Enterprise. If you remember it was a package that was supposed to be ejected on day six of your flight. You were not advised of the nature of this package in order to keep it secret. It is a device designed to destroy the nuclear bomb the Russians placed in orbit three-months ago. Their nuclear bomb's purpose we suspect is to threaten us when the Russians need leverage against us. We had planned to detonate their bomb as a non-nuclear explosion before they could launch it at us. The device you carried is a very sophisticated device. It contains rockets, maneuvering system and high explosives besides an operating system capable of being controlled by ground stations. I guess you can take it from there, John," Don said.

"We have picked up intelligence that the Russians are planning a rendezvous flight with the space shuttle and are hoping to retrieve the package in question. They would gain a lot of technical knowledge as well as being able to turn the world against us telling everyone that we are the warmongers, etc. You all know the drill. Don tells me that they have lost communications with the device and that it is no longer responding. If it was, we would explode it in the shuttle bay and everything would be destroyed including the shuttle. Since we can't destroy it, we need some input to decide what the solution may be. The device is too big and too dangerous to extract and return via an AFV so that's where you come in, Paul. The $10,000 question is can we retrieve the space shuttle?" John said.

Paul spoke first. "That would be some miracle. You rescued us and now you want to retrieve the shuttle. It's going to take some research and planning if it is to be done."

"I'm not even sure where we would start but what are our orders, boss?" Bob asked.

"NASA calculates the orbit of the shuttle is decaying at a rate which will put it in the atmosphere in about three weeks. If it reaches that point before the Russians reach her, we are home free. Anytime before that and they could possibly get the device. That gives us two weeks on the safe side to pull this off. I'll give you two a week to study it and come up with a plan. Meanwhile we will need some missions monitoring the Russian's launch site to see how far they have progressed on a launch to intercept the shuttle. We currently have no missile with a high explosive warhead with which we could destroy the space shuttle so this is our only alternative. Gentlemen, let's get at it," John said. "Don, did you want to add anything?"

"No, John, I think you about covered it all. I'm available with any help but not sure I can add anything," Don said.

"It looks like Paul and I are going to need to do a lot of research before we can give you an answer," Bob said.

"Just keep us informed of your progress, Bob. We know it is going to be a rough week of work for you two," he added. "It's about dinner time. Let me order from the galley and we can talk about this some more over a good steak."

They all agreed that a good dinner would set a good tone and relax them all so John Boland contacted the cook, Willie Sutton, and ordered dinner. Soon they were having French Onion soup and munching on filet mignon. The discussion was subdued a little with Paul being the skeptic that it couldn't be done in the time frame they were being given while Bob wasn't sure there was a capability to do it. After dinner they all said their farewells and departed. Bob and Paul were driven out to the Holiday Inn in Fairfax where a room had been reserved for them for the night.

Next morning they arose late and had a leisurely breakfast in the Inn's dining room. John Walker had given them a 2:30p.m. arrival at Dulles so there was no hurry to get there before that time. It was only a twenty-minute drive from their hotel so it would be a leisurely morning.

After breakfast they went back to their room and

began a discussion of what needed to be studied in order to make a decision. Paul would have to consult all the flight manuals for the shuttle to determine if it could be reactivated in space. He remembered when he left it he shut everything down and wasn't sure he could get it up and running again. Bob noted that he wasn't sure there was enough thrust in the AFV to slow the orbital speed of the shuttle to get it into the reentry profile. Bob said they would have a get together on the mountain when they returned to Kamas and hash it out. They determined to include Larry and Tori because the two of them were also most knowledgeable about the vehicles involved.

The black Ford SUV arrived at the hotel precisely at two o'clock. They had their travel bags and boarded for the short drive to the FBO at Dulles. John Walker taxied in on time and shortly they greeted him as he entered the building. He indicated all he needed to do was file his flight plan and they would be ready to depart. He had fueled up in Portland and was set all the way to Salt Lake City. Ivan Wheaton was John's copilot on this trip and he had all the paperwork ready to file.

They were airborne in about fifteen minutes and wending their way to Salt Lake City. After they reached their cruising altitude, Bob put on a headset and conversed with John about his Portland experience. John reported that the G550 he looked at was immaculate and the price was right. The owner was hurting because of the economy and had to liquidate assets in order to make payroll at his company. John indicated they should grab this one up as quickly as possible. Bob said he and Bill Grammercy would take care of it as soon as they could have a meeting with John at headquarters.

They arrived back at Hangar 512 in plenty of time to

catch the 5:00p.m. helo to headquarters. Bob told Paul they would go up the mountain in the morning so he should go home and get some rest. It was going to be a busy week.

In the morning, Bob met John and worked out the purchase of the G550. Bill was currently on the mountain so he did not attend the meeting. However, Bill would handle the final details and advise john when he could go pick it up. John left all the paperwork and they adjourned their meeting.

Bob called Paul who was up in his cubicle and told him he was ready to depart. Paul came down and the walked back to the security doors which was their gateway to the mountain.

When they stepped out on the hangar deck they saw Larry and Bill Grammercy standing under an AFV. They walked over and struck up a conversation.

"I don't like this," said Larry. "Anytime the big boss shows up it has to be serious."

"Larry, we've been around each other long enough that you can read me like an open book. Yeah it's important. Is Jack really busy?" he asked.

"Right now Jack's monitoring two flights," Larry said.

"Okay, let's have a meeting. We'll catch Jack up when he's recovered the flights. Is Tori available?" he added.

"She's up in the cockpit of number six doing a little studying right now. Do you want her at this meeting, Bob?" Bill asked.

"Yeah, we're going to need her input on this one," Bob said.

Bill went over and told Tori to climb down, that there was going to be a meeting. Bob, Paul and Larry headed for crew quarters. They all sat down at the kitchen table. Tori and Bill joined them there.

"Here's the deal," Bob began. He retold the story Don Rumsford and John Boland related on their trip to Virginia.

"You're not putting us on another nail biter are you, Bob?" Larry joked. "That's some scenario you've laid out. I guess it's going to take a lot of study before we have an answer."

"Here's the way we're going to handle this. Paul and Tori will research whether this is practical from the shuttle standpoint. Larry, Bill and I will research the problem from the standpoint of the capability of the AFV. Let's get a timeline written down and the tasks we need to solve along that timeline. Zero on the line should start with a rendezvous with shuttle Enterprise. As I see it, Paul and Tori will be the best pilots available to bring the shuttle back to earth. Next the shuttle will have to be powered up mainly so we have hydraulic power to the flight controls. Without maneuvering fuel and retro engine fuel, the AFV will have to substitute for those functions. How much do we have to slow the shuttle in order to bring it back safely to earth? Is there a satisfactory landing place based on the shuttle's current orbit? If there is not a suitable landing site is the AFV capable of changing the shuttle's orbit. We need to designate a suitable landing site where we can get away with retrieving the pilots and not exposing the AFV program. Anybody have anything to add?" he asked.

"Oh no big problems to solve just some petty bullshit," Larry joked.

Everyone laughed but nobody had any questions. They all had their assignments and each group went off separately to discuss the problems.

Paul and Tori began by discussing powering up the

shuttle. At least one of the fuel cells had to have enough oxygen and hydrogen to put power to the shuttle. If they had that capability, all the heaters could be turned on to warm the hydraulic fluid and help in powering up the other two fuel cells. They would need hydraulic power for the flight controls and landing gear. Electricity would be needed for the flight instruments and computers to give them calculations for the approach pattern for wherever they decided to land.

Larry and Bill discussed what needed to be done to get the shuttle into approach mode. They would need to slow the orbital speed that they were sure they could do with the AFV. Changing the orbital path might be possible but there was no way to gauge that maneuver. They determined if they were to accomplish orbital change it would need to be done before slowing the shuttle. In orbit the weight of the shuttle would not be as big a factor but once gravity started to effect it the weight would be a large factor and the AFV might not be able to move that much weight. They decided a discussion with Paul and Tori was in order to help with the problem solving.

In the meantime, Bob walked over to operations and chatted with Jack. Bob indicated that they needed to monitor daily activity at the Baikonur Cosmodrome. It could be included in their daily flight across North Africa and the Middle East.

Over the six days, the team discussed mutual problems and came up with possible solutions. They discussed, at length, possible landing sites and the consensus was the ice runway at McMurdo Sound in the Antarctic. It was still night there 24 hours a day and they could land the shuttle and pick up the astronauts without much chance of being seen.

Thursday's deadline was approaching and Bob journeyed back up the mountain for a final meeting with all concerned.

The team had worked together all week except for an occasional AFV flight but on Wednesday they finalized the plan.

They were sitting around the table when Bill suddenly shouted, "I hate this ridiculous operation. It's going to get us all killed," he said. The people that dream up this stuff never have to risk their ass or pay the consequences."

"Calm down, Bill," Bob said. "It's not as bad as it looks. Let's lay it out and then each one can give us an evaluation of this plan. Larry, since I'm assigning you as mission commander, give us your scenario, if you would."

"Okay, here is how I see it going down," he began. "Paul and Tori will be our shuttle crew. I will take them up in one of our birds. They will each be equipped with one of our EVA packs. Jack has calculated the ideal orbit to coordinate our flight with the shuttle's orbit. When it is one orbit short of the ideal orbit to divert it to McMurdo Base, Antarctica, I will attach our bird to the shuttle bay's tie-down. Paul and Tori will activate the EVA pack and proceed through the space lock in the cargo bay to the cockpit. Now, we picked McMurdo because it is the most secure landing spot where we can get away with attracting a minimum of attention."

"Once Paul and Tori are set and have established radio contact with us, I will detach and shadow them from five hundred miles away. During this one orbit they will power up the shuttle and ensure all systems needed for reentry are working. One orbit is approximately ninety minutes and we are all agreed that it should be sufficient time to get it done. When we come down across Asia again,

I will reattach the AFV to the shuttle. Here's the tricky part."

Paul chimed it at this point, "Once Larry is attached, we will close the shuttle bay doors and stop them at just the right space and time by pulling the shuttle bay door circuit breaker. We will leave just enough space for Larry to pull his landing strut clear when he detaches during reentry. We will then reset the circuit breaker and finish closing the shuttle bay doors."

Larry continued, "I will pull the shuttle into another orbit to take us over or close to McMurdo. Paul will have programmed the shuttle's computers to reflect the new orbit and as soon as we are in alignment, I will slow the shuttle the appropriate feet per second, then turn the shuttle around and position it for reentry. Again, Paul will advise me when we have achieved the appropriate angle of attack for reentry. I will remain attached to the shuttle until it gains about fifteen hundred pounds weight going from zero gravity to positive Gs.

We researched what we thought the AFV was capable of holding as far as weight is concerned. The Kalp Farm incident back in 1964 involved an auxiliary pod weighing approximately nine hundred pounds and was detached during a 4G pull-up of one of the earlier AFVs. We have not changed the propulsion system on the newer AFV so we knew it was capable of nine hundred pounds lifting capability.

We didn't leave it there. We researched the Coyame, Mexico, UFO incident from 1974. What we know is one of our newer model AFVs was carrying a drone. It was a sixteen-foot diameter disc and weighed in the neighborhood of fifteen hundred pounds. It too was lost in a 4G pull up at about 76,000' and 2000 miles per hour. So what we can draw from that is the AFV is capable of about fifteen hundred pounds additional carrying capacity.

Once we reach that weight we will detach from the shuttle and from there they are on their own for approach and landing at McMurdo. We checked the snow cover on the annual ice and it is less than two inches in most places so a landing at McMurdo is not a problem.

Once on the ice at McMurdo we will land immediately and retrieve Paul and Tori and get the Hell out of there. DOD will have to figure out how to retrieve their cargo bay package but then that will be their problem. That's how I see it, Bob. Anybody want to add anything?" Larry asked.

"Paul, what about powering up the shuttle? What do you think our chances are on that one?" Bob said.

"I think we have about a fifty-fifty chance of doing that," Paul said. "When I left the shuttle, I closed all the valves on the APUs and Fuel Cells. It's cold enough in space that the oxygen and hydrogen wouldn't evaporate at too fast a rate and I am confident there is plenty left to complete this mission. Getting one of the cells on line is another story but we will give it our best if we decide to go ahead with it," Paul added.

Tori piped up, "I think once we enter the shuttle, Larry should take up a position alongside the shuttle where we will be able to see him. No telling what can happen during power up since we've never done it before. If we don't get it powered up we can use hand signals to pass messages just in case the EVA communications system is shielded by the shuttle."

"That's a sound suggestion, Tori. I will add it to my notes and procedures," Larry said.

"Anybody have anything more to add before I get each of your assessment on this mission?" Bob asked.

Nobody added any comments so Bob started around the table.

"Larry, you're up. What's your assessment?" Bob said.

"I think what we have planned is a sound plan but I give us about 75% chance of success," he said.

"Bill, give us your honest opinion," Bob said in jest. He knew Bill was steaming on this one.

"Seriously, this whole mission is a disaster waiting to happen. Don't get me wrong, the plan is the best we can come up with. I think we have done our homework but it still feels tenuous and I'm not all that confident about our success. I rate it at about 25%," he said.

"Well, that's an honest assessment, Bill. Paul what's your take on this thing?" Bob asked.

"Bob, with all the experience we have at this table and my wanting to bring Enterprise home, I give us about a 75% chance of success," Paul said.

"Okay Paul, thanks, Tori you're up, what's your take on this thing?" Bob said.

"I see communications as our biggest stumbling block. Shuttle's radios need to work, EVA packs comms need to work, and especially split second coordination via radios is going to be critical. I'm with Larry on this one, 75% if we're lucky. Bill's right, however. The guys that dream up these things never have to put their lives on the line for it," she said.

Qatar, Arabian Peninsula

John Walker had a special charter for the State Department. Publicly they were scheduled to fly to Baghdad, Iraq. He had the Secretary of State, Navy Seal Team 4 leader, Commander Josh Freeman and two other Navy seals who were providing security for the secretary. As they approached Baghdad, John headed east towards the Iranian city of Ahwaz and the International Airport where, coincidentally, Iranian President Mahmoud Ahmad had previously landed on an "unscheduled" visit. On final approach, John could see a huge sandstorm approaching and knew he needed to put the G550 on the ground as soon as possible. He made a beautiful landing despite heavy turbulence on final from the approaching storm. He reached the gate about the time the storm hit the airport. It was all he could do to get the people into the terminal before zero-zero conditions obliterated the landscape.

John and his crew buttoned up the aircraft. They installed the engine covers, front and rear, covered the pitot tube and all other intakes to prevent the dust from entering.

The Secretary, Oscar Franks, was met by some high-ranking Iranian government officials and whisked off for a meeting. It was presumed he was meeting with President Ahmad.

The storm outside was really blowing. It lasted for about six hours and around 2:00p.m. visibility began improving and the sun started to shine. By 3:00p.m. the weather was clear and sunny with visibility better than 25 miles. One of the subjects being discussed at the meeting was the recent launch of a long-range missile by the Russians for the Iranians. Also the talks centered on secret talks about Iran's nuclear program, namely their weapons program.

An AFV made a pass over Ahwaz on its way to photograph Baikonur Cosmodrome for manned launch activities. He reported back to operations of the status of John's aircraft and the observed weather after the sand storm.

Secretary Franks returned to the airport and the aircraft was loaded and they departed for Qatar.

Secretary Franks had also met with the Russian Foreign Minister. He laid down the U.S. position and chastised the Russians once again for fomenting dissension in the Middle East. The Russian Military Intelligence (GRU) presence was duly noted at the Ahwaz airport and in the official delegation. The Russians and United States had been at loggerheads since the beginning of the Arab Spring in the Middle East and the Russians were becoming more militant as each day passed. John made some notes to be passed on to Bob when they returned to Utah. General Dimitri Zukov was a member of the Russian delegation. John was sure he had run into him before but couldn't remember where, so he put it in his report.

John made his way back to Utah via Afghanistan, The Philippines, Formosa and Anchorage, Alaska. A relief crew took the Secretary on to Washington, D.C., while John and Tom Harger deadheaded commercially back to Salt Lake City.

By the time John arrived in Salt Lake City, he remembered Dimitri Zukov. They had crossed paths in Vientiene, Laos, when he was flying his DC-3 for the CIA. Dimitri was helping the communist faction in Laos that was attempting to keep the Chinese influence out of the region. He later moved over to Vietnam to fly the Mig-21.

Naval Station Rota, Spain

The Iraeli Air Force had been directed by their Defense Ministry to fly their C-130E to Rota, Spain, to take delivery of some Mark 83 General Purpose bombs.

They arrived and were taxied to the parking area where weapons were handled for the base. It was isolated from all activities for safety reasons. As they pulled, in they were parked next to a United States Air Force C-130H. The base weapons department was charged with transferring and loading weapons on the base. The pilots of each aircraft went over to base operations while the enlisted crews stayed to load the weapons.

Pretty soon weapons carriers were seen towing 1000 lb. bombs out to each aircraft. The bombs were covered with bright yellow tarps so they were not visible to the naked eye.

The pilots returned to the aircraft and loading was complete. The crews manned their aircraft and departed Rota. The Israelis headed southeast while the USAF C-130 headed up the coast for the United Kingdom.

The flight back to Israel took about three and one half hours and they landed at Ramon Airbase, home of Wing 25. As the aircraft was parked, a truck with Israeli Air Force markings on it met them. Three young men exited the truck and boarded the aircraft. They talked with the Aircraft Commander who then escorted them to the cargo compartment where they methodically looked under each yellow tarp. At the sixth bomb when they lifted the tarp they saw the inscription "HPM E-BOMB WARHEAD (GBU-31/MK.84 FORM FACTOR)." They quickly replaced the yellow tarp and by then the crew of the C-130 had the ramp down for ground off-loading. Another man in their truck who had never left it backed it up to the C-130 and the three men on the plane pushed the bomb off and loaded it on their truck. They turned, thanked the aircraft commander, and departed the ramp.

Once off the base they entered Highway 40 and drove up to Sde Boker where they branched over to Highway 204. On the outskirts of Neve Nof they pulled into a compound with a house, two-car garage and an out building. It looked like a normal home but was in actuality a Mossad planning and operational control site. The three men opened the doors to the garage and backed the truck into it. Once inside they began to offload the bomb. Erik Selfridge had been taken off being Davita's handler and had been assigned to babysit the ebomb. Moshe Evans, Director of Mossad, had personally talked with Erik shortly after he found out indirectly from John Boland how he would receive the bomb. Everybody had deniability and it was so easy. Moshe found out that the USAF C-130 headed for the United Kingdom would have to shutdown two engines and jettison their bomb load into the ocean. No one would know of the switch in the bomb load and how Israel got the ebomb.

Now the technicians would have their day striping the outer shell of the bomb and building a nitrogen Dewar around the bomb. They attached a battery and two-cell phones to the wiring in the bomb. One phone to arm it and the other to detonate it. The plan now was to add some liquid nitrogen to the Dewar and then transport it into the underground complex at Natanz. Detonating it within the complex would do minimum physical damage but would disable and destroy all electric motors that would shut down all the centrifuges, destroy all computers, telephones and electrical devices with the complex. It would cripple uranium production at that facility for a couple of years maybe forever. Now it was up to Erik to carry out this diabolical plot.

Moshe directed his agent at the embassy in Washington, D.C., to send an anonymous thank you card to John Boland. John would know whom it was from and what it was for.

14

"Success in the Desert"

Sde Boker, Israel

The conversion of the ebomb into a combined bomb/Dewar package had been completed. It was crated and labeled "Nitrogen Dewar". It was put on an EL AL flight headed for Frankfort, Germany, and paperwork attached directing it to be delivered to Seimens Corporation, AG in Munich. It was addressed so the Mossad agent inside the company could redirect it with new paperwork to be delivered to the Natanz Iranian nuclear site without arousing suspicion.

The crate was loaded on a Lufthansa Flight out of Munich headed for Teheran, Iran. It was offloaded and delivered to the Seiman's representative at the airport. From there it was transferred onto a large company van and soon was headed for the nuclear complex at Natanz.

Erik Selfridge was positioned in the hills some two miles to the southwest of the complex with a clear view of the gate and the entrance to the underground complex. He had infiltrated overland from Kuwait City two days earlier. He also had a three bar signal on his cell phone from the local tower. He was observing activity in the complex when his phone rang. It was one of their agents in Teheran. He reported the truck carrying the bomb had departed the Seiman's airport facility about twenty minutes ago and should be in Natanz in four hours. Erik and his partner were well camouflaged on the hill and both had binoculars to observe activities in and around the complex. There was little movement above ground, just a few security guards and some people coming up from underground to have a smoke. During the four-hour wait there were only a few vehicles moving in the complex. The terrain around the complex was typical scrub. Lots of rock interspersed in the soil with a few small shrubs growing in it. There were hills to the southwest of the complex but flat rolling country as far as the eye could see to the north and east. Erik's partner nudged him and pointed to the northeast. He had spotted a dust cloud stirred up from a truck moving up the road from the town of Natanz. Both men shifted their gaze to the vehicle. Soon it was close enough that they could read the lettering on the side and recognized the Seimen's logo. It was right on time so this was it. As it approached the road to the complex it slowed and turned in. It was stopped at the gate where the paperwork was checked for accuracy and approval for entry into the base. The security guard was on the phone momentarily and then raised the bar allowing the truck to pass. It moved ever so slowly and finally disappeared down the entrance to the underground complex.

Erik and his partner checked their watches. From their observations previously it had been determined a wait of thirty minutes was recommended before they should detonate the bomb.

They looked at each other and mentally calculated the time. Both fidgeted and grew more nervous by the second. Not being able to see what was going on inside the underground complex was frustrating. As thirty minutes got closer they checked their watches more and more. Finally one minute was remaining and they both took out their phones. At thirty seconds Erik's partner dialed the number to arm the bomb. He checked and had three bars of signal strength. He got back an indication the bomb was armed. Erik now dialed his cell phone and it started to ring on the other end. Of course the phone in the bomb was not physically ringing. As quickly as it answered, the ground above the complex shook and dust was observed. At the tunnel entrance a plume of black smoke began to rise and people who were on the surface started to run down the tunnel while some of those underground began to appear running up the ramp to above ground. Erik had a number within the complex and he dialed it. If someone answered, the mission was a failure. The phone did not ring nor did anyone answer. They both picked up their binoculars and observed the people coming up from below. More than half of them had a cell phone in their hand and were dialing. Just as quickly as they dialed they appeared to hang up and redial. It appeared that no one's phone was working. Erik smiled and all he could say was success. He and his partner picked up their equipment, packed it in the bag they had toted into the country and started down the hill out of sight of the complex and road. At the bottom they exited a ravine and headed for the road to Natanz. When they reached Natanz they waited for a southbound bus going to Basrah, Iran.

Salt Lake City, Utah

Thursday Bob and Paul found themselves back on the road to Washington, D.C. It was a repeat of last week's excursion. John Walker was going to Portland, Maine, to pick up the Gulfstream 550 the company had just pur-chased. The plane was crowded with the crew scheduled to fly the G550 back to Salt Lake.

They arrived just before noon at the Dulles FBO and a black Ford SUV was there to pick them up. John and his ferry crew departed for Portland. Before he left, John indicated he would be back at Dulles by 9:00a.m. tomorrow to fly them back to Salt Lake City.

Bob and Paul relaxed as the SUV took all the back roads to the CIA in McLean. On arrival they checked in with security and after being issued their identification tags they were escorted to the director's office. Judy Burns greeted them and escorted them into Admiral Boland's office.

"Welcome back, gentlemen," he said. "I hope you had a good flight?"

"We had a good flight, sir. John Walker is the best we have and he's always there when we need him. He delivered us on a smooth flight all the way from Salt Lake," Paul said.

"I see Don Ransford's not here, admiral. Is he coming?" Bob asked.

"Don has a Presidential briefing he is prepping for so I don't expect he will make it," John said. "Most of what we need to talk about centers around our operation so he couldn't add too much to the discussion. Come on in and sit down. Anybody want a drink or anything?"

"I'm fine, sir," Paul said.

"Coffee, black, would be great John," Bob said.

John called out to Judy and ordered one black coffee. Within minutes she brought it and set it on the coffee table in front of Bob.

"Well, give me your analysis of what we proposed last time you guys were here," John asked.

"Paul will give us the analysis of his side of the equation," Bob answered.

Paul began, "Sir, we looked at this thing everyway we could. What it boils down to is electrical power to the shuttle. What we don't know is if we will be able to restart at least one fuel cell. If we can do that, we feel we have a 75% chance of completing this mission. There may be a few glitches along the way but electricity is the key to the whole situation."

Bob picked up the conversation, "John, we picked out your favorite place for landing the shuttle."

"Okay, Bob. Where's that?" John said.

"My team picked McMurdo. It's isolated and still dark 24 hours a day. We can sneak the shuttle in and pick up the crew before anybody realizes we've been there," Bob said.

"Doesn't surprise me, Bob. I think McMurdo is Larry Beck's favorite place," John said.

"Yeah, he has a lot of pleasant memories from that place," Bob responded.

"Well, what is your assessment of the mission over-all then?" John asked.

"My team evaluates a success rate between 60-75% at best. Tori Croft was very astute and pinpointed that communications was the critical factor once we had a fuel cell on line," Bob said.

"Well, I know this isn't a perfect mission and a probable high success rate but it is a go. DOD, National Security advisor and the Director of National Intelligence all advised the President that if the Russians obtain the technology contained in this cargo package in the shuttle, the safety of our nation is in jeopardy, one caveat I'm sure you all will not be happy about. Paul can't go on this mission," John said.

It was received as though Bob's wingman had been shot down. Paul and Bob were speechless for a few seconds then Paul broke the silence. "What's that all about sir? He asked.

"You are too close to the shuttle program, Paul," John offered. "When the media starts investigating how the shuttle returned to earth they will associate you with Omega Aviation and that will attract too much attention and tend to pinpoint the source of the UFOs. We can't afford that close scrutiny and even have the program exposed to the world. We still have to do everything we can to keep it secret. We have come up with a plan to ensure you don't attract attention on this one Paul. We will arrange for you to appear on the Hannity show the evening we are carrying out this mission. That way you and Omega can't possibly be tied to this mission. I hate to have to do that, Paul, but there is no other way. So that brings up the $100,000 question. Can Tori Croft handle this mission with one of our people assisting her in the shuttle?" he asked.

Without hesitation Paul answered. "Yes, sir. She's ready for it. When we were at NASA she was ready to command a shuttle mission and if there had been more after Enterprise I know she would have lead one," he said.

Bob chimed in, "We'll need to figure out whom to put in the shuttle with Tori, but whoever it is, they will be able to handle it. What's our window for this mission, John?"

"From your daily reconnaissance missions over the Baikonur Cosmodrome, we believe from the activity observed that the Russians intend to launch a mission to retrieve the package in question in about eight days. That means you need to get the shuttle back before then," John said.

"Okay, John. Give us a couple of days. I will advise

you of our schedule so we can coordinate all facets of this situation," Bob said.

The Admiral invited them to stay for lunch and they accepted. It was 2:30p.m., a little late for east coast time but their biological clocks were still on Mountain Standard Time. After lunch they departed the CIA and their trusty black Ford SUV took them to the Holiday Inn they had previously stayed at near Dulles. John Walker said he would pick them up at 10:00a.m. on Friday so they relaxed in their hotel and planned for an early morning departure for the FBO. They instructed their driver to pick them up by 9:00a.m.

After breakfast they packed their travel bags and walked down to the lobby and waited for their transportation. He arrived on time and they were off to the FBO as planned.

John Walker pulled into the chocks about 9:30a.m. and greeted Bob and Paul. He confirmed his flight plan with the FAA so they loaded up, taxied out and were off to Salt Lake City. Flight time was about three and one half hours and at 11:30a.m. they were on short final for Salt Lake City Airport.

When Bob and Paul arrived back at headquarters, they decided to go up the mountain and brief the remainder of the team. When they stepped off the tubes things were quiet in the hangar complex. A few technicians were working on the AFVs but the flight crews were all snug in the quarters. The last AFV flight for the day had arrived an hour earlier so everybody was just relaxing.

Bob gathered the mission team and they all sat down at the kitchen table to hear the results of the Washington trip.

Bob began, "Let me preface my remarks with something we all need to keep in mind. Let's take a positive attitude toward this mission. It's probably one of the most difficult we will ever attempt. The only lives on the line are ours so let's all look after us. The mission is a go and we need to attempt it within the next five days. Here's the bad news. Paul has been scrubbed from the mission."

You could see the reaction by all-hands. They were aghast. Why would anybody scrub their best shuttle pilot from this important mission?

Bob continued, "MJ-12 feels his participation would be detrimental to the AFV program. He would be the first one suspected of participating in the mission and he would be closely tied to Omega Aviation. That would put too much scrutiny on us and the AFV program could be compromised. I can see the reasoning so Paul will appear on the Hannity Show the night we are carrying out this mission. It's something we will have to live with. So that brings us to the decision of who will replace Paul. Obviously Tori now becomes the primary shuttle pilot and someone moves over in her seat in the shuttle. Let's hear your recommendations."

"Let me nip this discussion in the bud, Bob," she said. "My choice for this position is Bill Grammercy. He has studied all the manuals with me getting ready for this mission and he knows more about the space shuttle than anybody else here besides Paul and myself. He is a former naval aviator and can fly the shuttle should I be incapacitated during the mission. He is the obvious choice."

Everybody at the table looked at each other and nobody voiced objection nor suggested a replacement.

"You all know I will do my best and I thank you for your confidence, especially you, Tori," Bill said.

"Well, that settles that," Bob said. "What say we plan

on doing this thing on Tuesday? Jack you have been quiet for too long. Can you give us readout on the orbit of the shuttle? We will need to know when the best orbit for diversion to McMurdo will come up so we can activate that damn thing on the previous one. That's going to determine our flight schedule."

"I can do that, Bob," Jack said. "Do you want me to check on the McMurdo weather forecast for Tuesday?"

"That's a good idea," Bob said. "Let's get Mike Brenner in on this mission as a backup for you, Larry. He seems to thrive on these kinds of situations. While everybody is here, let me brief all of you on the new policy which I think you will like. Starting on Monday, we are going to a duty crew. Our missions have decreased in numbers since the end on the space shuttle program and we don't need six crews on a two-week schedule so I am instituting a three-crew schedule with only an overnight stay. We will have three crews come up here every day and stay overnight. Everybody will report on workdays to headquarters and fly the G550s as required. We will just have a daily duty crew of three AFV crews. I think everybody including our families will like it better. If we need more AFV crews, we will just play it by ear. Larry can find us a flight schedules officer who can coordinate things."

The reaction from the crews was a resounding agreement. The two weeks on the mountain were tough on everybody. This would be a great improvement and help morale.

"Larry, you and your team work out the final details of this mission. We'll brief on Monday. Besides your crew, Mike Brenner's crew, and Tori's crew, we will need three other standby crews to cover the normal missions we will have on Monday. Let's start down the mountain in small time intervals. Larry, Mike, Tori and Paul take your crews down the mountain. Jim you, Bruce and Pete are the duty crew until Monday morning. Does anybody have any questions?" Bob asked.

Nobody had any questions. Bob and Paul were the first to depart the mountain. The remainder of Paul's crew took the other tube and all departed for headquarters.

Bob told Paul to go home and relax and have a great weekend. He reminded him that he would have to fly to New York for his television interview with Hannity on Tuesday.

Bob went into his office and opened his desk and took out the emergency phone. He picked up the receiver and pushed the button for CIA. Admiral Boland came on the line.

"What's happening, Bob?" John asked.

"We have determined when we will fly the mission, John. I don't know what time yet but it will be sometime on Tuesday. I figured I had better give you a heads up so you can work your magic and get Paul scheduled for his television interview for Tuesday. Also, Bill Grammercy has been selected to replace Tori as pilot on the shuttle while Tori replaces Paul as the mission commander. Bill has been mentoring her and has been studying the entire shuttle operating manuals helping Tori bone up on her procedures. I believe that is going to work out just fine and Tori has all the confidence in Bill," Bob said.

"Okay, Bob. We're on for Tuesday. Keep me up to speed. We will also need to add some missions to monitor happenings at Natanz, Iran. It looks like they are having a problem or something untoward is going on. Let's put two flights a day with two passes each until we determine what's happening. I'll be in touch," John said.

McLean, Virginia

Admiral Boland hung up the red phone with Bob and asked Judy to call Lacy Harvey over at Mercury Group. Lacy was a CIA operative whose cover was in the media business and she was perfect to contact the Hannity people. Within a few minutes the Admiral's assistant advised him that Lacy was on line one.

He picked up line one. "Lacy, John Boland here. How you doing?" he asked.

"I'm doing great, Admiral. What's on your mind?" she said.

"You know how the Hannity show has been begging to get Paul Anderson on their show for an interview. Well, I just found out he will be available for an interview on Tuesday next week. Do you think you could arrange an interview?" he asked.

"Oh, that's no problem. They will be more that happy to have him. Do I need to call you back on this one?" she said.

"No, I don't think so. Let me give you Paul's home phone so you can pass it on to the Hannity people," he said.

"That will save everybody a lot of time, Admiral," she said.

John gave her the number.

"I got it, sir. I will take care of it," she said and hung up the phone.

The Admiral then asked Judy to get Don Ransford at DOD on the phone for him. He reminded her to get him on his secure line.

Don Ransford came on the line. "What's up, John?" he asked.

"Just wanted to give you a heads up. The mission you asked for is scheduled for next Tuesday. Retrieval will need to be made at McMurdo in Antarctica," John said.

"Thanks, John. I understand. Keep me posted if at all possible," Don said.

"Will do, talk to you later," John said.

Kamas, Utah

Bob had a little time on his hands so he put out a memo to all-hands to check-in with Larry before proceeding with their assigned duties on Monday morning. Larry would reiterate the new duty policy by word of mouth to all flight crews.

Tori had made her way down the mountain and walked gingerly over to the house she shared with John Walker. John was already home and he greeted her with a huge smile and welcomed her happily.

"Hey, lady. Long time no see," he said.

"Yeah, John. I guess it's been a couple of days at least. Bob has a new policy and he let us off early. No more two weeks away from home except I have to fly a special mission on Tuesday but after that it will be a duty crew each day for only one night away from home. We should see more of each other. When you get sick of me just say so and I will get a new set of quarters," she said.

"Well, that's a nice policy but don't worry about me getting bored with you. I think we have a good working relationship but feel free to move if you wish," he said.

"I was only kidding, John. I enjoy your company. Neither of us seems to have an agenda and I like it that way," she said.

"I was just getting ready to fix dinner. Do you want something?" he asked.

"Hey, that would be nice. Let me take a shower and I'll feel better," she said.

"Good. I was going to fix lasagna from scratch and it will take about an hour to cook. Take your time. I'm going to get busy," he said.

Tori grabbed her bag and made her way back to her bedroom. It was going to be a relaxing evening, she thought, after all the drama up on the mountain. She knew the upcoming mission was going to be dicey but tonight she didn't even want to think about it.

Natanz, Iran

Confusion was now the norm at the underground complex. Mohammad Hajad-Aeled, the director, and his staff were trying to access the damage from what appeared to be a small bomb explosion. He was not yet aware that it had included a non-nuclear EMP. The fire crews had put out a small fire that had occurred just outside the main centrifuge laboratory. Electricians were attempting to bring electrical power and lighting back on but were being unsuccessful. Operating under flashlight power, a rescue operation was in progress. The director couldn't figure out why the emergency lighting had not come on and why it had failed. Without power, all the computers and machinery were inoperative. He had tried to phone out but had no success. Soon reports began coming in that all cell phones were inoperative. It slowly dawned on him that an EMP weapon had been exploded in his complex and they were now suffering all the ramifications of it.

It was determined there was one dead and three injured from the explosion. These four people had been in close proximity to the crate containing the bomb or in fact had been moving it into the lab where it was destined to be used.

The director moved up the tunnel to the surface and

asked around to try to find a working cell phone. He eventually made contact with a security officer who had been on the surface making a perimeter check when the bomb went off and his cell phone was working.

The director took the phone and dialed his boss at the Atomic Energy Organization. Deputy Director Aji Esfanjani answered and Mohammad filled him in on what just happened. He advised him that a complete assessment had not been completed because the power had not been restored so he was not sure of the status of his computers and centrifuges. He did report the deaths and the sequence of the past events of the last half hour. Aji told him to keep him advised as things changed at his facility.

When he hung up the phone, Aji Esfanjani dialed the office of the President. He spoke to his chief of staff. He explained who he was and the situation at Natanz. The chief of staff thanked him and asked for his phone number and told him he would call him back.

Meanwhile Mohammad continued to assess the situation and was being given minute-by-minute updates. He decided not to allow anyone back in the complex until power was restored and the fresh air ventilation fans were back in operation.

When President Mahmoud Ahmad was briefed on the Natanz situation, he exploded in a verbal rage. He shouted that those vile filthy Jews were behind this attack and he would destroy their country, no matter how long it took.

When he calmed down, he directed his chief of staff to appoint a commission to evaluate what had happened and what it was going to take to get the facility back up and operating as quickly as possible. Then he directed his chief of staff to place a call to his Russian friend, General Zukov.

General Zukov and President Ahmad had a long discussion on the situation. The President wanted Dimitri and the Russians to retaliate against the Israelis. Dimitri tried to be as diplomatic as possible, telling the President that there was no positive proof that the Israelis were responsible for the Natanz attack. The President was making the point that who possibly could make a weapon like the one used on his facility. Rhetorically only the Russians, Chinese or Americans. Dimitri did say they would send a team to help evaluate the situation at Natanz and would help the Iranians rebuild it. That seemed to placate Ahmad somewhat and he calmed down just a little.

At Natanz, the electricians determined that they had power restored to the facility but couldn't get the lights to come on until they realized that all the bulbs in the facility had been shorted out when the bomb went off. They also could not get the circulating fans working and determined that all electrical motors were burned out. This recovery was going to take a long time and to get the facility up and running even longer.

15

"Secrets Lost"

Tel Aviv, Israel

The Russians were publicly getting more vocal about Iran and the possibility that Israel would attack their nuclear sites. Clandestinely they were investigating the e-bomb attack which had just been perpetrated on the Iranians and literally wiped out their Natanz uranium enrichment facility. Israel had already outed the Russians to the United States concerning the missile in polar orbit and now it was time to bring the Chinese into the picture.

Mossad drafted a coded dispatch to its embassy in Ulan Bator. They directed them to contact one of their agents in the People's Republic of China and brief them on the mission. Derek Goldberg boarded an Air China Airlines from Ulan Bator to Beijing. On arrival he made his way to the Israeli Embassy. The next day he traveled out into town and stopped for lunch at a local restaurant. While eating his lunch he caught the eye of his contact and gave him the sign to meet him out behind the restaurant. When he finished lunch, he left by the back door and started walking down the alley. As he walked, his contact, Chi Tran, caught up with him and in the few seconds they were close. Derek passed instructions to Chi. At the first corner, Derek went right and Chi went left. Once on the main street he flagged down a rickshaw for a ride back to the embassy.

Chi continued walking for a few more blocks, making sure he had not been spotted by the MSS. When he was sure he was in the clear, he stepped out onto the main street and stopped a rickshaw for a ride towards home. He changed rickshaws three times to ensure anonymity. When he was safely in his apartment he opened the paper Derek had passed him in the alley. It gave him complete instructions on what he needed to accomplish and how he should go about doing it.

In the morning he went out shopping. He purchased a used ten-inch Sony laptop computer, a used electronic Canon camera and some peasant clothing. His last purchase was a native douli hat. He had avoided the expensive shops and main streets in his trip, assuring he would not attract attention. The next morning he would board the train for Inner Mongolia and the city of Jiuquan.

Inner Mongolia

Chi Tran had boarded the train in Beijing and, after two days of travel, arrived in the city of Jiuquan. He had slept part of the way there and was somewhat refreshed as he stepped off the train onto the arrival platform. It was hot and dry on the edge of the Gobi Desert and even though it was early morning, the temperature was already over 95ºF. He was dressed in clothes which helped him blend in with the poorest of the population. His beard was long and he kept his douli hat down to cover his eyes that were shaded by his dark gray sunglasses. He was trying to be less visible and this would help him. He carried a small khaki cloth travel bag on a shoulder strap that contained a couple days change of clothes, his camera and his 10" Sony laptop computer. He moved quickly up the ramp and into the street. Jiuquan had a population of 962,000 people and it seemed like every one of them was on the street this morning. Cars and bicycles were everywhere and the huge busses slowed traffic. Chi needed a room and wanted to stay close to the train station so he walked a block before he came across a small boarding house with rooms to rent. The desk clerk spoke to him in Gansu Mandarin dialect. Chi was fluent in Northern Mandarin Chinese but understood the clerk and asked for a room. The clerk asked how long he needed the room and after Chi told him four days the clerk had him fill out a registration form then gave him a key to Room 6. The registration form was obviously for the local police and military district office. Chi indicated on his form he was there to visit the Jiuquan ancient tombs.

He entered his room and after unpacking his computer he took off his shirt and sandals then lay down on the bed to rest. Sleep in this heat was out of the question.

As the sun was setting and the temperature began to cool, Chi arose and stripped down to take a shower. The shower was down at the end of the hall and he stepped into the room. It was empty and he removed his shorts and sandals and turned on the water. There was no hot water but he didn't care. It was so hot a cold shower would be refreshing. When he finished, he returned to his room and put on his peasant's clothing once again. After combing his hair, he put on his douli hat and went back to the lobby and out onto the street. He spied a small mom and pop restaurant across the street and when traffic slowed he ran across. When he entered, the proprietor greeted him and offered him a seat. Once seated, the proprietor's wife came out of the kitchen and brought him some hot tea. He ordered dinner, which consisted of brown rice, and sweet and sour pork. She soon appeared with his dinner and he picked up his chopsticks and began his meal. He had a good view of the hotel entrance and no one entered or left while he was eating. He almost expected the local police to pay his room a visit but they had probably been warned that he could see the entrance from the place he was eating so they would wait for a more opportune time to check him out.

Chi finished his dinner, paid his bill and strolled back across the street to his hotel. He entered his room and booted up his Sony computer. He called up his mail program and began composing a new email. It was addressed to an Israeli Mossad agent who was known to the Ministry of State Security (MSS), Chinese Intelligence, located at the Israeli Embassy in Ulan Bator, Mongolia.

"Arrived Jiuquan. Will be heading out to Jiuquan Satellite Launch Center (JSLC) tomorrow. Will determine Chinese capability to shoot down Russian nuclear missile now in polar orbit," signed Ajuan.

He put the cursor over send and the email was off into cyberspace. He left the mail program open and closed the cover so the computer would go to sleep.

In the morning, Chi grabbed his travel bag and walked out of the hotel to the train station leaving the computer on the desk in the room. He caught the 8:10a.m. train going north to the Jiuquan Satellite Launch Center (JSLC). On the train he had a cup of tea and a sweet cake. The trip took about one hour and Chi exited the train into the heat and sun. He went into a local restaurant and ordered breakfast. The breakfast consisted of a warm bowl of congee, a watery rice gruel that bears a marked resemblance to porridge and a couple of crullers washed down with hot tea.

During breakfast he struck up a conversation with two older middle-class looking gentlemen. He knew they worked at Base 10 as they had IDs around their neck. He started asking questions about their anti-missile capabilities. Chi knew it would raise a red flag and they would report it to their supervisor. The supervisor would then alert base security that would send a team to find him and question him. It had to be planned just perfect for his plan to work otherwise he would spend a long time in a Chinese military prison.

Chi finished his breakfast and walked out toward the base. He stopped along the road and took some pictures with his telephoto lens on his Canon camera. He kept checking his watch and at exactly 10:37am he headed toward the train station. As he approached the small rural station a train from the north pulled into the station. He boarded the first car and made his way to the vestibule between the first two cars. Just then a train on the east track headed north pulled into the station. He opened the door, jumped off the train and stepped up onto the platform of the rear car and entered. Within fifteen minutes the train pulled out headed north.

The local police had entered Chi's hotel room in Jiuquan. When they entered his room the police lieutenant saw his computer sitting on the desk. He lifted the cover and the computer came to life. He opened the mail and checked the last incoming and outgoing messages. When he saw the last email to the Israeli Embassy in Ulan Bator he stopped and called the local MSS officer. He was directed to pack up the computer and bring it to the ministry office. On arriving he was directed to the office of Zee Tse Chaing. Chaing took the computer and opened it and began screening the emails, as had the lieutenant. He printed a copy as well as forwarding it to his own email address. He then asked the lieutenant to acquire the description of the owner of the computer and call a phone number he gave him at the space center. He also sent an email to alert the MSS office there.

The two employees who had been approached had also alerted base security. They had given a description of the individual and security and MSS teamed up to search for him. They questioned people at or near the train station. An old lady who had been there since early morning waiting for a relative to arrive stated she saw him board the southbound 10:45am train.

MSS placed a call to Jiuquan and alerted them to watch for the suspect returning to Jiuquan.

Meanwhile Chi had switched trains at the spaceport station. When he entered the rear car he immediately went to the bathroom. There was only one person in the car at the time and he went unnoticed. In the bathroom he retrieved his razor from his bag and shaved his face. Then he changed clothes and donned what appeared to be middle-class tourist garb. He put on a blue baseball cap with the spaceport logo over his black hair. The train was now moving north at sixty-five miles per hour and he opened the little window in the bathroom and threw out his peasant clothes and douli hat. He turned his khaki bag inside out and it became a blue travel bag. Inside he replaced the change of clothes he had along with some dirty laundry. Chi double-checked his camera to ensure he had pictures only of the Jiuquan Ancient Tombs should he be stopped and questioned. He placed the camera in his travel bag.

At the next stop Chi stepped off the train onto the platform of the rural station. It was a bare bones structure with only a ticket office, bathrooms and a waiting room. It was not crowded and Chi went around the building stopping to wait until the northbound train left the station. He then entered the station from the non-track side of the building walked over to the ticket window and purchased a one-way trip to Jiuquan.

Chi had studied the schedule before he started his mission and determined that a train would be in the station within ten minutes and would reduce his wait time. This would also reduce his exposure to being sighted to a minimum.

The train pulled into the station. Chi boarded, found a seat in first class seating and relaxed for his trip to Jiuquan.

On arriving at the Jiuquan station, Chi moved quickly to catch a rickshaw to the bus station. There was a 3:00p.m. bus to Jiayuguan Airport where Chi had a reservation on China Eastern Airline Flight MU2417 to Lanzhou departing at 4:50p.m.. It was only a twenty-five minute drive so Chi had plenty of time. His flight was in a fifty passenger Bombardier CRJ200 and his flight time would be forty-eight minutes. He would have thirty-five minutes between flights and would board Air China flight AC3546 departing at 6:07p.m. for Beijing.

His planning and execution had been perfect. He deplaned in Beijing at 7:34p.m. and faded into the depths of the massive population.

Jiuquan Satellite Launch Center (JSLC), Inner Mongolia

Execution of Chi's mission had been a complete success. MSS agents and Base 10 security had failed to locate and apprehend the mysterious suspect who left his computer in the hotel room in Jiuquan.

Chaing placed a call to his superior in Beijing to report the developments in Jiuquan. Li Koenig answered the phone. Li was head of the department and also held several other leadership positions, including head of the Central Investigation Department, deputy chief of General Staff, and vice minister of foreign affairs, and he attended meetings of the Political Bureau as an observer.

Li listened to what Chaing had to say and thanked him for his vigilance. He directed him to try to determine who the suspect was and for whom he worked. No matter, he had done China a great service by warning them of the Russian nuclear missile orbiting in space. He knew it was going to be difficult to find out why the Russians had done this and he devised a plan. He hung up the phone and determined that he needed to notify the Secretariat and the Prime minister as well as General Wang, head of the PLA. When he contacted these people he expressed to them that he would continue to investigate and would keep them posted on any new developments.

Li decided as part of his plan he would share this information with the North Koreans and the Iranians. He was certain that either one or both of their intelligence organizations knew about it already and were working with the Russians. His plan was to let the Russians know that China was aware of their action and was highly upset with this development.

Li directed one of his senior agents to meet clandestinely with an agent from the State Security Department assigned to the North Korean Embassy in Beijing. He also sent a message by diplomatic pouch to the Chinese Embassy in Teheran to question the Iranian Ministry Of Intelligence and Security (MOIS) to determine whether they knew about the Russian Missile. Li worded his message so his agents would express extreme concern and agitation now felt by the Chinese government.

Within days, reports were put on Li's desk with answers to his inquiries. The North Koreans expressed deep concern for this action but indicated they were unaware of this situation. The Iranians on the other hand said they were aware of the Russian's actions and said it was relayed to them that this was done as a deterrent against the Israelis to prevent them from attacking Iranian nuclear sites.

Teheran, Iran

General Zukov's mission to Iran was nearing and end. Iranian intelligence contacted his chief of staff and asked for a meeting. It was scheduled for the next morning.

Heydar Moshei was ushered in to the General's suite in the Leleh Hotel.

The general greeted him, "Heydar, how are things in the agency?" he asked.

"Things are fine, General, but we have a situation which I feel we need to discuss. My agents had a secret meeting with their Chinese counterparts. The subject of the conversation concerned the missile that you launched three months ago and placed in the 300 mile high polar orbit. The Chinese have information that it is a nuclear tipped missile and are highly agitated and concerned about its purpose. We tried to calm their agitation but were unsuccessful. Based on that meeting, I believe you need to know that and maybe try to calm the nerves of the Chinese. As you know we have not been told specifically the purpose of the missile but only in general terms. Can you share anything concerning this situation?" he asked.

"Heydar, we have placed that weapon in orbit so we have a quick response time should the Israelis launch a strike at your nuclear capability. We have also the capability to strike the United States should they attempt to protect Israel when they launch. You can take that back to the Chinese and try to assure them that we are not threatening their personal safety," the General said.

"Well, that really assures us, sir. I will pass that on to my contacts with the Chinese MSS. I am sure that will calm things down some. We can only hope the Chinese believe our answers," Heydar said.

"That will lower the tension some and when I return to Moscow I will have the Minister of Defense meet with the Chinese Ambassador and reassure them of the situation. Thank you for helping us with this, Heydar. We will be in touch," he said.

Heydar shook hands and departed the hotel. He hoped this message would calm the world situation.

16

"Media Relations"

Tel Aviv, Israel

Mossad had been monitoring the traffic between Russian, Iranian, North Korean and Chinese embassies. Their agents in the field had also been reporting the chatter on this subject. It was clear from the volume of traffic that Chi Tran had been successful and the Chinese had in no uncertain terms let the Russians know, be it indirectly, that they were pissed off at the whole situation. The chatter between Russia and Iran also was beginning to indicate that Erik Selfridge's diabolical mission with the e-bomb had also been successful.

The Israeli Prime Minister had been advised of the package carried by the space shuttle Enterprise on its last mission. It had been designed to destroy the Russian missile in space and resolve the situation in the event of an Israeli raid on Iran's nuclear capability.

There was a lot of discussion within Mossad and the government on what the next step should be to slow or stop the Iranians from obtaining a nuclear weapon. The Stuxnet virus had been successful and slowed development on a weapon in Iran but they had been on track to have a weapon within a year or two. With Natanz shutdown they may now be delayed for as much as four years. However the other Iranian nuclear sites needed to be slowed down and the upgraded Stuxnet virus may be the vehicle to do so. Work on an upgrade to the stuxnet virus was an ongoing project in cooperation with the United States intelligence community. The question remained, would it do the job? Siemen's corporation had developed a software program to remove it from any computer or controller board that was controlling their equipment. The upgrade would have to target other companies' equipment including nuclear power plants and other electrical controlling equipment.

Moshe had his assistant place the call. He finally had John Boland on the line.

"Good morning, John," he said.

"Good afternoon, Moshe. What can I do for you?" John asked.

"I wanted to personally give you a head's up on the Russian missile situation," Moshe said.

"Tell me what you have as we're a little thin in that area," he said.

"We leaked the facts on the Russian nuclear weapon and made sure the Chinese picked it up. They spread it to the North Koreans and Iranians. The North Koreans were in the dark but the Iranians told the Chinese they thought it was to threaten us and have a quick response time in case we launched a strike on Iran's nuclear capability. They in turn relayed that information to the Russians and at this point the Russians are trying to assure the Chinese that they have nothing to worry about," Moshe said.

"Our Secretary of State got an earful when he met with President Mahmoud Ahmad in Ahwaz. General Zukov also was there and he commuted veiled threats of retaliation at us should your Air Force launch a strike against Iran," John said.

"I guess your plan to destroy the missile is now out of the question since Enterprise was abandoned in space," Moshe said.

"Yeah, it looks like it's dead, Moshe," John said. That was intelligence related to AFVs and was a forbidden subject with anyone, so John lied to him.

"What is the status of the Stuxnet upgrade?" Moshe asked. "Our members of that task force have finished their part of the software and should be contacting your chairman in a day or two."

"I haven't had a report in a day or two, Moshe, but I am sure they are close to finishing the upgrade and integrating it into your portion," John said.

"I have another thing, John. What do you hear about a possible problem at the nuclear site at Natanz, Iran? We hear a few things between the Iranians and Russians but nothing definitive. There is more vehicle activity than normal but less cell phone traffic from the employees there," Moshe said.

"We are getting about the same Intel that you are, Moshe," John answered. "Thanks for the heads up on the Chicoms. We appreciate that."

"Okay, John, I will be in contact in a few days. Thanks for the information. Take care," he said as he hung up the phone.

John was counting on the Stuxnet upgrade to be ready in a week and to get it into the Iranian computers and controllers within the month. It would then take about six months to be effective and maybe shutdown some of the Iranian power-plants, especially the nuclear plant at Bushehr. That plant provided power to two of Iran's nuclear production sites. Stuxnet as now configured could also shutdown any Iranian electrical components that controlled production machinery and environmental controls with computer software in their systems. As always it would be a crapshoot on what was infected.

John called his deputy into his office whom he had charged with developing a plan to get an e-bomb to the Israelis with complete deniability. He told him the delivery had been successful and it looked like the Israelis had also been successful in delivering and detonating it. He told him Intel should be coming in from the four daily over flights the AFVs were making and he would like a briefing when we could make a definitive decision on the Israelis success.

Moscow, Russia

General Sergei Kovolov, Head of the Russian Federal Space Agency, scheduled a meeting with the Chinese ambassador. They met on a Friday morning at the agency's Moscow office. It was a cordial meeting and General Kovolov attempted to sooth the feelings of the Chinese and to assure them that their nuclear missile now in orbit was not a threat to them. He explained in detail what they were trying to accomplish. Both the Chinese and Russians were involved with helping the Iranians with their military and civilian infrastructure. The two countries wanted to keep their sphere of influence and would hardly ever agree on anything. The ambassador was polite but projected his distrust of what the Russian was saying and assured him that any damage to the Chinese would result in retaliation in kind. After the meeting they smiled and shook hands as the ambassador departed.

Dimitri Zukov entered General Kovolov's office.

"Well, Comrade. How did things go with the Chinese ambassador?" he asked.

"Dimitri, it was a cordial meeting but they are still

suspicious of our motives and what we intended with launching that missile. After this crisis with the Iranians is over, what are your plans for it?" Sergei said.

"Sergei, we have built in a program which we can activate and bring the weapon back to earth without a problem. If you believe we can relieve this situation by doing that now just say the word and I will activate the recovery plan," he said.

"Let's study this for a week or so and then we can make a decision. It may calm down and we will not need to do that until the Iranian/Israeli situation is solved," Sergei said.

"We can do that Comrade. I will keep it on hold until you give me the direction we will take," Dimitri said.

"That sounds good, Dimitri. Meanwhile I will brief the Prime Minister and the Secretary General. Have a good day," he said.

Dimitri shook hands and departed for his office. He would spend a few days in Moscow and then return to his command in Sary Shagan, Kazakhstan.

Salt Lake City, Utah

Betsy Moore of the Salt Lake City Tribune who was an investigative reporter decided to do a warm and fuzzy piece about the new Aviation Corporation at the Salt Lake City Airport, namely Omega Aviation. She contacted John Walker's office and asked to do an interview. John cleared it through Bob Avery and a time was scheduled.

Betsy arrived at the scheduled time and Ginny Wulf announced her to John. She was ushered into his office where he greeted her.

"Good afternoon. I'm John Walker and you must be Betsy," he said

"Pleased to meet you, John. I hope this isn't inconveniencing you?" she said. "I'm working on a story similar to what we do occasionally that is introduce our readership to new businesses in our city. I know you have been here awhile but we thought we owed it to you to do it," she said.

"That's okay. Come in and have a seat and we can get started," he said. "Would you like a drink?"

She took a seat on John's sofa, "No thanks. I'm fine." She began the interview, "First could you tell us what you do?"

"Sure, that's simple, we are an aviation charter corporation. We have six Gulfstream jets and six Bell 412 Helicopters. We book charters from anyone who needs to go somewhere," he said.

"And how many employees do you have?" She asked.

"We have approximately fifty flight personnel and about forty ground personnel," John answered.

"What made your company decide on Salt Lake City for your base of operations?" she asked.

"We studied the location of most charter services in the country. There are not too many out west and very few between the Pacific coast and the eastern slope of the Rockies. In addition we studied the tax structure assessed on corporations and Utah appeared to give us the best tax situation. Air traffic here is also not congested like say Los Angeles so we don't run into the delays and other things associated with heavy air traffic," John said.

"That's interesting and why did you establish your headquarters out in Kamas?" she asked.

"That's an interesting question. Most of our personnel are former Navy. We also have two NASA astronauts who are former Navy pilots. Many of them are well known publicly and are heroes. In order to maintain some privacy, we decided on Kamas because it is still part of the Salt Lake City complex while maintaining a certain isolation and a controlled atmosphere. Also the schools in Summit County are noted for their excellence. Let me add, we don't avoid the media, when asked, but we maintain our housing so we are all guaranteed no cameras searching in our windows and TV trucks parked on our streets. We have been open and granted interviews when the media has approached us but all of them are held in this hangar. That's why we have the large conference room in the attached structure to our hangar. Another factor in our isolation is our personnel have lived in, on and around military bases in urban settings all their career. We wanted our people to have a beautiful country setting yet still have the airport and city amenities available. Thus we chose Salt Lake City," John offered.

"That sounds reasonable. Tell me what kind of flights are you famous for?" she asked.

"Me personally or do you mean the company?" John said.

"Both would add some flavor to the story, John," she added.

"Well, let me see. We were selected by NASA to retrieve their astronauts after they were rescued from space. One reason was most of our pilots have flown in the Antarctic and Captain Paul Anderson was dropped at McMurdo Sound in Antarctica and NASA needed pilots who were Antarctic qualified. On a personal note I was directed to pick up the two astronauts who were set down in Mongolia. It was pretty much a routine flight. The Antarctic pickup was coordinated with two astronauts from Australia and the other two from Pitcairn Island. As it worked out we both arrived in Houston about the same time and reunited the astronauts on the ramp there. That was exciting," he said.

"How about your helicopters. What kind of flights do they conduct?" she asked.

"Our helos do a lot of flying within one hundred-fifty miles of Salt Lake City. Quite a few of our flights are ferrying businessmen to mines and logging camps. By us taking them, they don't need to rent a car and our guys land right on the property they are interested in so we save them a lot of time. We have a good working relationship with the federal government and, with our reputation of good service spreading, more and more agencies are booking flights with us. Many are overseas and to multiple countries. It makes the agencies operate more efficiently," John said.

"Well, your story has been an interesting one John and I hope we can tell it in our Sunday addition next," she said. "Would it be possible to interview one of your heroes? That would give our story more flavor so to speak."

"Sure, I think Doc Kealy is in our readyroom. Let me check to see if he wants to do an interview," John said. He called on the intercom to the readyroom. Doc Kealy was the only one there and he responded, "Yeah, John. What do you need?" he asked

"Doc, there is a reporter here from the Tribune who is doing a story about Omega Aviation and wants to interview one of our personnel. Would you be available to do an interview?" he said

"Yeah, John. I have about an hour to kill before the afternoon helo departs for headquarters. Send her down and we can do it right here," Doc said.

"Betsy, go out my door to the balcony, turn left and at the end of the balcony is the readyroom. Doc is waiting for you," he said.

Betsy found her way to the readyroom and entered. Doc was seated at one of the tables. "Come on in," he said. "Have a seat here or would you prefer a comfortable chair over there." He pointed to a couple of soft chairs with large cushions against he wall.

"No, this is okay at the table," she said.

"Okay, where do you want to start?" Doc asked.

"Tell me how you got mixed up with this bunch of Navy pilots in the first place?" she said.

"Well, after medical school I was commissioned as a doctor in the Navy. I volunteered as the station medical officer wintering over at the South Pole Station, Antarctica. During that tour we were supplied strictly by aircraft, namely the LC-130, a plane equipped with skis. I learned to appreciate what these guys were doing everyday and the conditions under which they were operating. After my thirteen months on the ice I was transferred to Christchurch, New Zealand, as the base doctor. It was a tour for me to come down from the high-pressure job of isolation from civilization all those months. I had a small clinic and the VXE-6 personnel used to come regularly to me for treatment. I learned to appreciate aviation personnel so I applied for and was accepted to flight surgeon's school in Pensacola, Florida. When I got my wings I had a choice of duty stations and chose to become the flight surgeon for VXE-6. So that's how I got mixed up with this bunch." Doc said.

"Did you do anything special or extra while you were attached to that squadron?" she asked.

"During the first summer back in Quonset Point, Rhode Island, I signed up for the Para-rescue Team. I went to jump school at Fort Benning, Georgia, and received my jump wings. The next season when we deployed to Antarctica, I made a free-fall jump at the South Pole from 16,000'. I was the first Navy man to do that, but remember it was only a 5000' jump since Pole Station is at ground level of 11,000'. Later that year the team made a jump in East Antarctica to the Gadout Glacier where we rescued two USARP scientists from a crevasse. I set the broken leg of one of the scientists after we retrieved him and then put them on a homemade sled and dragged them eight miles to Palmer Station. There was no airstrip for our Hercs to land so we stayed there until August and then a ship called at Anvers Island and took us back to civilization. We were in Antarctica only eleven months that time. We stayed home for two months before we were needed back in Antarctica. When the squadron was decommissioned, I resigned my commission and was hired by Omega Aviation. I am still their flight surgeon as I look after their aviation needs and ground them when necessary. I have a small clinic on the headquarters compound where I conduct sick call usually two times a day for all employees and their dependents who live on the headquarters compound. I don't have appointments. It's first in first out. So there you have my life story," Doc said.

"That's quite an interesting career," Betsy said. She thanked Doc and then departed back to John's office.

"That was a very nice interview. He is an interesting study," she said. "Could I get some pictures of your operation?"

"You sure can but let me get one of our people to accompany you for safety reasons. TSA doesn't like us to allow individuals wander around our ramp without an escort from the company," John said.

John activated the intercom. "Ginny would you have Ray Nunnally come up to our office? Tell him I want him to escort a guest though our facility," he said.

"Ray is our public relations man and can answer any more questions which you may have concerning your tour," John said.

Ray knocked on John's door and was welcomed into his office.

"Ray, I'd like you to meet Betsy Moore from the Tribune. She is doing a feature story on Omega Aviation and would like to get a few pictures of our operation," he said.

Ray extended his hand, "Pleased to meet you, ma'am," he said.

"Likewise, Ray." She turned to John shook his hand and departed with Ray for her tour of the facility.

17

"Risky Business"

Kamas, Utah

The red emergency phone in Bob's desk was ringing as he entered his office. It was only 7:30a.m. and he thought it must be really important for John Boland to be calling him this early. He rushed over to the desk and reached down to retrieve it.

"Good Morning, John," he said as he placed the receiver to his ear.

"Good morning, Bob. I know it's early but we have a rapid response mission that only you and your crew can handle," John said.

"Anything for the boss," Bob said in his normal humorous fashion. "What can we do for you today?"

"Well, Bob, our analysis of our total intelligence concerning the Russians is frightening. We knew they were going to try to rendezvous with space shuttle Enterprise and attempt to steal the DOD package we had discussed earlier. Our analysis tells us that they are almost ready to launch their space capsule from Baikonur Cosmodrome. We know from your reports that an AFV mission to Enterprise won't be ready for a couple of days so we need to slow the Russians down a little bit," John said.

"What do you have in mind, John?" Bob asked.

"We have devised a simple plan requiring a landing

party designed to sabotage their launch vehicle enough that their launch will be delayed at least four days, hopefully a week. Our Russians space experts have identified a valve on the vehicle which, if found faulty, would require them to obtain a new one. We are sure that the only replacements are at Plesetsk Spaceport up near Mirny. It will take three days to move it from Mirny to Baikonur and another day to install it. The valve is easily accessible from the ground and will not require any climbing. We are shipping, same day delivery, the tools necessary to remove and reinstall the valve by FedEx to Hangar 512 along with a detailed photograph of the launch area at Baikonur. We want you to launch a mission as soon as possible after you receive the package from us. Is that doable?" John asked.

"Yes, John. I believe we can get it done on that time frame. I have Terry Richardson and Wally Glennon who have been specially trained to handle this kind of mission. We haven't had a landing party since we had the one to ARO Corporation in Cheektowaga, New York, although we didn't need to be clandestine for that one. I will keep you informed as to our timeframe when we receive the package and have a little planning time. Let me get back to you on that one," Bob said.

"That sounds fine to me. We will be in touch. Thanks Bob," John said.

"You're welcome," Bob responded and they severed the connection.

The intercom sounded and Ginny told Bob that Jerry Elliott was in the outer office and wished to see him. Bob directed her to send Jerry right in.

"Hey, Jerry. Good to see you. What's going on?" Bob asked.

"I was getting ready to schedule my retirement from

the Navy and wanted to consult with you about a few things. For one, when do I need to move out of my quarters?" Jerry said.

"I was meaning to talk with you but things have been unreal around here and I was delinquent in doing so. Anyway here's my new offer to you. I know you have been doing this for thirty-two years but are you really ready to retire?" Bob asked rhetorically. "With our new schedule and with Jack and Choyce having to relieve each other much too regularly, I wanted to get another operations controller but have not found a suitable person. You fit that bill perfectly and with a new rotation, the duty would be three days on the mountain and six days off. I would also guarantee you four weeks vacation whenever you wish and still pay you a good salary that would be in addition to your Navy retirement. I think a starting salary would be in the neighborhood of $150,000 per year. How does that sound to you?" Bob said.

"Damn, Bob. Why didn't you offer that to me earlier? I wouldn't have needed to go though all this worrying about what I was going to do with myself. You bet I'll take you up on your offer. What's the timeframe we are looking at?" Jerry said.

"Well, you have to go to NAS Lamoore for a couple of days and complete the paperwork and get mustered out of the Navy. Why don't you take a week or so off and you and Susie head out for a much needed vacation. When you get back we can work you into the rotation with Jack and Choyce. I'll just put you on the payroll effective the day after your retirement," he said.

"You are too generous, Bob," Jerry said.

"Nah, you have been a member of this organization for too long Jerry, you rate it," Bob said.

"I appreciate your confidence in me and will not let you down. Thanks," Jerry said.

"It's the least we can do for an old friend. Thanks, Jerry," Bob said.

They shook hands and Jerry excused himself and left the office.

Bob placed a call to Larry Beck at Hangar 512. Larry was out of the office on a checkout flight for one of the pilots in the new G550 they had just received. It was the last of six John Walker had acquired and he had sold off all the G4s. Larry was also performing a test flight on the aircraft and checking for proper operation of all installed equipment. Ginny said she would leave Larry a message for him to call when he returned.

Within and hour, Larry returned Bob's call.

"Hey, old friend. What's going on?" he asked.

"I will brief you on the situation when you come back up here but for now we are expecting an important FedEx package tomorrow from the Post Office in Fairfax, Virginia so leave word with Ginger that if she gets it she holds it for you. Stop by my office this afternoon when you catch the helo coming to headquarters." Bob said.

"Okay, Bob. Will see you then," Larry said and hung up the phone.   Larry knew what the implications were when there was a package from Fairfax and also when Bob couldn't discuss something over the phone. Must be related to the AFVs, he thought.

Yesterday's Sunday Tribune ran Betsy Moore's story on Omega Aviation. Larry took that section of the paper, stuck it in his briefcase and decided he would discuss it with Bob when he saw him this afternoon.

Larry worked on his G550 flight schedule for the remainder of the week. They had six charters and he lined up the crews needed to fly those flights. He took a break for lunch with John Walker and discussed the new fleet of G550s John had acquired. They were some fine airplanes and the last one Larry had just test flown would be re-painted in the Omega Aviation's colors and the logo painted on the tail. It would then be ready for it's maiden flight with the company. Larry spent most of the afternoon updating his computer base inputting new qualifications, flight phys-icals and recent trips by all concerned flight crewmembers. FAA was coming for an inspection soon and would be re-newing their certificate, so his records needed to be up to date and accurate, otherwise the FAA might not renew it.

Time approached and Larry secured his computer and office and made his way to the helo pad to catch the af-ternoon flight back to headquarters. He climbed in and the helo departed the pad for headquarters after receiving clearance from the tower for liftoff. The twenty-minute flight over the mountains was smooth. Weather had been reported clear and winds westerly at five to ten miles per hour. Not enough to create turbulence, he thought.

They arrived at the headquarters helo pad and Larry wended his was up to Bob's office. Cindy announced him and he went right in to the inner office.

"Have a good flight?" Bob asked.

"What a beautiful day out here," Larry said. "What's happening?

"Sit down for a while, Larry. Talked with John Boland this morning and he put a priority landing party mission on us," Bob said.

"So what else is new? There's always a priority mis-sion for us. Doesn't surprise me in the least," he said.

"This one is going to be tricky," Bob said. He re-peated John Boland's request to place a landing party into the Baikonur Cosmodrome and perform the sabotage. When he finished, Larry said, "Whom do you have in mind to do this?"

"I want you to fly the mission and Terry Richardson and Wally Glennon will do the ground portion. I have already alerted Terry and Wally. I want you to go to Hangar 512 tomorrow on the morning shuttle and we will have the helo standing by to bring you back up to headquarters as soon as the package arrives. I will send Terry and Wally up the mountain first thing in the morning and then you and I can take the package up when you get here. We will need to do some planning. We need to shoot for a 3:30p.m. liftoff. That will put you in Kazakhstan about 4:00a.m. local time. That's probably our best time to infiltrate Baikonur without being seen and getting back out of there before dawn. Secrecy is the most important factor in this mission. Not getting caught is primary. You will have to improvise should anything untoward come up," Bob said.

"Okay, I got it. It never gets any easier in this business does it?" Larry surmised. "Listen, Bob, I wanted to discuss the article about us in the Tribune yesterday. First of all John did a nice job with it but I think we're looking for trouble. This Betsy Moore is an investigative reporter and some of the innuendos she has in her article infer that we are more than what we appear to be. Perhaps discuss it with the Admiral. I'll bet he or MJ-12 have a plan to deal with this."

"Thanks for the heads up on this, Larry. I always appreciate your input on these things. Go home and get a good night's sleep and I'll see you when you return from the airport in the morning," he said.

"Later, buddy," Larry mused as he got up and departed Bob's office for home.

Next Morning

Larry caught the morning helo shuttle to the hangar and was drinking his first cup of morning coffee by 8:05am. He stopped to talk with John Walker and gave him a copy of the upcoming schedule of flights for the rest of the week. He was becoming a little antsy because of the tight schedule but about 9:20a.m. he spied the FedEx delivery truck approach and stop just outside the hangar door. By the time the driver stepped out to make delivery, Larry was standing there ready to sign for it. He accepted the package and walked towards the waiting helicopter that Gary Sheen had scheduled to take him back to headquarters as soon as possible. It lifted off immediately and within nineteen minutes was coming to a hover over the pad at headquarters.

Bob met him outside his office and they strode quickly towards the security doors and went up the mountain. They stepped off into the hangar bay and quickly made their way to crew quarters. Choyce was on duty and he met them there. Terry, Wally, Tom Harger, Choyce, Bob and Larry gathered around the kitchen table. Bob tore open the package and removed its contents. Tools, photos and a map of the Baikonur Cosmodrome were placed on the table.

Bob began the briefing. The missile in question was on launch pad 81/23 which was located on the northwest corner of the base. Terry would carry a walking GPS and he entered the coordinates of pad 81/23, 46.074°N 62.978°E. Liftoff would be 3:30p.m. with Terry and Wally in the lower bay. Once over Russia, Larry would descend to about 15,000' and that would be the signal for Terry and Wally to shed their pressure suits. They were wearing their Russian street clothes under their suits and would be ready for insertion. As they approached Baikonur, Larry would descend to just above tree level and approach the base from the north. At approximately ¾ of a mile he would set down and Terry and Wally would continue on foot to the launch pad. There is no reported security fence due to the isolated area of the base so progress should be smooth. Roving patrols were to be found in pickup trucks with no set schedule. Once on the pad they would remove the valve on the missile indicated on one of the pictures that came in the package. They were furnished a tool to break the stem of the valve and then they would reinstall the valve after which they will make their way back north to the drop-off site for pickup. Maximum time allotted on the pad was fifteen minutes with another ten to reach the pad and ten more to return to pickup site. Larry was directed to loiter wherever he saw fit so he could react to the situation should he be called upon to do so. Tom Harger, Larry's systems operator, would be monitoring all known base security frequencies for any alert activity. In addition to tools, Terry and Wally had night vision goggles and very low light flashlights. The weather over Baikonur was forecast to be broken to overcast clouds so the moon would not give away either the AFV or the landing party. Bob finished his briefing and asked if there were any questions. Everybody was on the same page and ready for the mission.

Choyce went back to controlling the two AFV flights while the crews relaxed in quarters. Bob walked over to operations and picked up the emergency phone. He pressed number two and the phone in the Director's office rang. John Boland picked up and Bob spoke.

"John we are on for 3:30p.m. this afternoon. This will put us in Baikonur at 4:00a.m. their time tomorrow. We plan on being on the ground for thirty-five minutes.

Larry Beck is leading this mission so I know it is in good hands. Everything looks good," Bob reported.

"Okay, Bob. Keep me posted," John said.

"I am going to remain in operations for this one and will give you 'feet dry' when we're all safe," he said.

"I'll be here in my office until I hear from you. Tell your guys 'Good Luck'," John said.

"Roger that John. Will do. I'll be in touch," he said.

3:30p.m. that afternoon

Three-thirty rolled around quickly. Vehicle manned, Tom called operations for permission to launch. The claxon sounded and hanger door rolled out and down to form the landing pad. Larry rolled out the AFV, hesitated momentarily and lifted off smartly. He headed northeast climbing until he reached 105 miles altitude. He had accelerated to 15,000 mph and was coasting towards the North Pole. When he reached it, he turned southwest began slowing and descending to 15,000'. Tom called Terry on intercom and notified him they were below that altitude and Terry and Wally began to strip down from their pressure suits. Terry reported to Tom they were ready to land. Wally grabbed the canvas bag containing the tools, flashlight and night vision goggles while Terry had a similar bag containing night vision goggles, hand held GPS and flashlight. He had also thrown in wire cutters just in case they came across something unplanned and needed them. They both plugged in their earpiece and mike so they could remain in contact with the AFV.

Larry leveled off at treetop height and slowed too a couple hundred mph. As he approached five miles he was due north of launch pad 81/23. He slowed to 30 mph and alerted Terry. Terry switched on his GPS and he and Wally donned their night vision goggles. At ¾ of a mile Larry came to a hover, lowered his landing pads and set the AFV down. As advertised the cloud cover was overcast and the landing party scampered down the boarding ladder.

They moved out from under the AFV and Terry checked his GPS. The pad was exactly three quarter of a mile south by southwest and they headed due south. They crossed a ten-foot high earthen berm and just after came onto the dirt road that ran southwest directly to the pad. Next they crossed a streambed and there it was, directly in front of them. This missile had not yet been fueled so they moved quietly and quickly up on the pad. Wally found the valve and using the tools they had brought with them he took the stem out of the valve. With the other tool Wally broke the stem and put the first piece back in the body of the valve. Next he screwed the cover with the top of the stem back in place and signaled Terry he was ready to depart. As they stepped down they saw a night security patrol driving down the dirt road toward the pad. Tom Harger also gave them a heads up in their earpiece. The patrol was sweeping the area on each side of their vehicle with a searchlight. Terry pulled on Wally's sleeve and they hit the ground in the wadi they had first crossed. There was some brush that they used for cover and they lay completely still. The searchlight swept over them but kept on moving. When it was clear they began moving quickly up the road retracing their steps. After crossing the berm again they were only 200 yards from their drop-off point. Larry swooped in and with gear already down he set the AFV down gently. Terry and Wally climbed aboard and Larry was off once again clawing for altitude and speed to get out of Kazakhstan as quickly as possible.

Larry headed northeast towards the pole. Tom was

on the radio and broadcast in a burst transmission that they were clear of Russia and headed home. Mission accomplished, landing party safe and aboard.

Bob smiled at Choyce in operations and picked up the emergency phone.

Admiral Boland was quickly on the other end. "What's the word, Bob?" he asked excitedly.

"Feet dry. Mission accomplished, John. All-hands on the way home," Bob said.

"Wow, you guys know how to get things done," John said.

"Thank you, sir. I'll pass that on to the crew when we have recovered them," he said.

"Okay, Bob. Send me you final report after you debrief the landing party," he said and hung up the phone.

18

"A Rousing Success"

Kamas, Utah, Hangar complex

Larry set the AFV down on the hangar pad as gently as he always did. He slid the AFV into the hangar and the claxon sounded and hangar door closed. He shutdown the vehicle, extended the boarding ladder and all hands exited. Jeff Johnson, one of the maintenance people, asked the crew if there were any discrepancies. He didn't get an immediate answer because of the boisterous crewmembers and all the high fives going on.

Finally Tom Harger told Jeff that the UHF radio needed some attention as it had more static than normal.

Bob had come out of operations and greeted the crew.

"Hey you guys, great job," he said as he individually congratulated each man. "Get changed to your street clothes and meet me in the quarters for a debrief on the mission."

They all whined at him just to give him the naval aviator treatment. In their terms it was a gesture of love and respect but also a slight jab at is authority. It was all done in fun and was a ritual they had practiced over the years.

"Yap, yap, yap," said Tom Harger.

"Always has to show us whose boss," Terry chimed in.

"He still thinks we're in the Navy," Wally said.

"Come on you guys, give the boss a break. He's been under a lot of pressure for the past couple of hours," Larry said in a deep serious voice.

They all laughed. They were relieved and, with the pressure off, were all loose and completely relaxed.

Bob smiled at his crew of professionals and said in response to their badgering, "Get with it, you maggots. I need to debrief you. If we don't get it done soon I'll withhold your pay for the next quarter or force you to stay home for a month with your families."

The banter continued for a couple of minutes while they all made their way to the crew locker room. They were all laughing and slapping each other on the back. It was a successful mission and they were proud of what they had done.

The crew gathered in the kitchen and Choyce joined the debrief.

"I guess we better hear from the landing party first. You're up, Terry," Bob said.

Terry began, "Larry let us off in the exact spot we had planned. My handheld GPS was working great and Wally and I got to the earthen berm and climbed over it. About ten yards further we came across the dirt road we had expected and followed it to the launch pad. Along the way we crossed the wadi that was dry but had some low shrubs and bushes in it. We got to the launch pad where Wally and I jumped up on it and found the proper valve on the missile. Wally did all the hard work. The night vision equipment was invaluable and we couldn't have done it without them. Wally opened the valve and broke the stem, replaced the broken part and reattached the cover to the valve. We jumped down and started to head back to the pickup point when we spotted base security sweeping the area with a searchlight. Wally and I made in to the Wadi and crawled under some shrubs. The searchlight swept over us but didn't spot us. When we were clear, we went back over the berm and as we approached the pickup point Larry swooped in and picked us up. That's about all there was too it," Terry said.

"Larry or Tom, you have anything to add?" Bob said.

"I had Terry's GPS locked onto my ground display and when we saw him start to move after security passed, I told Larry we were clear to move in for the pickup. That's how we were able to coordinate precisely and not get there too early or leave them standing exposed for anytime," Tom added.

"The weather Choyce gave us was exactly as predicted. The overcast allowed us to move in and out undetected. Otherwise everything went perfectly," Larry said.

"Well, let me add to this discussion that if you guys didn't know what you were doing and weren't trained so well, this could have been a bad mission. The fact that it went so perfectly says everything about you guys and how professional this mission was executed. Well done. Admiral Boland sends us a Bravo Zulu," Bob said. "It's still early and you guys can stay on the mountain tonight and have a party or feel free to go down the mountain and spend it with your friends and family. I'll see you tomorrow as we have a serious mission coming up. Have a good night."

Baikonur Cosmodrome, Kazakhstan

The fueling crew was up early to begin fueling the Soyuz rocket first with oxygen and then with hydrazine. They pulled their refueling vehicle up to pad 81/23 and rolled out the hoses. After plugging into the rocket body they opened the valves at their truck and started pumping liquid oxygen into the rocket. After a few minutes they noticed excessive leakage of oxygen through the rocket motor and overflow valve. One of the technicians stepped up on the pad and turned the shutoff valve to the closed position. He gave the supervisor thumbs up that the valve was indicating closed. Liquid oxygen continued to flow from the Soyuz rocket and the supervisor signaled to shutdown the refueling. He called the cleanup crew and, as soon as the refueling truck was disconnected, the cleanup crew moved in and began tidying up the launch pad of liquid oxygen. This was a very dangerous situation and the safety of all concerned was paramount. When the pad was sanitized the rocket was defueled of its remaining oxygen and all lines and tanks were vented to the atmosphere to purge the launch vehicle of any remaining gas.

The rocket engineers were waiting for this process to be completed so they could troubleshoot the problem. It took them most of the morning before they pinpointed the faulty valve. The base had no spare valves so the senior engineer placed a call to Aviation Plant Number One in Samara, Russia, to see if they had one in their stock. They searched for more than an hour and called back to report they had none and had just shipped their remaining five valves to Plesetsk in Mirny, Russia.

General Spastek was the Baikonur base commander and he was contacted and advised of the situation. He placed a call to General Zukov base commander at Sary Shagan, Kazakhstan, to inquire whether he had any of these spare valves. They had a friendly discussion but General Zukov reported they did not stock that particular valve because it was only specific to the Soyuz and Proton rockets. General Spastek thanked him and hung up. He knew now his only source was the base at Plesetsk. He placed a call to General Vladimir Gorchinski. General Gorchinki answered the phone.

"Vlad, this is Boris down at Baikonur. How are things?" he asked.

"Boris good to hear your voice again. Things are doing great here. What can I do for you?" he said.

"Samara has recently shipped you some oxygen pressure relief valves for the Proton and Soyuz rockets. We have an important launch we are holding because we found a broken valve and need one to continue the countdown. Do you think you could get one to us as soon as possible?" he asked.

"Sure, we can do that for you Boris. It will take about three days however, but we will ship it out to Moscow this afternoon and mark it highest priority. Give me the stock number so we send you the correct valve. Anything else we can do for you at the point?" he asked.

The General gave Vlad the stock number. "No, Vlad. That will get us out of a serious bind. I owe you one, old friend. Take care," he said and hung up the phone.

Kamas, Utah

Bob was in his office early and picked up the emergency phone. He pressed the button for John Boland.

"John here. What's up, Bob?" he asked.

"John, I think we have a developing situation here which may threaten our security and I thought I better bring you in on it, but before we talk about that, what were the results of our two flights on our Baikonur surveillance?" he asked.

"This morning at Baikonur we observed their refueling crew begin to load liquid oxygen on the Soyuz rocket.

Shortly after we next observed their safety crew scouring the pad and defueling Soyuz. We can conclude that our landing party was successful and they are looking for a replacement valve. We have bought ourselves a four day window to get our mission to Enterprise accomplished so put that on your schedule," John said.

"We still have it scheduled for Tuesday, John. We should have all the planning and people in place by then. I don't know our exact time as yet but will have Choyce run the numbers again and see what our optimum time is for our best results, Bob said.

"That sounds good, Bob. Now what else did you call about?" he asked.

"John, we did an interview for the Salt Lake City Tribune for a reporter by the name of Betsy Moore. She did a nice article on Omega Aviation but she is best noted for her investigative reporting. Larry and I get the distinct feeling she's not finished digging into our operation," he said.

"Okay, Bob. We'll take the lead on this one. We have dealt with this type of situation before so let us worry about it," he said.

"Thanks, John. That takes a big load off my mind. Take care, we'll be in touch," and with that word Bob returned the phone to its cradle.

Salt Lake City, Utah

Since Betsy Moore had written the article on Omega Aviation for the Tribune she had been busy researching and gathering more information.

She had found that John Walker had been a pilot in Southeast Asia and had worked for Southern Air Transport. He had flown the C-130 and Boeing 737 for three years before he came to work for Omega Aviation. Other than that she could not find out much more about him. She did uncover that all the other flight personnel at Omega had been members of Antarctic Development Squadron Six and had resigned from the Navy to take jobs there. She found that to be strange. Sure enough she found that Bob Avery was indeed a hero and had rescued Swede Larson, the lost Antarctic explorer, only to have him die on the flight back to civilization. Larry Beck also was a hero as he had rescued the crew of the Maverick Explorer when the ship sunk in the Bay of Whales, Antarctica, after it was crushed in the ice. Almost all of the other flight crewmembers had been decorated for heroism while serving in the Antarctic.

She discovered Mike Brenner had also rescued an injured Argentine crewman from an Antarctic Base and had been decorated by not only the U.S. Navy but also the Argentine government.

John Walker certainly was correct when he said this was an organization of heroes.

Betsy's further investigation into Paul Anderson and Tori Croft brought out nothing but a squeaky clean record but did not answer how both of them moved from NASA to Omega.

She was still not satisfied and began digging into their financial situation. Phil Murphy's name came up as the CEO of World Security Associates, USA, Inc. and primary investor in Omega. She found that all the G550s had been purchased with money from his company and were 100% owned and paid for with no outstanding debt. Betsy thought this was strange as it was a lot of money to come out of the investment company.

Omega Aviation was becoming a strange entity. Why was their headquarters located in a restricted secure compound? John Walker had told her the reason but it just didn't make sense to spend that kind of company money when they were just organized and getting in business. She knew there was more money being spent than was coming in and that required an explanation. Betsy felt she was making progress and one day she got a call from a strange source. A Mason Williams called and told her he could fill her in on Omega Aviation. She made a mental note of the time and place but didn't record it in any of her documents or day planner.

The rendezvous was set for 9:00p.m. at a rest stop on Interstate 80. Mason described his car as a white Nissan Pathfinder with Utah license plates. Betsy drove out on the Interstate to meet Mason but was never heard from again. No trace was ever found of her car or her body.

A few months later there were reports that a Datu in Mindanao, Philippines, had a new concubine. A beautiful white woman probably an American.

Kamas, Utah

Bob was trying to catch up on his paperwork and drafted a letter to Phil Murphy at World Security Associates, USA, Inc. He laid out his decision to establish a branch office of Omega Aviation in Charlotte, North Carolina. A timetable was set out so as to take over World Securities maintenance and pilot responsibilities. Omega would find and hire, with his approval, a branch manager who would layout an organizational chart and begin to fill those positions with the approval of the staff at Omega. He made it clear that he wished to maintain the high quality of service Omega was noted for and whose pilots were some of the best in the world. John Walker would be charged with monitoring pilot qualification and currency. He would also ensure compliance with company FAA certification.

World Security Associates pilot's salaries would remain the responsibility of the parent company. Bob suggested that World Security Associates, USA, Inc., credit maintenance costs to Omega to assist in retiring any investment of capital, an amount to be determined at a later date.

Bob explained to Phil that by organizing in this manner the business could easily be expanded to manage and eventually buy more airplanes in the process thereby allowing the profits to be added to the bottom line for the whole company.

He asked Phil for assistance when time came to acquire a hangar for their operation at Douglas Airport. Bob indicated a spreadsheet and timeline plan would be forthcoming and if necessary he would schedule a Charlotte meeting, bringing John Walker, Larry Beck and Bill Grammercy to discuss the whole thing.

Bob thanked Phil for making this possible and assured him it would be profitable within a short time after establishment.

19

"The Ultimate Mission"

Kamas, Utah, Headquarters compound

Monday came quickly for the personnel at Omega Aviation. Paul caught the morning Helo down to Hangar 512. A shuttle was provided for him over to the commercial terminal and was soon winging his way to New York's JFK.

After a great weekend of crew R&R, Larry, Mike and Tori assembled their crews on the second deck of headquarters building. At various intervals they drifted down to the security doors and made their way up the mountain. As they arrived, one of the duty crews headed down the mountain.

Bob arrived just after lunch and they all sat down for the final briefing and last minute details on the mission. Larry once again went over exactly how the mission would run and covered the communications frequencies. At the end there were no questions as they had been over it so many times they all would know it in their sleep.

Jack looked at his notes and began his part of the briefing. He recommended they pick up the shuttle over central Russia and begin the mission from there. The shuttle would be in that position about 6:00p.m. Tuesday, mountain standard time (MST), over Russia 9:00a.m. Wednesday. Takeoff time in Utah should be about 5:20p.m. MST. Jack finished his briefing with the weather forecast for McMurdo for tomorrow evening. They were calling for clear skies, winds light and variable and temperatures in the -20 to -30ºF. Bill's comment was, "piece of cake."

With the briefing finished and no AFV missions, all-hands relaxed and settled down to watch a little TV. Mike Brenner's crew was elected to cook supper so they started fixing it. The time passed quickly and these professionals were relaxed and acting like they were going to a Knicks basketball game.

Tuesday rolled around and by mid-afternoon everyone was getting a little antsy. Bill took Tori back into the pressure suit locker room. He had set out two EVA packs and directed her to check out one while he checked out the other. The other crews entered the locker room and everyone began to don their pressure suits. Mike manned #6 and Larry took #3. Bill and Tori took the stations in the lower section of the AFV. Bill was on the right and Tori on the left of the entry ladder. Larry retracted the ladder and pressurized the spacecraft. The claxon sounded and Larry, followed by Mike, were given permission for departure. The adventure began.

Larry instructed Mike to follow him at a one hundred mile interval. They accelerated and climbed for altitude. Larry stabilized their speed at 20,000 mph and altitude one-hundred-six miles. Larry spotted the space shuttle coming up. He was approaching it from behind and began slowing to match it's orbital speed. Mike was directed to standoff at one hundred miles.

As they passed the north coast of Russia, Larry

moved into position and lowered his rear-landing strut. He locked into the shuttle bay tie-down and lowered his entry ladder. Bill and Tori had activated their EVA packs oxygen system and were proceeding down the ladder to the cargo bay interlock. The hatch was still open and unlocked, just as Paul had left it when he exited the shuttle previously. When they were clear, Larry pressurized as he retracted the ladder and closed the hatch. He retracted his landing strut and moved to a position at eye level with the cockpit where he could make eye contact with Tori. As Tori moved through the shuttle she opened the flow valves for the oxygen and hydrogen feeding the fuel cells and auxiliary power units. That done, she and Bill moved up to the cockpit. They began to monitor the electrical gauges, looking for an indication of electrical power. After thirty minutes with no indication of power, Tori told Bill through their EVA comm system that she was going down again to see if she could get oxygen and hydrogen flowing. In a couple of minutes she returned with still no indication.

Larry was getting irritated having no word of what was happening. He had been calling on the EVA comm frequency and suddenly Bill got through and Larry was relieved. Bill advised Larry of the problem and said Tori was still working on it. Time was fleeting and they were once again approaching the north coast of Russia. The space shuttle was now headed southeast when Tori reported she had an indication of electrical power beginning to build. Tom Harger calculated that one more orbit of the shuttle could still allow them to change orbit and land the shuttle at McMurdo.

Suddenly and without warning, the cargo bay package ejected from the cargo bay and its rocket ignited. Larry immediately recognized that the package had locked onto the Russian nuclear weapon which was just crossing the polar area. Without thinking Larry shouted into his microphone, "Tori and Bill get the Hell out of the shuttle now. We have an emergency and need to leave the area as soon as possible. I mean NOW. Do not delay." Bill jumped out of his seat and pulled the ring for the overhead window jettison system handle located forward of the flight deck in center console (C3). It activated the overhead window jettison system. After initiation, the outer pane was jettisoned upward and aft. A time delayed the pyrotechnic firing circuit which delayed the initiation of the opening of the inner pane 0.3 second after the outer pane was jettisoned. The inner windowpane then rotated downward and aft into the crew compartment aft flight deck on hinges which were located at the aft portion of the window frame. A capture device attenuated the opening rate and held the window in position.

Bill grabbed Tori and she held onto Bill's boot and they exited the window.

Larry had seen the window blow and quickly moved his vehicle over the opening, while extending the boarding ladder. By the time Bill and Tori were clear of the shuttle window, the boarding ladder was touching the overhead of the shuttle cockpit. Once again Tori followed Bill up the ladder and as quickly Larry began closing the hatch. He radioed Mike.

"Red Dog this is Husky. Break away southwest and get as faraway as fast as possible. All Hell is going to breakout at any moment." Bill and Tori were strapped in and Larry accelerated towards the southeast.

Without warning, the sky behind the AFVs lit up like the sun was coming up. The shuttle package found the Russian probe, which had been booby-trapped with proximity radar and triggered the nuclear explosion. It had occurred at three hundred miles altitude over central China. An electromagnetic pulse (EMP) was traveling out in all directions at 600 miles per second as was a high-energy explosive burst. Larry hoped to avoid both as he was still accelerating. He steadied the vehicle at 25,000 miles per hour. Mike Brenner had been doing the same. Out of the corner of his eye Mike caught sight of the International Space Station, which was a couple of hundred miles to the north, heading directly into the blast zone. They were less than 1000 miles from the blast center and Mike was concerned the EMP and the blast could affect them.

When Mike was sure he was clear of both he turned and headed back for the space station. As he approached he slowed to match the speed of the Station and was appalled at the condition of the station. The solar panels had been torn away by the blast and a couple sections of the station itself were broken apart. Mike moved around the station in hopes of seeing some human activity. Part way around the silence was broken by a weak voice through the static on UHF calling for help. Ivan Wheaton, Mike's systems officer, answered. There were two astronauts alive in the Quest section of the station. Ivan determined they could don their space suits. He instructed them to don their suits and move out through the space station interlock. Mike positioned himself over the interlock. Inside the astronauts donned their suits, entered the interlock and depressurized. They activated their emergency oxygen escape pack which was of fifteen-minute duration. Mike lowered his entry ladder and his flight engineer went down to assist the astronauts board the AFV. He strapped them into the seats in the lower cabin and reentered the flight deck. Mike retracted the entry ladder and pressurized the vehicle. He streaked away from the station to the south-west to avoid the radiation belt already present where the bomb went off.

Larry called Mike on the UHF, "Red Dog this is Husky. Report your status."

"Husky, this is Red Dog. Everything is A-Okay. I have rescued two astronauts from the space station which was almost blown to pieces by the blast. The astronauts are in bad shape and need immediate medical attention. Request instructions," Mike said.

Bob Avery had been monitoring the comm channel. He sent Mike a burst transmission, "Red Dog, we have a helo on the way back from Reno. Set down and discharge your passengers on the Bonneville Salt Flats. Turn on their survival strobes and return to base. We'll have the helo pick them up and drop them on the helo pad at the University Hospital in Salt Lake City."

Mike received the transmission, "Roger copied," he said.

Mike came about and headed east across the Pacific Ocean.

Meanwhile Larry had headed directly for Kamas. He was fifty miles out. Tom Harger keyed the mike, "Whisper, this is Husky for landing."

"Husky cleared for recovery," Jack said.

Larry brought the AFV in for landing and as quickly as he set it down he slid it into the hangar bay. The claxon sounded and the hangar bay door closed. Lights came back on and the vehicle was shutdown. The vehicle emptied with Tori down the ladder first followed by Bill Grammercy, Tom Harger and Larry Beck.

At the bottom of the ladder stood Bob Avery. His first words were, "What the Hell just happened out there,

Larry?" he asked.

"The God Damn Russians detonated the son of a bitch," Larry responded.

Bob had never seen Larry this angry. He knew the debrief was going to be a doozy so he directed the crew to change into their street clothes and then come into the crew quarters for a debrief.

Meanwhile, Bob had alerted Gary Sheen, who was piloting the Bell 412 back from Reno, to be alert and pick up the two astronauts and deposit them at the helo pad at the University Hospital.

Mike slowed his vehicle as he passed Lake Tahoe. He descended quickly and made a beautiful landing on the Bonneville Salt Flats. His flight engineer carried the astronauts down the ladder and set them on the ground. He turned on their survival strobe lights and reboarded the vehicle. Mike lifted off and headed directly for home. Everybody in the hangar complex heard the claxon and knew Mike was close to touchdown. Larry's group was just entering the crew quarters so they decided to wait for him to get there before they started the debrief.

Bob went out on the hangar deck just as Mike shut down his vehicle. The radiation warning horns were all sounding and a higher than normal reading was being sensed. Some of the other flight engineers in quarters knew what that meant and quickly ran out into the hangar bay along with a few other flight crew personnel. Jack reopened the hangar door and they slid the AFV out onto the landing pad. As soon as it was chocked and the crew clear the auto spray system came on and sprayed the vehicle from all directions. Mike's crew was stopped immediately in the hangar and a hand held Geiger counter was used to check their pressure suits. The suits indicated a small amount of radiation but well below the acceptable level. Bob asked the crew to give him their dosimeters, which they wore around their necks, and gave them to Jack. He told the crew to go change into their street clothes and meet in the crew quarters. Jack took the dosimeters into operations to check the exposure levels.

In quarters, the rest of the personnel were all talking practically at once. Everyone was animated and no one actually had the complete story but were all keyed up as to what had just happened.

New York, New York

Paul Anderson was in the middle of his interview with Hannity when Hannity stopped talking, turned pale white and announced a news alert.

"Ladies and Gentlemen, we have a news alert, It appears that there is some kind of emergency happening in China. Reports reaching Fox news at this time report that there have been numerous plane crashes and all communications have ceased. No further information is available at this time. We will continue to monitor the situation and bring you updates as we receive them."

Hannity wondered out loud what that was all about and that it appeared serious.

Paul just sat there dumbfounded. He knew full well what had just happened and he was concerned about the AFVs and their crews.

Kamas, Utah, Hangar complex

Mike's crew hurriedly changed clothes and rushed into the crew quarters. They entered a room in conversational chaos. All turned to Mike's crew and started to ask questions. Bob Avery came in and finally yelled for everyone to take a seat.

"Alright, something serious happened out there tonight and right now we are going to pay attention to us and our operation. First of all, is everyone okay?" he asked. Everyone indicated in some fashion that they were.

Just then the door burst open and the remaining crew from the hangar came in.

"Sir, number six is secure inside and has been de-contaminated," they reported.

"Okay, come in and find a seat. This is going to be a long night. Larry let's start with what you did and saw," Bob said.

"I rendezvoused with Enterprise and attached to her cargo bay tiedown. Tori and Bill exited my vehicle and I detached and moved to a spot alongside the cockpit from where I could observe. What happened next I think Tori or Bill can fill us in," Larry said.

Tori took up the narrative, "Bill and I made our way to the cockpit. As I moved up there, I turned on all the oxygen and hydrogen flow valves. We reached the cockpit and Bill and I began reading and executing the checklists. During this time, Bill tried and was eventually successful in contacting Larry's vehicle. We were monitoring the battery voltage gauges and we started to see the needle move off the peg indicating some voltage beginning to flow. Suddenly and without warning the cargo bay package ejected from the cargo bay. The next thing we heard was Larry telling us to evacuate the vehicle by emergency means. Bill activated the jettison sequence for the overhead hatch and he pulled me out of the cockpit. We made it up Larry's boarding ladder in record time and he quickly executed a breakaway maneuver and that's all I observed."

H.J. "Walt" Walter

Bonneville Salt Flats, Utah

Gary Sheen had spotted the two strobes and flew directly towards them. He and his copilot spotted the two figures sitting on the ground. They landed, exited and carried the two astronauts into the helo. Gary flew directly to the helo pad at the University Hospital. While enroute he radioed the hospital to turn on the landing pad lights and that it looked like he had two severely injured astronauts. The hospital turned on the lights and Gary landed. The astronauts were taken into the emergency room on gurneys. Gary left his business card with the hospital in case someone needed to talk with him. Before he departed he briefed the staff on how he came across the patients and all that he knew about their situation, which wasn't much.

Kamas, Utah, Hangar complex

Larry continued his narrative, "While in position alongside the cockpit of the shuttle, I saw the DOD package ejected from the shuttle, light off its rocket motors and speed away toward the north. I knew immediately that it had locked on to the Russian nuke and was headed in that direction. I immediately warned Tori and Bill and directed them to make an emergency evacuation of the shuttle. At the same time I directed Mike to get the Hell out of there. Then I saw the cockpit upper hatch blow off and I placed my vehicle over that hatch and lowered my ladder. Bill and Tori made a hasty exit and boarded the vehicle. I did an emergency breakaway towards the southeast. I knew there was going to be an explosion so I wanted to get away as far and as fast as possible. I had no idea there would be a nuclear explosion. When it went off, I was out of range of it and had no effects what-so-ever from it. I checked to see if Mike was okay and he reported he was fine. I guess he can take it up from there."

Before Mike could start, Jack entered the quarters.

"I am happy to report that Mike's crew did get a little extra radiation but it was at a low level and within limits. I guess you were far enough away from the explosion that it was a limited dose," Jack said.

"Thank God for that," Bob said.

Mike began his version of the story. "I was sitting on my perch listening to what was happening when Larry came up and warned Bill and Tori to get the Hell out of the shuttle. He also directed me to break away to the southwest at max speed, which I did. I was diving and at the same time passing two hundred miles altitude when I spotted the International Space Station off to my right. I continued on my heading and, when I was sure I was at least 1000 miles away from my perch, I turned back and that's when I saw the mushroom cloud and felt a little turbulence. I immediately knew it was an EMP high altitude burst so I went back to check on the space station. They were in a 56° orbit and headed southeast when I saw them so I knew they were not headed into the radiation belt. What I saw when I was about one hundred miles away really scared me and, as I moved even closer, it was worse than I expected. The solar panels were blown away. Three or four of the modules were heavily damaged and even partially separated. I made a fly by and did a 360° around the station. Ivan had switched one of the radios to their frequency and he heard a voice crying for help. I just couldn't leave them and do nothing so I waited while Ivan coaxed them into their pressure suits and somehow got them moving to us out of their space interlock. Ed moved down and out of the vehicle and assisted them into the seats in the lower section of my vehicle. From there I did as directed and dropped them off on the Bonneville Salt Flats. Ed carried them off and turned on their strobe lights. Believe me, guys, they were in bad shape. They had sustained some severe injuries both internal and external and got a pretty good dose of radiation when the EMP and blast passed them. They were both almost unconscious most of the time. Did we alert somebody to pick them up?" Mike asked.

Jack chimed in, "Yeah, Mike, I had a report from Gary Sheen on his way back from Reno. He saw them, picked them up and deposited them at University Hospital in Salt Lake City."

"That's good to hear. I hope I didn't compromise the whole program, boss," Mike said.

"Mike, don't worry about it. You did the right thing. That's what we trained for all these years. One of our jobs was to look after the astronauts in our space program. You did that tonight and I commend you and your crew for the bravery you showed in doing your job and having to make a decision in that split second. Now does anyone else have anything to add to this debrief? If not, break out the booze and beer and get calmed down from this hyper evening. I'll be back shortly to join you so don't drink it all before I get here. I need to report to the boss," Bob said.

Jack piped up. "Bob, there were three astronauts on the space station. I think we should send out an AFV to search for the third one."

Bob directed Jack, "Send Bruce Fleming and his crew to do a reconnoiter of the station and see if they can find the other astronaut."

Bruce was sitting there and quickly gathered his crew and was out the door headed for a search and rescue mission of the space station.

Bob walked over to operations. He picked up the

emergency phone and hit the button for John Boland. John picked up, "What the Hell just happened out there, Bob?" he asked.

Bob had taken copious notes and related the complete story of the mission. He emphasized that it was an EMP from the nuclear weapon that created the problem for the crews and added that the DOD package ejected prematurely. He said he didn't know if the rescue of the astronauts from the ISS was going to create a problem with the secrecy of the AFV program. He said they currently were mounting a search and rescue mission for the third astronaut. John Boland told him exactly the same thing he had said to Mike Brenner. Mike had reacted as he was trained to do. He had rescued astronauts from our space program and that is what we are trained to do. John assured him that was all the AFV program could do for now but further reconnaissance might be required after we access what was going on in China.

Bob went back to the quarters where a wake was being held. There was some drinking going on but the crew had not unwound yet from this harrowing evening,

Bill was talking to Larry. "I have never had a more near death experience than tonight, old buddy," he said. "If we ever volunteer to do this again, kick my ass, will you?"

"You were never in trouble, Bill. I was looking after you all the time," Larry said factiously.

"Yeah, that kind of watching my back I can do without. I know you scared the shit out of Tori," he said.

Tori piped up, "Bill that's what you call a controlled ejection," she offered. "It was close but honestly I wasn't scared. You and I reacted just as we trained for the mission. All I can say is that I'm glad you studied your shuttle emergency procedures or we might still be inside that thing. The only thing I regret is I didn't get to pilot the damn thing. Anyway, Larry did a great job and we're here, aren't we?" she said.

"Christ, don't make Larry out to be the hero in this or he will get a swelled head and want to take over Bob's job. That's all we need. We'd be flying missions like this every other day," Bill said.

Bob could see by the banter that things were loosening up a little. It was going to take more that this to shake up these guys and gal. He knew what would, a death in the family, and he was going to try to avoid that if at all possible. There had not been a death since the early sixties when they lost Lieutenant Paul "Flatspin" O'Dea over Kansas. He had made a fatal error by exceeding maximum speed at too low an altitude and the AFV broke up into little pieces.

An hour had elapsed and Bruce Fleming was returning to base. He reported no luck in finding the third astronaut. After landing and securing the AFV, Bruce was debriefed by Bob and Jack.

Bruce stated, "I did a visual 360º of the space station and saw no signs of life. I then sent my engineer into the station to search further.   Aaron Burkette chimed in, "I made my way through the debris of the station and my search was negative. I did notice that the third pressure suit was missing and the station was completely depressurized."

"That's an interesting observation Aaron." Bob noted, and wrote down the information to pass to Admiral Boland.

20

"The Aftermath "

Salt Lake City, Utah

The space station astronauts were now in the emergency room. From the flags and patches on their space suits, the emergency staff had determined that one was a Russian and the other an American. The Russian was in the worst shape. Tests were still being run but they had determined that he had a broken pelvis, hairline fractures of the left leg and ankle, and internal injuries. He was bleeding internally and was being prepped for emergency surgery. The American had a concussion and bruised ribs as well as a severe bruise on one of his kidneys. At this time he was unconscious and not able to communicate. The Russian was incoherent and wasn't giving anyone any answers as to how they got there. When the tests results were read, both astronauts would probably develop radiation sickness since it was determined they had been exposed to a large dose of Gamma radiation. Their dosimeters had revealed a large exposure.

The local sheriff had been called to investigate and, when he had assessed the situation, placed a call to the local FBI office. Sheriff Ponder soon met up with Special Agent Simon Calleder. They met in the lobby of the hospital and went back to the emergency room. The staff there briefed them on the condition of the astronauts and said they would appreciate it if they could put a name to each of their new patients. Simon made a note in his case notepad that he would call NASA for that information. The staff also gave them Gary Sheen's business card and told them how Gary had come to deliver the astronauts to the hospital. It was approaching midnight and Simon made more notes of things to do in the morning.

Morning came and Simon was up early and at the hospital by 6:00a.m. He checked on the patients and both were in ICU. He found an unoccupied doctor's office and placed a call to NASA Houston. He finally reached Winston Perry, Director of Manned Space Flight.

"Director Perry, this is FBI Special Agent Simon Calleder. I am calling concerning two astronauts from the International Space Station," he said.

"Oh my God where are they. How did they get there and what has happened to them?" he asked.

"They are currently in the University Hospital at Salt Lake City. They were picked up on the Bonneville Salt Flats and delivered here by helicopter. Both are in ICU and unconscious. One is Russian, the other American. Can you give me their names?" He said.

"The Russian is Yuri Shaminski, but which American do you have and where is the other one. How did they get to Bonneville from the space station?" he asked.

"We didn't know there were two Americans and don't know which one we have here. Please give me both the names and we will go from there," Simon said. "I have no idea how they came to be on the Salt Flats. We won't be able to determine that until we talk with the astronauts."

"Our astronauts are Jesse Oddo and Elmer Hudson. Wasn't there a name tag anywhere on the space suit?" he asked.

"If there was we didn't find any Mr. Perry. Can you send us a picture of both for ID purposes?" he said.

"Yes, we can do that. How would you like to receive it?" he said.

Simon asked Winston to fax them to the hospital and he gave him the number. He also passed on the phone number for the doctor charged with treating the astronauts so he could talk with him and receive updates on their condition. Winston thanked him for the information and hung up the phone.

Simon next called Omega headquarters and tried to locate Gary. He was told Gary had flown the morning flight to the Hangar at Salt Lake City airport. Gary figured someone would be investigating the incident so he made himself available at the hangar. Simon dialed Omega Aviation and Ginny Wulf answered. She located Gary in the pilot's readyroom and switched the call there.

"Gary, I understand you were the pilot of the helicopter that rescued the astronauts at Bonneville Salt Flats last night," Simon said.

"Yeah, I found them if you want to call that a rescue," he said.

"Can I come over and talk with you?" he asked.

"Sure but make it soon as I have an 11:30a.m. flight," Gary said.

"Okay, I'm on my way. Will be there in about fifteen minutes, he said.

"Good. I'll be in the readyroom. Check in with the secretary and she'll direct you," Gary said.

It was about twenty minutes when Simon entered the readyroom. He introduced himself to Gary and asked him how things happened the night before. Gary explained how he was coming back from Reno, spotted the strobes, went to investigate and found the astronauts and delivered them to the hospital.   Simon asked if he saw anything else, maybe how they got there. Gary assured him he had seen nothing except the strobes which caught his attention. The interview came to an end and Simon left his card with Gary in case he should remember anything else which might help with the investigation. Gary inquired about the status of the astronauts and Simon told him they were both in ICU and unconscious.

Simon went back to the hospital as he felt that was going to be the only source of information and help for his investigation. When he arrived the hospital administrator saw him and called to him. He was advised that the staff had identified the American astronaut as Jesse Oddo. That meant Elmer Hudson was missing. He made a note in his notepad.

Mclean, Virginia

News and Intelligence reports had been coming in like a tidal wave. It was more than the analysts could keep up with but the director was asking for a briefing every hour. He had known from Bob Avery that the blast had been an EMP from 300 miles up. What they needed to find out was how much China was crippled? Reports were slow coming with most of the reports currently from around the periphery of China. The latest briefing went around the edges, so to speak. The section chief for China started with Hanoi, Vietnam. A few computers were reported burned out, as were some electric motors. Hainan Island, China, reported a flickering TV signal and lights but no outages. Hong Kong had a lot of electric motors burned out. Lights were off for two hours and some electronics were inoperative. South Korea reported no interference, as did Pyongyang, North Korea. Finally Ulan Bator reported no effects from the EMP.

The thing missing were reports from mainland China. There were no reports what so ever. Apparently they had suffered the worst outages from the EMP. At the next briefing, not much had changed. The briefer summarized with the assumption that the EMP was centered and occurred over the city of Xi'an in central China. All analysts concurred that there had to be some lives lost. Airliners in flight controlled by computers would surely have gone down probably with loss of life.

It was evening in China and aircraft flying the periphery of the continent reported no air traffic communication and no lights visible along the coast. John Boland made the decision. Time for a couple of AFV missions over China. John alerted Jack in AFV operations and in a short time he launched a couple of missions. Within one half hour, intelligence data was flowing back to Utah and Langley. Analysts found a couple of things. There were no electronic communications going on in China. Night vision pictures showed people on the streets and roads but very few cars and no busses. There were still many rickshaws but that was about it. Around a few major airports they spotted many aircraft crashes and quite a few still burning. There were no lights at all. China had been relegated to the Stone Age or at least thirty years or more.

John received a call from the President's National Security Advisor. He asked John if he could brief the President in the morning. John said he could be there whenever the President wanted him. The National Security Advisor told him he would set it up for 9:15a.m. They discussed some of the latest reports the CIA was forwarding to the National Security Advisor.

The next morning John was in the White House before 8:45a.m. He checked in with the Secret Service agent who was required to check in all Oval Office visitors. At 9:15a.m., John was ushered into the Oval Office.

"Good Morning, Mr. President," John said.

The President responded, "Good Morning, John. I guess it's been a long night at your shop."

"Yes sir, it's been a long night but I think I have a handle on what's happening," John said.

"Well, give me the bad news, John. From what I've heard already it looks pretty grim for China. It that right?"

"Yes, sir. Let me begin at the beginning. At about 7:30 last evening the Russian nuclear tipped missile we have been tracking, exploded over Xi'an, China, at about 300 miles in the atmosphere creating an electronic magnetic pulse which appears to have affected China for about a 1000 mile radius from Xi'an. We have no firm intelligence but China is exhibiting all the symptoms of the EMP. There have been many aircraft crashes, no electrical power and very little road traffic. We don't yet know how many casualties. Somehow two astronauts from the International Space Station were found on the Bonneville Salt Flats seriously injured. One is the Russian who has since passed away and one astronaut is still missing. The surviving astronaut is in the Utah University Hospital in guarded condition. That's about all we know at this time, sir," John reported.

The President gestured and spoke, "The Assistant Secretary of State Susan Walsh is currently in Mindinao, Philippines. I am sending her to China, if she can get there, to size up the situation. The Communist Chinese are going to need a lot of help on this one."

"Yes, sir. That's a great idea. Her pilot is John

Walker and he is fluent in Chinese Mandarin so he will be able to communicate well with the people still running things. I will keep in contact with the Secretary.

His briefing over, John Boland excused himself from the Oval Office and went back to the CIA building in McLean.

Moscow, Russia

Publicly there was complete silence from inside Russia. The Prime Minister called an emergency meeting of all those involved with the decision to place the nuclear weapon into orbit. Present were the President Boris Petrovsky, Prime Minister Sergei Puchinov, Head of the Russian Federal Space Agency General Sergei Kovolov, Minister of Defense General Arturo Meechaim, Head of the GRU Petre Borginov, General Vladamir Gorchinski and General Dimitri Zukov.

The Prime Minister opened the meeting.

"Gentlemen, as I see this situation we are in deep shit," he said. After the Chinese found out about the weapon, we assured them they were safe and were not to be threatened by it. Obviously things happened which put them under the EMP explosion and if everyone remembers they threatened retaliation if they were in the least hurt. I believe that China is now in a disastrous situation and many lives will be lost because of our stupidity. My question is what are we going to do?" he asked.

All present in the room sat there with no response. It was obvious nobody had an answer.

Dimitri Zukov spoke, "One thing in our favor is their recovery will take many years if not a couple of decades and retaliation is a long way off, if ever. We need to come up with a plan to wipe away the memories of what we have done and maybe in twenty years it will be forgotten."

"Comrades," General Kovolov said. "It will never be forgotten. The civilized world will ensure we will go down in history as the warmongers and responsible for this epic disaster." He turned to General Zukov, "Not that it matters, but what happened, Dimitri?"

"Here is my best estimate of the situation. The weapon we deployed into space, when activated after it reached orbit, was equipped with proximity radar coupled to a detonator. If any object came within fifty miles of the weapon it armed itself and detonated within two seconds. It was capable of Doppler effect sensing and in this case must have detected an incoming object and activated itself. Unfortunately for us it detonated over central China and caused the catastrophic disaster they are now experiencing," Dimitri said.

President Boris Petrovsky had been silently listening then began to speak, "I am the one who made the final decision on deploying the nuclear tipped weapon and I take full responsibility for it. I will consult with the Federation Council as well as the Security Council. They will need to develop a plan to defend the homeland against any possible retaliation. Meanwhile we should send a delegation to Beijing and determine priorities on what infrastructure we are best able to help restore. It will take a continuing effort over a long period of time. As for now, I will have drafted an official statement expressing our deep sorrow for the situation the Chinese find themselves. We will offer whatever help we can to assist the Chinese recover from this disaster. This meeting is adjourned."

Salt Lake City, Utah
At the University Hospital their public relations di-

rector held a news conference. The auditorium was swarming with media people from all the major TV networks. The public relations director announced that Yuri Schaminski had passed away due to his injuries and the American astronaut Jesse Oddo was in guarded condition. She described his injuries and prognosis for recovery. She said it was too early to judge his chances of survival The staff had done everything humanly possible to save the Russian but he was too mortally injured. The FBI announced that Ed Hudson was still missing. Simon Calleder's investigation was at a standstill and if Jesse Oddo didn't survive no one would ever know what happened. The news conference lasted for over an hour with the main question still unanswered. How did the astronauts come to be on the Bonneville Salt Flats?

The hospital staff had been in contact with the Russian Embassy in Washington, D.C., and now advised them of Yuri's death. The embassy was making arrangements for transportation of the body back to Russia.

Winston Perry was also in contact with the hospital checking on Jesse. He also asked whether Simon had a lead on Ed Hudson and the answer was still no.

Word leaked back to Bob Avery and the crew on the mountain. It was all over TV. Mike's engineer Ed Hollins, who had helped the ISS astronauts, and Bruce Fleming's engineer each said they hadn't seen anyone else on the station. Ed Hudson must have been in another part of the station when the blast hit it. He was probably killed instantly and his body must still in the station. The status of the orbit would need to be determined by NASA and a Russian mission to the station could possibly recover the body.

21

"The Morning After"

New York, New York

Paul Anderson's Hannity interview surely was successful albeit unnecessary because the space shuttle was still in some kind of orbit and had not successfully returned to earth. Paul was worried about his fellow pilots who had been involved in the mission. He had heard about the EMP nuclear explosion over China but he was still in the dark concerning his compatriots. He boarded his American Airlines flight for Salt Lake City. His questions would be answered in a couple of hours

Paul stepped off the plane after it stopped at gate C7 in Salt Lake. He had advised Ginny Wulf of his arrival flight and there was an Omega Aviation shuttle waiting outside at the curb when he stepped out of the terminal. The shuttle dropped him at Hangar 512 and he made his way to John Walker's office. John was on a trip to the Far East but Ginny was there. He inquired with Ginny on the status of the helo shuttle to headquarters. Ginny advised that the usual schedule was in effect and it would depart at 11:30a.m. He checked his watch. It was only10:40a.m. so he checked out a company car and drove over to Juanitizo's for lunch. He made it back to Hangar 512 by 11:25a.m., turned in the car and boarded the helo.

The flight was an agonizng twenty minutes to headquarters. When it arrived, he jumped off as quickly as possible and hurried to Bob's Office. Cindy announced him and he went into Bob's office.

Bob could read the anxiety in Paul's face and without a welcome, said, "Everyone is fine, Paul, safe and sound and probably hung over. How was your trip?"

"I have been worried ever since I heard during Hannity's interview. It is an agonizing feeling not knowing what exactly happened and not knowing if everybody is okay," Paul said. My trip was okay except for the worrying."

"I know just how you feel, Paul. Been there, done that. I had that happen to me when I was in the hospital in Punta Arenas and the guys were flying a mission I was supposed to be flying. I had to wait only ten hours to find out whereas you had all night. My advice is go up the mountain, talk with everybody, and get the story straight from the your felow astronauts. It'll make you feel better," Bob said.

"I think that's what I need to do. Thanks, Bob. I'll see you later," he said.

Paul moved toward the security door for his trip up the mountain.

In Bob's office, the emergency phone from John Boland rang.

"Bob here, John. What's up?" he asked.

"Bob, I understand that John Walker is on a trip in the Far East and has Assistant Secretary of State Susan Walsh on board. The President is going to get the State Department to divert her to Beijing and find out how everyone is at the U.S. Embassy there. I want you to send John a code that we want him to conduct a visual reconnaissance of that area and make a written report to us when he gets back. I will also have our China section chief call him for an oral report. He's the only way we are going to get any Intel on China for the time being. Do you think he can get in there without radio communications?" John asked.

"John, if the weather's good he can get into most any-place without help. I'll send him a message immediately. Can we help in any other way?" Bob asked.

"No, Bob, not right now. Just keep those flights over China going. They have been very helpful. I'll talk with you later," John said and hung up the phone.

Bob hung up on his end and pulled his cell phone from his suit coat pocket. He brought up John Walker's contact information in text mode and composed a text message.

"Expect State Department diversion to mainland China. Observe and report upon return. Safety first. Signed Bob."

John would understand the message. He had been an agent with the company since his days with Southern Air Transport and he knew what an "observe and report" mission meant.

Paul arrived at the 6000' level and stepped out of the tube onto the hangar deck. There were two AFVs out on reconnaissance missions so he walked into the crew quarters where everyone was gathered. Even though it was afternoon, it was obvious there we a few hangovers.

"Hey, Paul, glad you made it back. You missed all the fun," They said.

"Damn, I have been worried sick about all of you since I heard the first reports. Couldn't confirm anything in New York. I was in the middle of my interview when the news broke. Asked Bob about how bad things were but he said I could get the straight story from all of you," Paul said.

Bill Grammercy was sitting at he table next to Tori.

"Come on over here, Paul. The two of us will tell you of our death-defying mission." Tori and Bill looked at each other and laughed. It was funny now but last night it really was a death-defying mission. They told Paul the story from the beginning to the end and he sat there practically with his mouth agape. He assured Tori and Bill he couldn't have done any better and that their procedures were sound and execution perfect. There had to be a glitch in the electrical protection circuit for the DOD package.

The most amazing part was Mike's rescue of the two space station astronauts. They all realized that once again Mike was truly a gifted leader. His snap decision judgments were always right on and he had the right stuff to carry them out safely. They were all proud to be in his presence. The down side to the story, which they had learned from the television reporting this morning, was the death of the Russian astronaut.

The discussion lasted for another hour when Larry piped up and said they should all make their way down the mountain, go home and get a couple of days rest before reporting back to headquarters for duty.

Tori went down the mountain accompanied by Bill. When they reached the front door of headquarters Bill reminded her, "We did everything according to the book. Don't look back. See you in a couple of days."

She walked over to the house and let herself in. It sure was lonesome and she wished John were there to comfort her.

Mindanao, Philippine Islands

John had just landed at the Davao Airport and he turned on his phone. It beeped at him. He read Bob's message and sent back a one-word text message, "Understood."

They were to spend a couple of days in Davao City as Susan was attempting to find out all she could about the reports of the Datu's new concubine. The Muslim community was located twenty to thirty miles north of Davao in the jungle. They had a primitive village and very few people had ever been there. Beni Guiang was the local crime boss and controlled almost everything in and around Davao and might be a source of information.

The Americans caught a taxi to town and established headquarters at the Mergrande Ocean Resort. It was located on the south beach and was a beautiful equatorial resort hotel.

After settling into their rooms, Susan called and set up a meeting to discuss their plans for the next day or two. After dinner they would meet in her suite and set it up. Her aide was the antsy type who hovered over every word but was just a yes man. John knew he would be worthless on this assignment.

After dinner John and his copilot Ken Pyle went up to Susan's room for the confab. Susan began by discussing a possible meeting with the local crime boss Beni Guiang. She proposed how they should meet him and questions she might ask. John was an old hand at dealing with Asian personalities, especially shady characters like Beni. He soon straightened out Susan's thinking by laying out how it should come down. Invite Beni to lunch on the patio overlooking the beach. Beni would insist on meeting in town but Susan should be persuasive and insist on lunch at the hotel. This would eliminate the possibility of any hanky-panky and intimidation on Beni's part. It would also be the safest since John who always carried his pistol on these trips could ensure her safety. Beni was always used to getting his way so she should be firm but calm in asking her questions. This would assure Beni he was being treated fair and respected.

If they received unsatisfactory answers or no information at all, John knew the local Constabulary officer who might be able to help.

The next day Susan was scheduled to meet and have lunch with Beni. Things went down as John had predicted and Susan had followed John's suggestions to the letter. Beni finally agreed to meet her and have lunch at the hotel. Beni arrived with two of his hoodlums all dressed in two-piece suits. They took seats in the lobby where they could watch while Beni met Susan on the patio. John lurked at a table over in the corner where he could watch all parties involved to ensure Susan's safety. He stationed Ken in the lobby by the exit to stop any quick escape should it be planned to kidnap Susan.

Susan and Beni had a nice quiet lunch and, after he left, Susan reported no information was forthcoming. She felt Beni was feeding her baloney all the time and that he actually knew nothing of the Datu's new concubine.

John and Susan had a meeting after lunch. John offered to meet with his old friend Colonel Bonnie Surrano, Philippine Constabulary Commanding Officer of the Davao District. Susan agreed and John indicated he should first meet with Bonnie and discusses the situation and see if he could add anything that would help in Susan's quest. He told Susan meeting him alone would be better as Bonnie would be more relaxed with his old friend. If necessary, John would arrange a later meeting.

John called his old friend and after renewing their acquaintances arranged a time to meet personally with his old friend. Bonnie said they should meet at his office and he gave John the address. He took a taxi to Bonnie's office and his secretary ushered him into his office.

"Bonnie, long time no see," John said.

"Great to see you again, John. How have you been all these years?" he asked.

"I have been doing well, I am the Vice President of my company now." John said.

"I think the last time we met I was just a Captain. You see now I am a Colonel. Not bad for a kid from the Manila slums," Bonnie said. "What's on your mind my friend?"

"Bonnie, I have the Assistant Secretary of State from the U.S. government. She is trying to find out some information about a newswoman reported missing from Salt Lake City. The report reaching her is that the missing woman is a concubine for one of the Datus here on Mindanao. She is hoping someone here can help her. She met with Beni Guiang and of course he was of no help. I suggested you because you and your men are always in touch with the Muslim albeit as enemies most of the time. Bonnie, confidentially we don't want you to find this woman but we need you to give the Secretary some hope. I know you can fake it. So what do you think?" John asked.

"You're still a spook aren't you, John?" Bonnie said.

"I guess you could say that Bonnie. I just can't get away from it," John said.

"Okay, I can do this for you. How do you want to proceed?" he asked.

"Let's have breakfast at 9:00a.m. tomorrow at the hotel. I'll invite the Secretary and we three can have a working meeting. I think you can just give her the vague answers and don't promise her anything. That should do it," John said.

"Okay. I'll see you in the morning," he said.

"See you in the a.m., Bonnie," John said and got up shook hands and left Bonnie's office.

John headed back to the hotel and met with Susan. He described his meeting and told Susan Bonnie wanted to meet with her so he made a reservation for breakfast in the hotel dining room.

The next morning Susan met John who was already seated and having a glass of pineapple juice. Shortly Bonnie entered the room. He had a commanding presence as he entered. He was six feet six inches tall, quite a bit taller than the average Filipino and was in his official uniform. Many heads turned to look. The locals all knew who Bonnie was and nodded in acknowledgement of his presence.

What John had failed to tell Susan was that Bonnie was the fiercest man he had ever known. Bonnie had served with the Constabulary in the Vietnam War as a Second Lieutenant. His men had run out of ammo while pinned down by a machine gun. Bonnie told his men to stay in position and he crawled on his belly until he had out flanked the enemy. He then attacked and single-handedly killed seven of them with an axe. For his heroism he was awarded the highest military honor, the Philippine Medal of Honor.

John stood and greeted Bonnie.

"Bonnie, I would like you to meet Susan Walsh, Assistant Secretary of State," he said

"I'm pleased to meet you, Ma'am," he said.

"Like wise, Colonel Serrano," she answered. "Won't you sit down and join us?"

"Thank you," he said as he took a seat across from her at the table.

This was a table for four and John sat between them.

"Before we get started, let's order breakfast," John

said.

"Good, John. I have been up since five and haven't had time for even a cup of coffee. I had to brief a patrol of my men going into the jungle today to arrest a few Muslim men. Always a dangerous assignment," he said. "I learned a few of their tricks over the years and I always pass them on to my men before they depart," Bonnie said.

The three ordered breakfast and so they began their conversation.

"Madame Secretary, John tells me you are looking for a missing American woman," Bonnie said. I have heard of a third white woman in the Datus harem. There's the Labbe girl who if you remember John was captured when you were at Sangley Point. Then there is Mindy Burke, the Australian who was kidnapped off the yacht. Those are the only three I know of.

"Yes, Colonel. She was a newswoman from the Salt Lake City Tribune when she disappeared. We later had reports that she had been sold into slavery and ended up as a concubine of one of your local Datus. I brought a picture which I can let you have so I had hoped you or one of your men might have seen her. If so we would then mount a delegation to attempt to obtain her release," she said

"I'm not sure how that will fly," Bonnie said. "Sultan Jamal Kieram of Jolo still has his people stirred up all over Mindanao and he's not ready to negotiate over anything. We have tried to integrate the Muslims into our political structure and have yet to be successful. The President has given the Sultan autonomous regions but that still had not calmed the situation. Leave the picture with us and we will see if we can at least identify her. That in itself will be an insurmountable task as it is difficult to get close to a Muslim village. I assure you my men will try and if we are successful we shall notify the American Embassy in Manila. That's about all I can promise you," Bonnie said.

"Thank you, Colonel. That's all I can hope for at this point," she said.

Breakfast was served and small talk continued through the meal. After coffee Colonel Surrano arose and shook hands and excused himself. He said he had an inspection team coming in from Manila and needed to square away some things. John walked Bonnie to the front door of the lobby and they said their goodbyes. John indicated he hoped they would meet again real soon.

22

"An Assessment"

Davao, Mindanao, Philippines

Departure was scheduled for the next day and the Americans wanted to get some relaxation and then head for home. They had been gone now for seven days and John and Ken looked forward to Kamas, some American food and television but he knew what was coming as he had already been alerted by Bob Avery.

While they were all enjoying some rays on the beach and a few Mai Tais, Susan received a phone call from Manila. She went into the lobby of the hotel to answer it. It was the Ambassador. He had received new instructions to pass on to her. Proceed to Beijing, China, assess the situation and advise the Secretary with a recommendation whether to maintain a presence in China or close the embassy and withdraw all personnel.

Arrival time in Beijing had not been dictated to her so she felt she should discuss it with John and then decide what to do. She returned to the beach and sat down next to John where he had stretched out to gather some rays.

"John," she said, to get his attention. He rolled over onto his side facing her. She was sitting in a chair, "I have new instructions from Washington and have been directed to a new destination."

"The Secretary has directed me to proceed to Beijing

and assess the situation on the continuing status of the embassy. Arrival time in Beijing has apparently been left to my discression. What are your thoughts," she asked.

He acted surprised even though he already knew that it was coming. "It all depends on the weather. There are no radio communication stations operating and no weather reporting. When we go it will be completely in the blind. I recommend we stop in Taipei, Taiwan, and get a weather briefing. They probably have a better handle on Mainland China's weather than anybody. If necessary, we can delay in Taipei until conditions look favorable then go for it. I don't know how much you are aware of how the EMP affected China but they are in the Stone Age right now. Nothing is working. Everything electrical and electronic is kaput, burned out or shorted out. Nothing is going to be working for quite some time," John said.

"John, I'm a history major," she said. I don't know a damn thing about EMPs or their effects. So you'll have to educate me along the way."

"I'll give you a rudimentary education before we get to Beijing. Let's plan on leaving early tomorrow and stop in Taiwan. If you would send a cable though the Manila embassy and have them relay to Taiwan, to advise the Chinese we are planning a transit of Taipei, that will alert the Chinese and we won't get shot down. It we leave here around 9:00a.m. we can be in Taipei by 11:30a.m. Let's plan on spending two hours on the ground and leave at 1:30p.m. It is about one hour forty minutes to Beijing so we could arrive by 3:10p.m.

Susan copied all the information and placed a call to the U.S. Embassy in Manila. The embassy personnel copied all and assured her they would pass it on to the American Embassy in Taipei.

John and Ken concluded their sunbathing and returned to their room for a little nap.

John and Ken were up early the next morning, had a
quick breakfast and John departed for the airport. He
needed to get the plane refueled and ready for departure.
He received a weather briefing and called Ken back at the
hotel with the winds aloft from Davao to Taipei. Ken would
do his flight panning at the hotel but most of all he was
there to provide security and escort Susan and her aide to
the Airport, ensuring nothing happens to them during the
trip. When he finished his planning he called John again
at the airport, gave him the route of flight and time enroute.
John filed his flight plan and after refueling was ready for
departure. All he needed was the passengers. While waiting he sent Bob a text message reporting a change in destination and a revised itinerary.

Susan arrived at 8:45a.m. and they were off to Taipei
on time. This was summertime in the tropics and early
morning saw few buildups or thunderheads. The rainy season had not as yet arrived so the flight was pleasant and
comfortable.

John set down at 11:20a.m. and by the time he
reached the parking area it was 11:30a.m., right of time. A
representative from the American embassy met them. John
suggested Susan and her aide travel into Taipei if she desired where she could relax, have a long lunch and return
to the airport by 1:15p.m. in time to depart on the half
hour. The embassy aide had greased the skids with customs and immigration so that was not a problem. Ken and
John walked over to the weather office which was in the
main terminal of the airport. When they walked in John
addressed the weather people on duty with his finest Northern Mandarin Chinese. Ken was taken aback. He didn't

even know John could speak Chinese. Southern Air Transport's headquarters had been in Taipei for a few years and working for them he had acquired a fluent tongue in Mandarin Chinese.

The weathermen smiled widely at John and answered him in a pleasant tone. John then switched to English, as he wanted Ken to hear the Beijing weather. Ken could see from John's addressing them in their native language that they were more attentive and appreciative of a foreigner being fluent in their native tongue.

They searched and researched the Mainland's weather. They told John it would be a wild ass guess, a WAG if you please, as they had no actual station reports from China in a couple of days. However from the satellite pictures they were able to give him a fairly complete picture of what to expect, summer weather in the upper latitudes. Scattered to broken clouds at 8000' with visibility over 25 miles decreasing to less than a mile approaching Beijing due to the smog.

John thanked them first in English then in Mandarin. Once again the weather people were appreciative of John. He and Ken walked out into the main terminal and searched for a restaurant. They found a suitable place and Ken acceded to John ordering lunch. While at lunch John observed through the window that the FBO as ordered was refueling the Gulfstream. John wanted enough fuel to be able to fly to Anchorage, Alaska, should Beijing be unable to pump fuel.

They finished their lunch and walked upstairs to flight service and filed a flight plan for Beijing. The controllers on duty warned them that there was probably no air traffic control in China and cancelling their flight plan after they arrived would be impossible. John assured them everything would be okay but that they would try to cancel it with Taipei flight service just before touchdown in Beijing.

Susan and her aide arrived just at 1:15p.m. and boarded the aircraft. After they were settled in the cabin John came forward occupied his position and started engines. They were airborne and headed for places and conditions unknown.

Ken checked out of Taiwanese airspace on the HF radio and was warned once again that they were on their own. They flew on for another hour. John had set the GPS system to the Beijing Airport coordinates. When he was about seventy-five miles out he began his descent remaining clear of all clouds just in case of other traffic. Ken checked out with a status report to Taiwanese air traffic control.

He and Ken kept a keen lookout for other traffic. As they approached within twenty miles of the airport and entered a lower layer of air the visibility decreased until finally it was less than a mile. John had set the coordinates on the GPS for the approach to Runway 27 left at Beijing. He turned to intercept a point on an imaginary extension of the centerline of that runway at ten miles from touchdown. When he intercepted that point he turned to the runway heading and completed the landing checklist. He slowed to approach speed with the gear and flaps set for landing. Both men were scanning ahead and at about one mile Ken shouted and pointed to the left at the approach to the runway. John banked left and when he was over the approach light stantions returned to the runway heading. John called out runway in sight and slowed to touchdown speed and landed. He braked and reversed engines until the aircraft was slowed to taxi speed. He displayed the airport layout on the middle screen of the instrument panel and taxied to the terminal. On arrival he shutdown and there was met by many people in different uniforms. As he deplaned an army Lieutenant accosted him. John eased the situation by speaking to him in northern mandarin. John made it clear who they were and that they were there to help and to check on the American embassy personnel's well being. The young army Lieutenant understood and was very accommodating. He ordered the other people to go back to what they had been doing and indicated he would handle this situation.

Susan and her aide deplaned and after John secured the aircraft they were led into the terminal. Talk about a deserted place. John observed no aircraft or vehicle movement whatsoever. No lights, computers, electric signs or air conditioning. There were very few people at the workstations. John overheard a conversation that his was the first plane to land there in four days. Arrangements were made for three rickshaws to take them to the American embassy. Two for the Americans and one for the security guards to accompany them.

When they arrived at the embassy gate two marines were there to challenge them. Susan showed her credentials and her party was admitted to the compound. The two Chinese military escorts took up positions outside the gates of the compound.

Susan was escorted directly to the ambassador's office while John and Ken chose to hotfoot it to the kitchen. Tea was brewing on a gas stove and John asked the Chinese cooks if he could have a pot of tea. He and Ken sat at a table nearby and waited. John extracted his small notebook from his jacket pocket and began to write. Ken asked him what he was doing. He told Ken he should write down what he had observed since they entered Chinese airspace and after they had landed. That is what he was doing. They would make a written report after they returned to Salt Lake.

John started a conversation in Mandarin with the Chinese help. It was very animated and he took a lot of notes for his report.

Word was passed down to the kitchen that they would spend the night at the embassy and depart the next morning for the states.

The next day found them winging their way to Anchorage, Alaska. After six and one half hours in the air, they were on the ground for one hour for some JP5 and then were off for another five and one half hours to Washington, D.C.

Susan and her aide were delivered to Dulles and John was off to Salt Lake City. It had been a long day when he finally touched down and taxied to Hangar 512. Time was approaching 3:00p.m. and he figured he would catch the 4:30p.m. helo flight to headquarters and home. He sat down and began to write his report. It had been a long eight days and he was ready for a break from the routine.

He stepped off the helo at headquarters and walked over to the house. When he walked in, Tori was back in her bedroom. She had been home for three days. She heard the front door open and rushed out of her bedroom and ran into John's arms. She was shaking and crying uncontrollably. "Oh, John. I think I started World War III," she sobbed. John said nothing but hugged her even closer and assured her he was there for her. He finally carried her over to the sofa in the den still holding her close he said, "Okay just this once tell me about the mission and what happened."

He already knew the final outcome of the mission but felt she needed to just talk about it. Tori described exactly what happened and by the time she finished she had calmed down some and stopped crying.

"Tori, it sounds like you and Bill did everything correctly and that a glitch in the way the package was wired into the shuttle was the cause of it being ejected prematurely. Let me ask you would you have done anything differently?" John said.

"I have reviewed our procedures over and over and I know we did it as it was set down but I still have doubts that maybe I did something wrong," she said.

"Tori you should know that in our business sometimes no matter how much you plan, study and execute, things happen that you have no control over it. This is one of those times. You did everything right so don't dwell on it and move forward." John said.

"Okay," she said. "Just hold me close."

"They just cuddled up close on the sofa and finally Tori went to sleep. She slept solid for seven hours and when she awoke John was still asleep but holding her. She gently slipped from his grasp and kissed him on the lips. She knew for the first time that she was deeply in love with this solid, reliable guy.

When John awoke he realized Tori and gone back to her room. He walked back and heard the shower so he called to her and asked if she was okay. She answered and said she was, and would be out in a little bit.

John went back to his room where he undressed. He was still in the clothes he had on since he left Beijing and he felt he really needed a shower. He stepped in and turned on the hot water. He brought the cold water on line and modified the temperature until it was comfortable. He just stood under the showerhead letting the water soothe his skin as well as his nerves. After some twenty minutes he found the hair conditioner and washed his hair. Then he finished up with the little soap to the body and turned off the water and stepped out.

He had slipped into his warm-ups and walked into the kitchen. Tori was already there fixing breakfast for both of them.

"I thought you were going to drown, I almost came in to check and see if you were okay," she said.

"Almost two days without a shower tends to make me a little rustic I guess is a polite word. Are you doing okay this morning?" he asked.

"Yeah, I just needed to talk and have someone listen. I was a little over melodramatic I guess but it was bothering me. I guess things in China are a disaster and people are struggling to survive," she said.

"Tori you wouldn't believe the conditions there. It's almost an eerie situation. There is no damage or visible physical disruption but with no electricity and absolutely nothing working, the people are struggling. There were no planes flying, no cars running. I mean I can't begin to describe the while situation. Food is going to start to run short pretty soon and then trouble is going to begin. I haven't written my trip report yet but when I do I will let you read it and you will get more of a prospective on what is going on."

John changed the subject as he felt she didn't need to get into the China situation until she was healed herself from the trauma she had just experienced.

"I have a couple of days off and so do you. Would you like to go camping up in Yosemite for a couple of days," he asked.

"That's a great idea, I would love it," she said. Tori walked over to John and put her arms around his neck and gave him a long lingering kiss. "I guess I'm your girl now and your stuck with me." John returned the favor and planted a loving kiss and held her ever more closely. "This will be a trip to remember for the rest of our lives."